PENGUIN BOOKS

The Templar Cross

Carefully fitted into custom-made Styrofoam slots was a row of five gold bars, each one approximately five inches long and two inches wide. Japrisot reached into the box and pried one of the bars out of its nest. It looked about half an inch thick. Holliday reached into the box and took another one out. It was heavy in his hands, almost unnaturally so, and it had an odd, greasy feel to it that was unaccountably repellant.

The bar was rudely made, the edges rounded and the surface slightly pitted. 'I KILO' was stamped into the upper quadrant, the letters *E.T.* in the middle and an instantly recognizable impression in the lower end of the bar: the palm tree and swastika insignia of the German Afrika Korps of the Third Reich. There was no serial number or any other coding on the bar.

'Fifty kilos a box, ten boxes, five hundred kilos,' said Japrisot quietly.

'One thousand one hundred and three pounds,' murmured Rafi. 'A little more than half a ton.'

'Dear God,' whispered Holliday, 'what have we stumbled on to?'

The Templar Cross

PAUL CHRISTOPHER

PENGUIN BOOKS

PENGUIN BOOKS

Published by the Penguin Group
Penguin Books Ltd, 80 Strand, London WC2R ORL, England
Penguin Group (USA) Inc., 375 Hudson Street, New York, New York 10014, USA
Penguin Group (Canada), 90 Eglinton Avenue East, Suite 700, Toronto, Ontario,
Canada M4P 2Y3 (a division of Pearson Penguin Canada Inc.)
Penguin Ireland, 25 St Stephen's Green, Dublin 2, Ireland (a division of Penguin Books Ltd)
Penguin Group (Australia), 250 Camberwell Road, Camberwell, Victoria 3124, Australia
(a division of Pearson Australia Group Pty Ltd)
Penguin Books India Pvt Ltd, 11 Community Centre, Panchsheel Park,
New Delhi – 110 017, India
Penguin Group (NZ), 67 Apollo Drive, Rosedale, Auckland 0632, New Zealand
(a division of Pearson New Zealand Ltd)
Penguin Books (South Africa) (Pty) Ltd, 24 Sturdee Avenue,
Rosebank, Johannesburg 2196, South Africa

Penguin Books Ltd, Registered Offices: 80 Strand, London WC2R ORL, England

www.penguin.com

First published in the USA by Signet, an imprint of New American Library,
a division of Penguin Group (USA) Inc. 2010
First published in Great Britain in Penguin Books 2011

2

Copyright © Paul Christopher, 2010
All rights reserved

The moral right of the author has been asserted

Set in 13.5/16.5pt Garamond MT Std
Typeset by Jouve (UK), Milton Keynes
Printed in England by Clays Ltd, St Ives plc

Except in the United States of America, this book is sold subject
to the condition that it shall not, by way of trade or otherwise, be lent,
re-sold, hired out, or otherwise circulated without the publisher's
prior consent in any form of binding or cover other than that in
which it is published and without a similar condition including this
condition being imposed on the subsequent purchaser

B-format ISBN: 978–0–241–95118–7
A-format ISBN: 978–0–241–95252–8

www.greenpenguin.co.uk

MIX
Paper from
responsible sources
FSC
www.fsc.org   FSC® C018179

Penguin Books is committed to a sustainable
future for our business, our readers and our
planet. This book is made from paper certified
by the Forest Stewardship Council.

Epworth Mechanics' Institute Library
Tuesday 10a.m – 12 Noon
Thursday 1.30p.m – 4p.m
Friday 7.30p.m – 9.30p.m

21. 3. 17.

Please return books as soon as you have finished with them so that others may read them

I

The United States Military Academy at West Point was deserted. There were no platoons practicing close order drill on the Plain, marching under the tarnished eternal eye of a bronze George Washington on horseback. There was no echoing sound of polished combat boots on asphalt in the Central Area as cadets did punishment duty. No barking orders echoing from stone walls. No drill sergeants calling cadence.

Graduation was over. Firsties transformed into newly minted soldiers were gone to their posts – plebes, cows and yuks all gone on summer training tours of one kind or another. No bands played, and the trees whispering secrets in the early-summer breeze was the only sound. The complex of old gray buildings was fading to a warm golden hue in the waning light of the sun. It was the last Sunday in June. Tomorrow was 'R' Day.

Lieutenant Colonel John 'Doc' Holliday walked

across the broad, empty expanse of the Plain in his dress whites, feeling just a little bit tipsy. He was returning home from his farewell dinner at the West Point Club on the far side of the campus and he was relieved that there was no one around to see him in his present condition. Drunk history professors in tailcoats reeling around on the grounds of the nation's premier military school didn't go down well with civilian cadet moms and dads; definitely not good public relations.

Holliday stared blearily into the gathering darkness, the scarred eye socket under his black patch giving him phantom pain probably caused by one too many single malts. The gloomy breadth of the Plain was as empty as the rest of the Point. Tomorrow the fathers, mothers, brothers, sisters and friends of twelve hundred new cadet recruits would swarm over the big, neatly clipped field like ants with video cameras recording the doomed twelve hundred's last hours of freedom before they were swallowed up by the U.S. Military machine.

Registration Day was like a circus and the end of the world combined. The new cadets, with their hairstyles still intact, had more than a few things in common with concentration camp inmates. They arrived, wide-eyed and terrified, in lines of buses and were shorn, poked, yelled at, given numbers and uniforms, then marched away into oblivion, like Hamelin's children following the Pied Piper.

After five weeks in Beast Barracks getting Cadet Basic Training – which would winnow out a hundred or so who just couldn't take it – and four grueling years that would winnow out a few hundred more, the same Pied Piper might eventually lead them onto the killing fields of Afghanistan or Iraq, or wherever else it was decided they should go by whoever happened to be occupying the White House that year.

Holliday had seen them come and seen them go and for years before that he'd seen them die in places the family and friends of the new cadets could never even imagine. The pomp and circumstance and hypotheticals of West Point would give way to blood and brains and severed limbs and all the other realities of armed conflict that never made it onto the evening news, let alone the pages of *The Howitzer*, the West Point yearbook. Proof of that, dating back to 1782 in the form of a soldier named Dominick Trant, lay in the old cemetery just along the way on Washington Road.

But that was over now. Ten months ago, following his uncle Henry's death, had found Doc Holliday following the trail of a Crusader's sword that led him and his cousin Peggy Blackstock halfway round the world and to a secret that had changed his life forever: a Templar treasure hoard that now lay securely hidden in an ancient castle in the south of France, the Chateau de Ravanche.

Now he was hostage to that treasure, bound as a steward to its awe-inspiring secret. For months he had wrestled with his obligations and finally realized that in good conscience he could no longer spend his time teaching history; it was time to live it. He had handed in his resignation to the superintendent and agreed to finish out the year. Now the year was done.

Holliday reached the edge of the Plain and turned down Washington Road. He went past Quarters 100, the old Federal-style house occupied by the superintendent, and headed onto Professor's Row. His own house was the smallest on the treelined avenue, a two-bedroom Craftsman bungalow built in the 1920s, all oak paneling, stained glass, twenties furniture and polished hardwood floors. Married quarters, even though he'd been a widower for more than ten years now, but when he signed on at West Point after Kabul and the idiotic accident that had taken his eye, the little house had been the only accommodation suitable to his rank.

Holliday fumbled with his keys, managed to unlock the front door and let himself into the dark house. As usual, just for a second, some small part of his heart and mind imagined that Amy would be there and a second later he'd feel the soft sweep of sadness as he realized that she wasn't. It had been a long time, almost ten years now, but some pain just didn't go away no matter what the philosophers said.

He tossed the keys into the little dish on the sideboard that Peggy had made for him when she was twelve and headed down the hall to the kitchen. He switched on the gas beneath a pot of cowboy coffee he always kept on the stove, then went to the bedroom and stripped off his uniform. Even tipsy he made sure he hung it neatly in the closet beside his Ranger Class A's and then slipped into jeans and a T-shirt. He went back to the kitchen, poured himself a mug of the bitter brew and carried it to the small living room, a book-lined rectangle with a short couch and a few comfortable old chairs arranged around a green-tiled Craftsman fireplace complete with the original Mother Oak keystone.

Outside it was fully dark now and Holliday felt a chill in the room. He laid the fire, lit it and dropped down into one of the armchairs, sipping his coffee and watching as the flames caught in the kindling and licked up into the larger logs. In ten minutes the fire was burning brightly and a circle of warmth was expanding into the room, the evening chill dissolving in the face of the cheerful blaze.

Holliday's glance drifted up to the object hanging over the fireplace mantel on two pegs, glittering almost sensually in the dancing light: the Templar sword that he and Peggy had found in a secret compartment in Uncle Henry's house in northwestern New York. The sword that had started it all, thirty-one inches of patterned Damascus steel, its hilt wrapped in gold wire, the wire coded with its remarkable message. A sword that had once belonged to a Crusader knight named Guillaume de Gisors seven hundred years in the past. A sword once possessed by both Benito Mussolini and Adolf Hitler. Twin to the sword that Holliday had used to kill a man less than a year ago. The deadly weapon hanging above the fireplace was *Hesperios*, the Sword of the West.

Before he and Peggy had embarked on their long journey of discovery almost a year ago, Holliday's attitude toward history had been absolute. Facts and dates and the timelines of events were literally written in stone as well as textbooks. Words like 'unqualified,' 'unassailable,' 'irrevocable' and 'immutable' were all part of his historical vocabulary.

But now, things had changed. A view of history could be upset as easily as a placid pond by a tossed pebble or a simple act of birth. Or, in Holliday's case, a sword.

Discovering *Hesperios* in Uncle Henry's house in Fredonia had altered not only his own history but others' as well. If he hadn't found it, good people and bad he'd never known would still be alive, some dead now by his own hand. Uncle Henry's past had changed as well as Holliday uncovered the circumstances and secrets that led to the sword being in his possession.

His understanding of Templar history had also changed. Once upon a time he'd taught his students at the Point that the ancient brotherhood was no more than an interesting footnote in the chronicles of medieval times, a group that had seen a ragged assembly of less than a dozen unemployed knights transform themselves from *routier* highwaymen on the Pilgrim Road to Jerusalem into an economic force that spread itself over thirteenth-century Europe like a cloud.

He'd also taught his cadet students that all of that had come crashing down in a single day, Friday, October 13, 1307, as Philip of France and Pope Clement's order for the arrest of all Templars in France and the confiscation of their property and wealth was carried out.

Every other country in Europe soon followed suit, seeing an easy way to rid themselves of crippling royal debt to Templar banks. According to accepted history the Templars had simply disappeared, erased from history, a brief phenomenon that had come and gone. Holliday had taught all that as fact. And he'd been totally wrong.

On that particular day in 1307 King Philip's bailiffs cut off a thousand Templar heads, but Philip forgot that there were also a thousand Templar tails. The knights, or at least most of them, were gone, but the accountants, many of them Cistercian monks, survived. By the end of World War II Germany was a rubble-strewn wasteland, but when the smoke cleared it was the same men running the trains, policing the streets and teaching the children. In the United States, presidents came and went every few years like a revolving door, but the bureaucrats remained. So it was with the Templars.

Long before King Philip sent out his edict, the lower echelons of the Templar Order saw the potential for disaster and took steps to avoid it. Deeds and testaments were quietly rewritten, titles to properties changed and notes in hand for enormous sums were transferred to supposedly innocent hands in distant places, far from the clutches of Philip and his English cousins. It was no accident that the man who invented double-entry bookkeeping was a monk. The concept of keeping two sets of books wasn't far behind.

When Philip arrested the Templars he confiscated their visible wealth but their *invisible* wealth had long since been spirited away. As Jacques de Molai, the last official Grand Master of the Templars, said shortly before he was burned at the stake in 1314: 'The best way to keep a secret is to forget that it exists.' And that was precisely what the Templars did.

For the better part of seven hundred years, under scores of different names and identities, the Templars' hidden assets had grown to almost unbelievable proportions, doubling and redoubling over time, diversifying into every walk and facet of everyday life in virtually all the nations of the earth.

Consolidated into a single force, the power of that much wealth would be almost overwhelming, capable of toppling governments with ease. Forged into a mighty hammer the influence of the Templar fortune was capable of doing enormous good or unspeakable evil. It was the key to the kingdom of heaven or to the burning gates of hell.

And the key lay in the small, blood-spattered notebook now locked in a desk drawer in Lieutenant Colonel John Holliday's study. The notebook was the gift of an ex-priest named Helder Rodrigues, dying in Holliday's arms on the island of Corvo in the distant Azores.

The gift came with a codicil, however: use it wisely, use it well or use it not at all. The Templar treasure Rodrigues had revealed to Holliday and Peggy that day in the furious rain had been great enough; the secret revealed within the bloody notebook was a million times greater. The neo-Nazi Axel Kellerman had forfeited his life for it, run through by *Aos*, Sword of the East. The anonymous assassin from the Vatican's Sodalitium Pianum had died for it on the narrow midnight streets of Jerusalem.

All of which lay behind Holliday's decision to leave West Point. He knew the menace inherent in the notebook from Rodrigues wasn't over and there was no way he was going to imperil the cadets or anyone else at the Point; if there was danger ahead, it would be his alone.

Holliday dozed, warmed by the fire, then fell into a dreamless sleep. When he awoke it was almost dawn, the first pink light creeping up over the trees along Gee's Point and the Hudson River. The fire had burned to cold ashes in the grate and Holliday's joints ached after a night of sitting up in the chair. Something had awakened him. A sound. He blinked and raised his wrist, checking the old Royal Air Force Rolex he'd inherited from his Uncle Henry. Ten to six. Too early for reveille by forty minutes.

He levered himself out of the armchair and crossed the room to his front window. There was a blue Academy Taxi from Highland Falls idling on the street in front of the house. A figure climbed out of the taxi and started up the walk. He carried only a flight bag for luggage.

Holliday recognized the handsome dark-haired man immediately. It was Rafi Wanounou, the Israeli archaeologist he and Peggy had befriended in Jerusalem. From this distance he looked fit and well, and the only evidence of the savage beating he'd taken on their behalf in Jerusalem was a slight limp. The expression on his face, however, was grim. He climbed the steps, favoring his right leg. Holliday went to the front door and threw it open.

'Rafi,' he said. 'This is a surprise. What on earth are you doing here?'

'She's gone,' the archaeologist said. 'They've taken Peggy.'

2

'Talk,' said Holliday, busying himself by making a fresh pot of coffee. Rafi sat slumped at the kitchen table. His face looked pale and exhausted. He made a little groaning sound and sat a little straighter in his chair.

'You knew how it was between us,' Rafi started tentatively. It was almost a question.

Holliday shrugged. 'You were a couple,' he said. 'She went back to Jerusalem after we were in the Azores and she stayed there.'

'That's right,' Rafi said and nodded. 'At first it was so she could take care of me after I got out of the hospital, but later . . .' He let it dangle.

'Later it turned into something else,' said Holliday.

'Something like that,' said Rafi.

Holliday found two mugs in the cupboard above the counter, then went to the refrigerator and brought out a container of cream. He kept his hands working, fetching spoons. He'd never felt comfortable talking about his own relationships, let alone anyone else's, particularly Peggy's. With Uncle Henry gone, he and his much younger cousin were orphans together. It was a special bond. Now this young archaeologist was in the mix.

'Did you have a fight or something?' Holliday asked, taking a stab in the dark. He took a handful of coffee beans and poured them into the little grinder on the counter. The machine whirred for a few seconds and the dark, rich aroma of the freshly ground beans filled the air.

'No,' said Rafi, shaking his head. 'No fight. Nothing like that. In fact we were talking about making things a little more . . . permanent.'

'Marriage?' Holliday asked, surprised. Peggy was a self-described serial monogamist, a committed bachelorette, or spinster, or whatever the hell the politically correct term for it was these days. It seemed out of character.

'We were getting there,' said Rafi bleakly.

'So what happened?'

'She got a call. *Smithsonian* magazine. They had an assignment for her. They knew she was in Jerusalem, so she seemed like the obvious choice.'

'They wanted a photo story?' Holliday asked.

He dumped the coarse ground coffee into the Bodum French press on the counter and poured in boiling water from the kettle. The cowboy coffee on the stove was for himself; the Bodum was for guests.

'A photo story and a written one as well. A journal of the dig. She liked the idea of writing; she'd been thinking about it for a while. This was a break for her, or that's what she thought,' added Rafi bitterly.

'What dig?' Holliday asked.

'The Biblical Archaeology School of France in Jerusalem had underwritten an expedition into Egypt and Libya. One of their senior people, a man named Brother Charles-Étienne Brasseur, had stumbled onto a cache of old Templar texts while he was doing research in the Vatican Archives.'

'The Vatican? The Roman Catholics had the order disbanded and the last grand master burned at the stake,' said Holliday.

'The texts Brasseur discovered had been confiscated by King Philip's marshals during the dissolution,' replied Rafi. 'They came from an obscure abbey called La Couvertoirade in the Dordogne region of France.'

Holliday pressed down the plunger in the Bodum and poured out two mugs. He brought them to the table and set one down on the table in front of his friend, then took a seat himself.

'What was in the texts that set this Dominican Brasseur off?' Holliday asked.

Rafi took a grateful sip from the mug. He was visibly unwinding, sitting straighter in his chair and looking more alert as the strong brew seeped into his system.

'The texts were written by a Cistercian monk named Roland de Hainaut. Hainaut was secretary to Guillaume de Sonnac, the grand master who led the Templars at the Siege of Damietta in 1249.'

'Where's Damietta?' Holliday asked.

'The Nile Delta, east of Alexandria.'

'Okay, I'm with you.' Holliday nodded, visualizing a map of Egypt and the fan-shaped delta of the Nile not far from Cairo, which lay just below it.

'According to Hainaut he traveled to a Coptic monastery somewhere in the desert, and while he was at the monastery he heard rumors about the location of Imhotep's tomb. Imhotep was a polymath, sort of a Leonardo da Vinci of his era. Imhotep was the man who invented the pyramid and founded the art of Medicine.'

'I know who Imhotep was,' said Holliday. 'Does this story have an ending or should I be thinking about fixing us dinner tonight?'

'Sorry,' said Rafi. 'It's complicated and I'm tired.'

'Go on,' said Holliday.

'Anyway, the Hainaut text gave fairly clear directions on how to get to the monastery but said nothing more about the tomb's location. The expedition was supposed to make a preliminary test dig at the monastery location. Finding the tomb would be an extraordinary coup all by itself, but this archaeologist, Brother Brasseur, has some kind of wild theory that Imhotep was the archetype for Noah and the biblical flood. In my opinion it's a little thin scientifically, but the press was eating it up and the expedition got financed.'

'So what happened?' Holliday asked. He got up, brought the Bodum coffeemaker back to the table and divided what was left in the pot between them. Rafi continued.

'They set out from Jerusalem and rendez-voused in Alexandria, where the outfitters met them with their vehicles, supplies and hired help. Somewhere between El Alamein and Mersa Matruh they were kidnapped by a group called the Brotherhood.'

'Who the hell is the Brotherhood?' Holliday asked sourly, an ugly sensation curling in his gut and putting bile in his throat.

'Their full name is the Brotherhood of the Temple of Isis. According to them they're the Muslim version of the Templars and they were around long before them. Supposedly they date back to the cult of Imhotep at Memphis on the Nile around 600 B.C. The Brotherhood worship Imhotep as the god Ptah. Ptah was the god of craftsmen and of reincarnation. He was immortal. In other words a carpenter who comes back to life and lives forever. The Christian parallels are obvious. The Brotherhood feels that the Christians, particularly the Roman Catholics, hijacked Imhotep as Jesus Christ. They also cite themselves as the direct descendants of both the Copts and the Assassins, or *Hashasheen*, a sect of drugged-out Shia Muslims and the original fedayeen – "freedom fighters" in their terminology.'

'Terrorists,' said Holliday.

'Lunatics,' Rafi said and shrugged.

'Same thing. And these are the people who've got Peggy?'

'Yes.'

'How long ago did this happen?' Holliday asked.

'What's today?'

'The twenty-sixth. Monday.'

'Thursday, then. Four days ago.' Rafi ran his fingers through his wiry hair and yawned.

'What are their demands?' Holliday asked.

'They haven't made any,' said Rafi. 'At least they hadn't when I left from Ben Gurion yesterday.'

'That's not good,' said Holliday.

'No,' said Rafi. 'That's what my friends in the Mossad said.' He gave another jaw-cracking yawn.

'When was the last time you slept?' Holliday asked.

'On the plane. What I need is something to eat.'

'Let's get you some breakfast, then.' Holliday stood up. 'You up for a walk?'

'After fourteen hours sitting in the cheap seats of an El-Al 777? Sure, I'm up for a walk. Where to?'

'Grant Hall. The cafeteria's open this early. You need kosher?'

'Right now I'd eat a bacon sandwich with a side order of more bacon,' answered the archaeologist.

'Hang on,' said Holliday. 'I'm going to change and then we can get going. Bathroom's down the hall if you need it.'

Rafi headed for the bathroom and Holliday went to his bedroom. Five minutes later he reappeared dressed in a worn, comfortable set of chocolate-cookie camouflage BDUs that dated back to the First Gulf War. Five minutes after that a freshly scrubbed Rafi reappeared and they left the house. The morning air was cool and pleasant as the sun rose over the trees. It was going to be a nice day. As Holliday locked up the cannon thundered on Trophy Point half a mile down Washington Road. He paused and snapped a quick salute as reveille sounded, the rat-a-tat bugle notes echoing across the entire installation.

'Another "R" Day begins,' said Holliday, joining Rafi on the walk. 'God help us all.'

'What's "R" Day?' Rafi asked.

'The arrival of the freshman recruits. Twelve hundred kids with their moms and dads and their kid brothers and their sisters, maybe a girlfriend or boyfriend, sometimes even the next-door neighbors. The whole place turns into a circus.'

'At six thirty in the morning?'

'The Army likes to get an early start on its insanity,' Holliday said with a grin. 'If we're lucky we'll escape most of it.'

They walked down Professor's Row. A lot of the houses had that locked-down deserted look. Most of the officers and civilians who taught academic courses at West Point had already left on vacation or were on summer courses of their own somewhere else.

The two men reached the junction of Professor's Row and Jefferson Road, then turned west, passing Quarters 100 and the Thayer Monument. In front of them the gray bulk of Washington Hall loomed with the Washington on horseback statue in front of the giant twin-armed building and the Cadet Chapel rising on the hill behind. Doorways were leaking new recruits now, most of them wearing the black and white gym strip that would be their slightly demeaning costume until they were given their uniforms later in the process. Here and there Holliday could see uni-formed, red-sashed second-year cadets herding the bewildered-looking new recruits into some kind of order.

'They look like they're in hell.' Rafi grinned, watching the frightened young men and women as they tried to keep their expressions blank.

'That's the idea,' said Holliday. 'Alienation and separation from the past. Shock treatment; like cutting the umbilical.'

'Better them than me,' said the Israeli.

'You got that right,' agreed Holliday.

They stepped onto the broad concrete mall in front of Washington Hall, threading their way through pods of new recruits that darted nervously like small schools of fish, moving this way and that. On the wide expanse of the Plain to the left parents and friends were beginning to congregate like witnesses to an execution.

As they passed in front of the Washington statue, a cadet got up from where he had been sitting and stepped forward. He was in full uniform, complete with the six gold chevrons of a Cadet Regimental Commander and an ugly pair of BCGs – Birth Control Glasses, named that because you weren't going to get any while wearing them. He looked older than the average firstie and he had a dark stain of five o'clock shadow on his cheeks and jaw. There was a West Point ring on the second finger of his left hand. The right hand was digging into the pocket of his uniform trousers. The young man was smiling sheepishly.

"Scuse me, sir, but I seem to have lost my . . .'

Holliday reacted almost without thinking. He shoved Rafi hard, sending him sprawling. At the same time Holliday lashed out, punching the cadet in the face as hard as he could, feeling cartilage crack under the impact. He grabbed for the young man's right wrist as it came out of the trouser pocket, then put his heel behind the cadet's forward-stepping left ankle, simultaneously twisting the right hand back on itself, the wrist snapping like a twig.

The cadet screamed and fell with Holliday still gripping the wrist. Rafi struggled to his feet as a small crowd began to gather on the pavement around them. Out of the corner of his eye Holliday saw several red-sashed cadets running toward them. The man on the ground struggled briefly, then fell still. He stared darkly up at Holliday, his jaw working as though he was grinding his teeth.

'Who the hell are you?' Holliday barked. 'I know you're not a cadet.'

The man on the ground began to shudder, his heels rattling on the pavement. His eyes rolled back in his head until only the whites showed and a foamy froth slipped out from between his lips.

'Dear God,' whispered Rafi, staring down at him. 'He's dying.'

Holliday nodded to a black carbon-steel object on the ground beside the man in the cadet uniform.

'And that's a military-grade switchblade,' said Holliday. 'He was trying to kill me. He's an assassin.'

3

They stood around the table in one of the emergency cubicles at the Keller Army Community Hospital and looked down at the naked body on the gurney. Less than an hour had passed since the events in front of Washington Hall, but the corpse already had a gray, washed-out appearance. It looked like a frighteningly realistic store mannequin. There was a complex tattoo on the left side of the dead man's chest above the heart: crossed keys behind a shield showing a lion and an anchor with a miter over the shield. Holliday used his cell phone to take a picture of it. It was clearly the coat of arms of a Pope, but he had no idea which one.

'I'm no pathologist,' said the doctor, a captain named Ridley. He was young, under forty, with dark hair only just thinning back from his forehead, the temples barely fuzzed with gray. 'But from the foam at the corners of his mouth and the stiffness of the limbs I'd say it was some sort of neurotoxin. Quicker than hell.'

'He didn't have time to take anything,' said Holliday.

'That's right,' said Rafi.

'I found bits of plastic on his tongue and in the throat,' said Ridley. 'Some kind of capsule. It must have already been in his mouth.'

'A suicide pill?' Rafi asked, astonished.

'It looks that way,' the doctor said.

A representative of the West Point Garrison Provost Marshal's Office was also on hand, a husky thirty-something woman in BDUs, combat boots and a ponytail. She wore a sidearm on her hip, and her face was white as a sheet. She was a sergeant. Her name was Connie Sayers.

'I'm just a Military Police Investigator,' she said. 'This is way above my pay grade.' She shook her head, never taking her eyes off the dead man. She looked as though her throat was full of barely contained bile. When she spoke her teeth were clenched.

'Have you called in CID?' Holliday asked, referring to the Army Criminal Investigations Department.

'Yes, sir. They're sending us up a pair of detectives from Fort Gillem.'

Fort Gillem was in Georgia, which meant six to eight hours of waiting, maybe even longer. Holliday knew that the more time he spent at the Point the deeper he was going to sink into bureaucratic glue. The entire Academy was in an uproar over the situation and it was just going to get worse.

'Do we have any ID on him?' Holliday asked, knowing what the answer would be.

'No, sir,' said Sayers, shaking her head. 'Nothing but the tattoo.'

'Whoever he was he was nuts,' said the doctor. 'A crazy.'

Holliday picked up the knife from the stainless steel tray on the examining table. It was a carbon-steel Microtech Troodon with a five-inch out-the-front blade. A stiletto. A split second later and it would have been Holliday on the table with the blade buried in his heart. Not the kind of weapon a crazy person carried.

'Presumably we can agree that I didn't kill the guy,' said Holliday.

'I can vouch for that,' said the doctor. 'There's no doubt that it was suicide.'

'Good,' said Holliday. 'Because Rafi and I have business to attend to in New York.'

'The investigating officers from Fort Gillem will want to talk to you,' said Sergeant Sayers. 'They'll have questions. Homeland Security, too, I'll bet. Maybe you should stay on base . . . uh, sir.'

Holliday gave her the hard eyeball of a much senior officer.

'Is that an order, Sergeant?'

The young military cop got the message loud and clear. That kind of rank-pulling intimidation went against the grain for Holliday, but right now it was necessary.

'No, sir.'

'Good. I'll leave my cell phone number with your boss.' Holliday took a last look at the body, then turned on his heel and walked out of the cubicle, Rafi hard on his heels.

Holliday whistled up a motor pool car and they drove to the Burger King out by Mitchie Stadium on Stony Lonesome Road. True to his word Rafi packed away two enormous Double Croissan'Wiches loaded with eggs, ham and bacon, washed down with several cups of black coffee. Holliday managed to work his way through a single

English muffin with egg and sausage. He could still feel the last shakes of the adrenaline rush through his blood from his incident with the killer.

'You reacted so quickly. How did you know?' Rafi asked. A sobbing mother came in with her husband and a young girl, probably the sister of a new recruit they'd just said good-bye to for the next few months. Apparently Mom was going to drown her sorrows in hash browns.

'He was all wrong,' said Holliday. 'The uniform was right but any real senior cadet would have shaved better on "R" Day and the ring was on the wrong hand – always on the right, never the left. The glasses were wrong, too. You're only required to wear Army Issue BCGs during the first few weeks of Basic – Beast Barracks. After that you're allowed to wear your own.' Holliday took a swallow of coffee and felt it sour in his stomach on top of the sausage and egg. 'Our friend Sergeant Sayers snoops long enough, she's going to find a firstie in barracks who's missing a uniform.'

'What the hell is going on, Doc?' Rafi asked. 'First Peggy and now this.'

'They have to be connected. It would be too

much of a coincidence otherwise. The tattoo is the clincher.' Holliday frowned. 'Reminds me of Lutz Kellerman and his neo-Nazi friends.'

'You think the Templars are part of it?'

'Beads on a string,' said Holliday. 'According to you, Peggy was part of an expedition based on Templar texts. It would make sense.' He shook his head. 'It doesn't really matter. What matters is finding Peggy and getting her back.'

'Where do we start?'

'By heading for New York.'

'I was wondering about that,' said Rafi. 'What's the business we have there?'

'Catching a ride to JFK,' said Holliday, standing up and putting their garbage on a tray. 'We're going to France.'

They returned to Holliday's quarters, and Rafi waited while Holliday quickly packed a bag and retrieved the precious notebook the monk Rodrigues had given to him. Then they called a cab and headed into Highland Falls. Rafi rented a car there in his name and Holliday drove to New York City. They left the car at the Avis Park and Loc behind Penn Station on Thirty-first Street, then took a shuttle to JFK. By four in the afternoon they were boarding an Air France Airbus

330 direct flight to Paris. They went through security and passport control without incident, which meant that so far no one back at West Point had noticed their departure.

They sat in the rear AB seats on the port side of business class just in front of the galley. There were only two other passengers in their section – an overweight man in an expensive suit who broke wind in his sleep and an icy cold woman in a Chanel outfit and four-inch Prada heels who drank white wine steadily from the moment it was offered. Beside him Rafi dozed, fighting off jet lag that was in the process of reversing itself. For the first two hours of the flight Holliday stared out the window, watching as the Atlantic Ocean unrolled beneath the big wide-body's wings.

'I'm an idiot,' he muttered finally.

'What?' Rafi said blearily.

'I'm an idiot,' repeated Holliday.

'Why would that be?' Rafi asked, stretching and yawning.

'Motive,' answered Holliday. 'I should have been thinking about motive.'

'What are you talking about?'

'Why was this Brother Brasseur of yours

doing research into Templar texts in the Vatican?'

'I have no idea. Probably doing research into the Templar invasion of Egypt. He's an archaeologist.'

'A year ago an assassin from the Vatican attacked Peggy and me in Jerusalem. Now a tattooed freak tries to kill me at West Point.'

'Your point?'

'Why? What's the motive? I'm a history teacher. Peggy's a photographer. Why us?'

'Your connection to the Templar sword. The treasure trove of scrolls you found in the Azores.'

'This isn't some whacko story about religious conspiracies and whether or not Jesus had a sex life. People don't kill each other over bits and pieces of history, no matter how historically valuable.'

Rafi shrugged. 'Okay. Why?'

'Money,' said Holliday firmly. 'This whole thing has been about money right from the start.'

'Explain that.'

'We followed the trail of the sword from my uncle Henry's house all the way to that cave on Corvo in the Azores. Rodrigues showed Peggy and me a hundred thousand gold-cased scrolls from the Library at Alexandria and half a dozen ancient storehouses. A wealth of history, enough to keep scholars happy for a hundred years. Longer. A treasure.'

'The treasure of the Templars,' agreed Rafi.

'For years now I've taught my students that the Templars, at least initially, were really no more than an organized troop of highwaymen, preying on pilgrims more than protecting them. Carrying the banner of the Templars was an excuse to kill and plunder in the name of Christ. They were thugs; gangsters in shining armor.'

'And you were wrong.'

'No. I was right. Dead right, and I should have remembered that. The scrolls in that cave on Corvo weren't the treasure at all.' Holliday reached into the inside pocket of his sports jacket. He took out the thick notebook given to him by Helder Rodrigues as the old man lay dying in his arms. It was a tan, suede-covered, 240-page moleskin notebook with a tattered strap. It looked very old. There were water stains on the cover and spatters of dried blood: the blood of the dying ex-priest. 'This was the real treasure,' said Holliday, handing Rafi the notebook. 'A thousand names and addresses that Rodrigues copied

33

down sometime back before World War Two and kept updated until he died. Companies, families and individuals all with allegiance to the original Templar fortune dating back to the thirteenth century. Templar Incorporated. *This* is what the killer in Jerusalem was after. *This* was what Kellerman and his Nazis were after, and the assassin at West Point as well.'

'AstroEur,' said Rafi, reading the first name on the list.

'Hotels all over the world, four thousand of them. Catering for every major passenger rail company in Europe. Three billion euros a year.'

'Atreal et Cie?'

'Real estate all over Europe and Southeast Asia. Even bigger.'

'Breugier Telecom. Cell phones?'

'And cable TV,' added Holliday.

'Crédit Alliance SA?'

'The second-largest retail bank in France.'

'And these are all Templar operations?'

'One way or another. I've barely touched the surface but it's pretty clear how it works. A dozen small companies, companies that no one would ever notice, invest in a larger company, eventually securing a majority control. I took a company called Aretco, a huge multinational, and traced it all the way back to a company called Veritas Rochelle, a shipping insurance underwriter going back to the early nineteenth century. Veritas Rochelle was owned by a single Cistercian monastery in the Dordogne region. According to the head of the monastery, ownership of the company had been willed to the monastery by one Guy d'Isoard de Vauvenargues, a count from Aix-en-Provence. As it turns out the Count de Vauvenargues family on his mother's side goes back to Robert de Everingham, one of the early Norman Templars in England. It's like a huge, endless jigsaw puzzle.'

Rafi shrugged. A blonde flight attendant in a natty suit and kerchief asked him if he wanted a drink. He shook his head and she shimmered off. 'Okay,' he said. 'So all these companies, or at least their financing, all have their origins with the Templars. That was then. This is now. What does it mean in the present? I mean, *so what?*'

'I ran through a hundred of the interconnecting companies for the first five names on that list. The majority share holdings of all one hundred companies are held by Pelerin and Cie, Banquiers Privés. Does that name ring a bell?'

'Castle Pelerin in Israel. Where we found the Silver Scroll.'

'The very one,' said Holliday grimly. 'It is, or was, a private bank. Private banks are owned by individuals and they don't have to declare their assets. Pretty good cover if you're trying to hide old Templar money. There are only three people on the board of directors of Pelerin and Cie, none of whom I had ever heard of: Sebastien Armand, Pierre Pouget and George Lorelot. Between them it looked as though they controlled about a hundred billion euros in assets. That's a whole hell of a lot of euros, pal. And *that's* enough to kill for.'

'You used the past tense – "it *looked* as though" they controlled a hundred billion euros.'

'That's because all three people on the board of Pelerin and Cie are dead. Armand in 1926, Pouget in 1867, and Lorelot in 1962. The only thing they have in common is that they're in the same row in a cemetery in the village of Domme in the Aquitaine district of France.'

'So Pelerin and Cie is a front?' Rafi asked.

'I don't know yet. The estates of all three men are handled by an *avocat* – a lawyer in the village named Pierre Ducos. It took almost eight months to track Ducos down after I started trying to decipher the notebook. He's the person we're going to see in France.'

'You think he'll be any help?'

'I think he's the only lead we've got.'

4

Driving a rental Peugeot 407, Holliday and Rafi rolled across the Dordogne River on the centuries-old stone bridge at Cenac-et-St-Julien and found themselves in a landscape that had changed very little since the time it had been the realm of Richard the Lionheart's mother, Queen Eleanor of Aquitaine, eight hundred years before. It was early afternoon, a day after their arrival in Paris, and the sun shone down from a perfect blue sky. Summertime in the south of France was a storybook come to life.

With the exception of the odd highway here and there the valley of the Dordogne was the same patchwork of fields that had existed since the Middle Ages, dotted about with walled villages, hillsides dark with forest, the earth itself as black as pitch and capable of growing almost anything.

Ahead of them the steep cliff rose from the banks of the winding river, cloaked in a protective skirt of evergreens. At the top of the cliff on a long angular plateau they could see the walls and the castle keep where more than seventy Knights Templar were imprisoned after the sudden dissolution of the Order in 1307.

Just before the little village on the far side of the bridge they turned sharply to the right. The fields and the river were lost to view as the car plunged into the forest and began the long switchback climb up the escarpment. Craning his neck and looking up through the windshield, Rafi could barely see the base of the old city walls. In the twelfth century any attack on the fortified village would have been next to impossible without a long siege and the complete deforestation of the hillside.

'Strange to think what the world was like when this place was built,' Rafi said as they continued upward.

'Full of violence and superstition,' said Holliday from behind the wheel. They had been driving since leaving their Paris hotel early that morning, going due south for the better part of three hundred miles, making only bathroom stops and a half hour halt just outside Limoges for a quick sandwich-and-coffee-to-go lunch at an Autogrill on the highway. 'For all the talk of knights in shining armor, I wouldn't give you five cents for life in the Middle Ages. Smokey rooms, bad hygiene, rotten teeth and the plague. Not my idea of a good time.' They drove on in silence, the forest on both sides dark and gloomy.

'I'm still not sure that this isn't all a waste of time,' said Rafi, finally. It had been a theme he'd been harping on ever since they'd arrived in France, and his chafing arguments were starting to irritate Holliday. 'I can't see how talking to this Pierre Ducos is going to get us any closer to finding Peggy.' The Israeli shook his head. 'We should be talking to the police in Alexandria.'

'That and five dollars at Starbucks should be just about enough for a cup of coffee in Egypt,' Holliday answered, negotiating yet another hairpin turn on the tree-covered hillside. The Peugeot was beginning to strain and he dropped the transmission into low. 'You really think the Egyptian authorities are going to give much time and energy to an Israeli and his American friend trying to track down a bunch of Catholic priests?' He glanced over at his companion. 'Or do you have friends in the Mukhabarat that I don't know about?' he asked, referring to the Egyptian version of the CIA.

'I've told you a hundred times, Doc: I went to school with a guy who works for Mossad now. As far as I know he does something with computers. That's my only connection with spooks and spies, really.' He shook his head again, his expression tense with worry. 'If I had pull with Israeli Intelligence I would have used it by now, believe me.'

'Whatever,' Holliday answered wearily. 'We'll see what Ducos has to say and take it from there.'

'What makes you think he'll even talk to you?' Rafi asked.

'I know the secret handshake,' replied Holliday.

They made a final turn and drove through the twin-towered, high-arched gate in the fortress wall that surrounded the town. The streets were narrow, stone buildings on either side almost a thousand years old, windows shuttered, roofs slate, doors with iron strap hinges. There wasn't a modern building to be seen. They found the French lawyer's office in a small building next to a bistro named Godard with a sign showing a plump goose waddling across a village street.

Directly across from the office there was a tiny hotel called the Relais des Chevaliers. The street was so narrow Holliday had to park the car with the offside wheels up on the sidewalk to give another vehicle space to pass.

'Built for horses and carts, not cars,' commented Holliday. He knocked on the heavy wooden-planked door and waited. Nothing happened.

'Maybe he's not there,' Rafi said.

Holliday rapped harder. Still nothing.

'Maybe he doesn't exist,' said Rafi, his tone a little acidic.

Holliday ignored the comment. He tried the latch and the door opened. He stuck his head into the doorway. The interior of the building was dark and cool. Holliday stepped into a cramped, low-ceilinged hallway. Rafi followed. The walls were plaster, mottled with age. There was a wrought iron chandelier above them that looked as though it had been designed for candles. 'Hello?' Holliday called out. Somewhere there was a rasping cough.

'*Viens*,' called out a thin voice. Come. The voice echoed from behind a door on the left side of the hallway. Holliday opened the door and stepped inside the room, Rafi on his heels.

The office was from another time, like something out of *Les Misérables.*

An ancient case clock ticked away loudly in one corner. Rows of wooden file cabinets lined one wall and a spindly looking secretary's desk with pigeonhole cubicles above it stood against another. Light leaked into the room through cracks in the shutters over the large window, dust dancing in the broad beams of sun. The floors were wide yellow oak planks worn smooth of any varnish. Looking out from across an enormous desk, a large man with wavy snow-white hair sat in a high-backed velvet chair. There were two identical chairs on the other side of the desk.

The man appeared to be in his late seventies or early eighties, fat but well preserved. His skin had the faintly translucent look of parchment. His nose was a beak and the eyes were large and gray behind half-lens reading glasses framed in bright blue plastic. He was wearing a wide-lapel blue suit that had gone out of style half a century ago.

The front of the jacket was speckled with bits of ash from the fuming curved stem pipe held between the large man's lips. From where Holliday stood it looked as though the pants were drawn up almost to his elbows. The shirt was as white as the man's luxurious head of hair and obviously starched.

'Mr Ducos?' Holliday asked.

'*Oui,*' said the fat man. '*Je suis* Ducos.'

'Do you speak English?'

'Of course,' said Ducos. 'Several other languages as well, including a little Hebrew.' He smiled pleasantly at Rafi.

'I didn't know it showed,' said the archaeologist.

'It doesn't,' said Ducos. 'But I'm well aware of who you are, Dr Wanounou, and you as well, Colonel Holliday.'

'And how's that?' Holliday asked.

'On the telephone you said you knew Helder Rodrigues, Colonel,' said Ducos. 'That is sufficient to catch my attention.'

'You knew him?' Holliday asked. The south of France was a long way from the remote island in the Azores that had been the old man's home.

'For many years.' Ducos paused. 'Do you know what I seek?' he asked obscurely.

'You seek what was lost,' answered Holliday. Rafi gave him a long look.

'And who lost it?'

'The King lost it.'

'And where is the King?'

'Burning in Hell,' said Holliday with a smile.

'Do you mind letting me in on your secret?' Rafi asked. 'I'm feeling a little bit out of the loop.'

Ducos explained. 'After the dissolution of the Templars under the aegis of King Philip in 1307, fugitive members of the Order needed a way of recognizing each other safely. They devised a number of secret exchanges.'

'The secret handshake,' said Holliday.

'That particular one was used between Father Rodrigues and myself,' Ducos continued. 'It was written in the back of the notebook he kept.' He looked at Holliday. 'You have it?'

'Yes.' He took it out of the inside pocket of his jacket and slid it across the desk towards the old man. Ducos's large, age-gnarled hand reached out and he laid his palm over the notebook. Holliday saw that a tear had formed in the corner of one eye. Ducos made no move to wipe it away.

'His blood?' Ducos asked.

'Yes. He died protecting the secret of the scrolls,' said Holliday. 'He died in my arms.'

'So Tavares told me,' Ducos said and nodded.

Manuel Tavares, the captain of the fishing boat *San Pedro* and the other gatekeeper of the Templar hoard on the island of Corvo.

'We have a problem,' said Rafi urgently.

'Do you refer to the disappearance of Miss Blackstock in Egypt or the recent attempt on the life of Colonel Holliday?' Ducos asked.

'You know about that?' Holliday said, startled. 'It's barely been forty-eight hours.'

Ducos took the pipe out of his mouth and smiled, the thin lips opening to reveal a neat row of large, pure white and obviously false teeth, made in some long-ago era.

'One of the advantages of belonging to an order that has been in existence for close to a thousand years is the number and the extent of the ears to the ground which are available,' said the old man.

'The man who tried to kill me isn't important now; we have to find Peggy. Quickly,' replied Holliday.

'Tell me everything you know,' said Ducos.

In the end it wasn't very much. The Frenchman listened to what there was, leaning back in his chair and puffing on his pipe. When Rafi was finished, Ducos asked Holliday a few questions about the attack at West Point, then fell silent, staring at the ceiling thoughtfully. Finally he spoke, the words measured and precise.

'The man who attempted to kill you was almost certainly a member of La Sapinière, the French arm of Sodalitium Pianum, the Vatican Secret Service. They were first written about in fiction by the late Thomas Gifford and more recently by your Mr Dan Brown in his *Da Vinci Code*. The tattoo is sure evidence of this – it is the sigil, or crest of Pope Pius X, who instituted the original group in the early nineteen hundreds. They are also known as the Assassini and sometimes as the Instrument of God. They are willing to sacrifice their very souls as martyrs to a higher cause.'

'But why try and kill me?' Holliday asked. 'What's their motive?'

'And what does it have to do with Peggy's disappearance?' Rafi asked angrily. 'We're sitting here talking about theological voodoo and she's in danger. What possible connection is there?'

'I suggest that the shared motive is a sense of imminent danger. The Vatican obviously sees Colonel Holliday as a threat. I would say the same holds true for Miss Blackstock. Either she alone or the expedition as a whole discovered something that the Brotherhood of Isis perceives to be a threat as well. The connection is quite clear. Brasseur must have triggered La Sapinière's interest while he was doing his research at the Vatican and whatever he found in the Templar documents in the Secret Archives led to the kidnapping of the group in the desert.'

'That's insane,' argued Rafi. 'It's oil and water. Islamic terrorists and the Vatican?'

'Oil and water indeed,' said Ducos calmly. He paused for a moment, took a kitchen match from the pocket of his ancient suit jacket and scratched it alight on one yellowed thumbnail. He relit his pipe, sucking noisily and blowing clouds of smoke into the air, swirling into the broad sunbeams coming through the shutters. 'Oil and water indeed,' he repeated. 'And since oil and water do not usually mix, Doctor, as a scientist I would suggest that you search for an emulsifier, some common cause.'

'Could it be something as simple as territory?' Holliday asked. 'The expedition crossed into the Brotherhood's turf?' He shrugged. 'Maybe they were affronted by a bunch of Catholic priests defiling their sacred land or something.'

'Possible but unlikely, Colonel. I was born much closer to the nineteenth century than the twenty-first but I have kept up with events, I think. There are few true believers anymore. Terrorist organizations are like political campaigns – they're always in need of money and volunteers. There are the cynical among us who believe, with good reason, that 9/11 was nothing more than a publicity stunt by bin Laden to raise his stature among his peers. In the nineties all he could be blamed for was a failed assassination attempt and some complicity in the Dar es Salaam and Nairobi embassy bombings. Instead of being the rich, favored son of an Arab sheik he was a nobody and a poor one at that. Just prior to 9/11 his family had cut off his seven-million-dollar-a-year allowance. He needed a fund-raiser. The Brotherhood are no different.'

'Then Doc is right – it's really all about money,' Rafi said.

'The Brotherhood is a small group and it has no real backer,' Ducos said. 'With Qaddafi in America's bed once more they have been cast adrift. The Brotherhood's territory ranges from

Qare on the edge of the Qattara Depression to Jaghbub on the far side of the border.'

The old man levered himself upright, wincing as he did so, palms flat on the desk. He lumbered over to the filing cabinets, opened one of the drawers and withdrew a buff-colored file. He brought the file to his desk, sat down again with a little sigh and pulled an eight-by-ten photograph out of the folder. He slid it across the desk to Holliday.

The photograph showed a young man in sunglasses wearing shorts and a black T-shirt that read *I Was There: Solar Eclipse 2006-03-29*. Directly behind him two turbaned men were talking beside a battered Toyota Land Cruiser. On the right edge of the picture Holliday could see some pale-colored ruins of what might have once been stone huts.

'This photograph was taken by a Canadian tourist chasing the 2006 eclipse. It was taken at the ruins at the small oasis of Tazirbu in the central Sahara. The two men talking in the background are Sulaiman al-Barouni on the left and Mahmoud Tekbali on the right.' Holliday looked closely. Al-Barouni looked much older than his companion. His face was drawn and deeply lined, skin drawn tightly over his bladelike cheekbones. Tekbali was younger, his face darker, his eyes covered by expensive Serengeti Driver sunglasses.

'Exactly who are they?' Rafi asked, looking over Holliday's shoulder.

'Tekbali is a senior officer in the Brotherhood, second in command to Mustafa Ahmed Ben Halim, the founder and leader of the group.'

'So what's the significance of the photograph?' Holliday asked.

'It is significant because Sulaiman al-Barouni is the chief go-between for a man named Antonio Neri. Neri is the boss of an Italian criminal organization known as La Santa. Neri's specialty is smuggling women, drugs and valuable artifacts. Contrary to the Great Leader's press releases concerning the satanic evil of the American drug culture, Libya has long been an alternative location for the Marseilles morphine labs. As well there is always a supply of village women looking for broader horizons, and Libya and Egypt have been doing a thriving business in tomb raiding and artifact smuggling for thousands of years.' The old man lifted his sagging shoulders in a Gallic shrug. 'The Vatican. La Santa. The Brotherhood.'

'Oil and water,' said Rafi.

'A common cause,' said Holliday.

'Indeed,' said Ducos, and smiled.

5

It was like stepping into a Humphrey Bogart movie; any minute now you expected a sloe-eyed Lauren Bacall to appear with a cigarette in her hand, looking for someone to light her up. The interior of the Bar Maritime in the Vieux Port of Marseilles was all brown wood and thirties-style, down-at-the-heels and I-don't-give-a-damn décor complete with a sleepy bartender and just as sleepy patrons nodding on their high stools over their pastis and Stella Artois, with hungrier patrons chowing down on *escargots* or *petit quiche* or a big bowl of local steamed mussels, the *coquillage* that formed the mainstay of the *bouillabaisse* that was the foundation of every menu on the Azure Coast.

Holliday and Rafi Wanounou were sitting at a small round table at the front window, soaking up the atmosphere. The remains of lunch were still on the table as well as their coffee cups. Seated with them was Louis Japrisot, a captain in the Police Nationale de France, formerly known as the Sûreté. Japrisot was short and stocky with a broad, jowled face, a lot of gray-stubbled five o'clock shadow and a bristling salt-and-pepper Stalin mustache, of the soup strainer variety. He appeared to be in his late fifties.

He had fierce black eyes, eyebrows like his mustache and a military-style short back and sides crew cut. Somewhere along the line he'd had his nose broken and he had a bull neck. Underneath the wrinkled brown suit the muscles of his arms and shoulders flexed like a boxer's. Sitting still was something he didn't do very well. He smoked Gitanes continuously, the harsh cigarettes disappearing into his big butcher's hands.

'Been a cop long?' Holliday asked, looking for something to say. Japrisot wasn't the most voluble person he'd ever met, even though his English was excellent.

'Thirty-one years. Before that the Prévôtales in Algeria.'

'Prévôtales? Provost Corp? Military Police?'

'Yes, Le Légion étrangère, what you call the Foreign Legion.'

'Bad times,' commented Holliday.

'Very bad,' said Japrisot. He shrugged. 'Better for me than others however,' he murmured.

'How so?'

Japrisot's heavy shoulders lifted again.

'I wasn't at Dien Bien Phu.'

'There is that,' Holliday said and nodded. The Battle of Dien Bien Phu had been the last encounter of the war in Indochina for the French and a ghastly preview of the coming war in Vietnam for the United States. More than a thousand soldiers died during the prolonged battle and several thousand more were taken prisoner, never to be heard from again.

Japrisot stared out the window and smoked. Across the quay the Vieux Port was a forest of masts. Once the central port of the city, the Vieux Port was now reserved for pleasure craft and the local fishing fleet. On the far side of the narrow harbor a line of pale yellow seventeenth- and eighteenth-century buildings rose in a solid wall. At the far end of the harbor was a narrow plaza where the daily fish market was staged, and rising away from it was la Canebière, a broad triumphant avenue that led up the steep hill the old city was built on, leading to the basilica on the summit. The only thing Holliday remembered about Marseille was that King Alexander Karageorgevich I of Serbia had been assassinated there in 1934, the first political murder ever caught on film.

'All I know about Marseille is *The French Connection*,' offered Rafi.

'Popeye-goddamn-bloody-Doyle,' muttered Japrisot, stubbing out his cigarette in a big enameled Cinzano ashtray in the middle of the table. 'He put a curse on this place. *Connard!*'

'Things aren't as bad as the movie made out?' Holliday asked.

'They are actually much worse,' said Japrisot. 'Sometimes I think the film made it that way with all the publicity it was given. Still, the tourists come and ask if they can see where the heroin is made. *Merde!* It gives the place a reputation, yes? Not a good one. We have Disney cruise ships and you hear them talking, Gene Hackman this, Gene Hackman that.'

'They don't smuggle drugs here?' Rafi asked.

'Of course they smuggle drugs here. They smuggle everything here,' answered Japrisot. 'Morphine, pornography, girls, Africans, toothpaste, cigarettes. Cigarettes. A great many cigarettes. Le Milieu smuggles anything to make a profit. Last year it was false teeth from the Ukraine.'

'Le Milieu?' Holliday asked.

'Marseille's version of the Mafia, the under-world,' explained Japrisot. 'They started off mostly as stevedores, controlling the waterfront in the late forties and early fifties, then moved from there. After the war they got into drugs in a big way.'

'Is our guy Valador one of this Milieu?' Rafi asked.

Japrisot let out a snorting laugh, smoke rushing out of his nostrils like an animated bull in a cartoon.

'Little Felix!?' Japrisot said. 'Felix Valador barely knows his mother's name, let alone anyone in Le Milieu. He's strictly small-time. Sometimes he brings a few hundred cartons of cigarettes in for the Corsicans, sometimes knockoff Rolexes from a Hong Kong freighter. Connecting with La Santa is a big step up for him, believe me. We got lucky, my friends – of that, I have no doubt.'

A boat came through the narrow entrance to the Vieux Port. It was an old-fashioned harbor trawler, perhaps forty-two feet long, the high deckhouse set far back towards the stern. Once upon a time she'd been painted blue and white;

now she was just dirty, rusty tear tracks running down from her ironwork, dark stains everywhere from bilge runoff, her brightwork dull under a layer of grease. Her license number was painted in large figures on her bow and there was a name-plate on her transom as she passed, heading towards the tent-covered fish market on the plaza at the end of the harbor.

'That's her, Valador's boat, *La Fougueux*,' said Japrisot. 'In English, *Tempestuous*, I think.'

'Now what?' Rafi asked.

'Perhaps we should go for a little stroll,' suggested the French policeman. He lit another cigarette, stood up, flicked ash off his bright yellow tie and stepped out into the sun-dappled afternoon. Rafi followed. Sighing, Holliday dropped three fifty-euro notes on the table to cover their tab and went after them. Japrisot hadn't shown the slightest sign of paying for his own lunch even though he'd been the one to order wine. Apparently whatever his obligation was to the old lawyer Ducos it didn't include cash.

The Rive Nueve, the New Side of the old port, seemed to be wall-to-wall restaurants and bars. There was everything from a Moroccan place called Habib's to an Irish pub and a German beer garden called Kanter's. They made their way down the broad quayside, keeping on the shady side, threading their way around café tables full of patrons finishing lunch and enjoying the weather.

Holliday watched as *La Fougueux* tied up at the dock, nestled beside the little double-ended, black-hulled ferry that took tourists from one side of the harbor to the other for a few euro. A blond-haired man stepped out onto the foredeck wearing a bright red nylon shell. He looked tall and athletic, somewhere in his thirties. Another man appeared, shorter, heavier and older. Together they started hauling fifty-kilo rope-handled fish boxes up on deck.

Holliday, Rafi and Japrisot walked across the Rive Nueve and stood looking out over the water, leaning on the beige metal fence that ran around the seawall. Japrisot flicked the butt of one cigarette down into the oily water and lit another. A young woman was sunbathing topless on a sailboat almost directly below them. The boat was a Contessa 32, named *Dirty Girl*. The sunbathing woman was much larger than that, at least a 38. Japrisot paid no attention.

'The one in the red shell is Valador,' he said.

'The older man is Kerim Zituni. A Tunisian. Some people say he was Black September once upon a time. Others that he was one of the Tunisian Black Suits – their secret police.'

'Is that signifigant?' Holliday asked.

'He's old enough for it to mean that he probably worked with Walter Rauff,' answered Japrisot.

'Never heard of him.' Holliday shrugged.

'I have,' said Rafi, his voice dull. 'He murdered my grandparents. He was one of the men who invented the mobile gas trucks the Nazis used in the sub-camps. He was also in charge of the Final Solution in North Africa. He rounded up all the Jews in Morocco and Tunisia and exterminated them. If Rommel had taken Egypt, Rauff's next step would have been Palestine.'

'What happened to him?'

'He died in Chile in 1984. Peacefully, in his sleep,' answered Japrisot. 'He was seventy-eight. He was an intelligence advisor to Pinochet.'

'So we take it this Zituni is not a nice man,' said Holliday dryly.

'And potentially very dangerous,' Japrisot said and nodded.

They kept watching the ship as Felix Valador

and his Tunisian companion continued to stack fish boxes on the deck. At forty boxes they stopped and Valador began humping the boxes down onto the narrow plaza and loading them into a bright red boxy old Citroën HY van with corrugated sheet metal sides. A sign on the side of the van read *Poissonnerie Valador* in gold with a phone number beneath. He loaded the first ten boxes through the side door and the rest through the doors at the back of the van.

'Notice the order,' commented Japrisot, watching as Valador loaded the boxes one at a time.

'Last ones out of the hold went into the truck first,' said Rafi.

'Remember that,' said Japrisot.

'He's almost done,' said Holliday.

'*Bien,*' murmured Japrisot. He flipped yet another cigarette butt into the greasy water, nodded pleasantly to the young lady on the deck of the *Dirty Girl* and turned away. '*Attendez-moi,*' he instructed. He climbed into an angle-parked, dark blue Peugeot 607 four-door sedan, probably the most ubiquitous car on the highways of France. This one was almost ten years old and looked like a well-used taxi, which was probably the point.

Rafi got into the back and Holliday slid in beside Japrisot. He wrinkled his nose. The inside of the car smelled like an ashtray and the windshield was fogged with a slightly yellow film of old nicotine. Japrisot lit another Gitane and switched on the ignition. The car chugged to life. The French cop watched as Valador finished loading the fish boxes into the rattletrap van and then had a brief conversation with Kerim Zituni. Conversation over, Zituni climbed back onto *La Fougueux* while Valador started up the Citroën and drove off. Japrisot followed the square-nosed little truck. They headed east, staying well behind the van, moving steadily away from the center of town.

'He's not going on the Autoroute,' commented Rafi. On their right hand the Mediterranean glowed like an immense blue jewel, bright light bursting off the sun-dazzled facets of the waves sweeping in to crash against the base of the craggy limestone cliffs.

'No,' answered Japrisot, 'he's following the coast.'

'You've done this before,' said Holliday.

'*Bien sûr,*' answered Japrisot. 'Several times.'

They spent the rest of the afternoon and into

the early evening tracking the Citroën along the length of the Côte d'Azur, stopping to make deliveries in the towns of Cassis and La Ciotat, then bypassing the larger city of Toulon before stopping again in Hyeres, Bregancon, Le Rayol and Frejus.

In Cassis the van stopped in front of Chez Nino's on the harbor front, delivered a box of fish and then moved on. It was the same each time they stopped. In Ciotat it was Kitch and Cook; in Hyeres it was the Hotel Ceinturon. Bregancon was a motel-style place called Les Palmiers; in Le Rayol it was a rustic-looking old winery called l'Huître et la Vigne – the Oyster and the Vine. In Frejus it was a gaudy Moroccan dining room called La Medina. In none of these places did he leave more than three of the boxes and usually only one. By the time the sun was beginning to set they had reached suburban Cannes and the huge Florida white slab of the Royal Casino Hotel in Mandelieu-la-Napoule, complete with a six-story-high blue and yellow flashing neon image of a slot machine on the side of the building. A little bit of Vegas on the French Riviera.

The Casino Hotel was part of a complex of

interconnected buildings right on the beach beside a river estuary that led back to the Cannes Marina and the Mandelieu Golf Course. Japrisot parked the Peugeot in the fifteen-minute lot in front of the hotel and they watched as Felix Valador took a dolly loaded with two boxes of fish around to a side entrance. Presumably he was going to the hotel kitchen.

At the main entrance a good-looking, well-dressed European with a neatly trimmed Vandyke beard climbed out of a blue Audi Quattro with his beautiful companion and slipped one of the car jockeys a folded bill. The valet parker looked at the bill, saluted the bearded man and climbed into the Audi.

'He paid him not to park the car in the big lot under the overpass,' explained the French cop, nodding toward the busy Avenue General de Gaulle behind them. 'It's blackmail, really. Local boys sneak into the parking lot and sometimes roll cars right into the water. *P'tit loubards!* Little hooligans. Worse than the English football yobs sometimes.'

The elegant couple strolled into the hotel and the car jockey drove the Audi a hundred feet up the driveway. A few minutes later Valador reappeared with the empty dolly.

'That's eighteen boxes of fish spread over almost a hundred miles,' said Rafi from the backseat. 'He can't be making much money.'

'It's the last stop that's the important one,' said Japrisot obscurely.

Valador climbed wearily up into the Citroën and drove off. He headed for the service road that led to the parking lot on the other side of the overpass. The little truck disappeared.

'Where the hell is he going?' Holliday asked.

'Watch,' murmured Japrisot.

A few minutes later the van reappeared. The gold lettering on the side of the truck had been covered by a magnetic sign that read *Camille Guimard – Antiquaire, 28, rue Felix Faure Le Suquet, Cannes.*

'Who's Camille Guimard?' Rafi asked from the backseat.

'Felix is,' said the French policeman. 'In Marseille Valador is a smelly fisherman. In Cannes he is a sophisticated antique dealer named Guimard. *Une grandes blague, n'est-ce pas?* A neat trick, yes?'

'And Le Suquet?' Holliday asked.

'Like El Souk in the Kasbah of Marrakech,' explained Japrisot as Valador's transformed Citroën rattled by. 'The old quarter of the city, up on the hill.' He put the Peugeot in Drive and followed the van at a discreet distance. Ten minutes later, driving along the Boulevard du Midi at the water's edge, they reached Cannes and Le Suquet, a rabbit warren of narrow, twisting streets that rose up from the stone quays of the Old Port to the formidable square tower of the eleventh-century castle built by the Cistercian monks of Lerins.

'Cistercians again,' said Rafi after Japrisot explained the geography. 'They're everywhere.'

'Pardon?' the Frenchman asked, frowning.

'A private joke,' said Holliday.

They followed the Citroën around the harbor then turned up the lush treelined boulevard of rue Louis Pasteur and started to climb the hill. Valador turned right onto rue Meynadier. They crossed the wider rue Louis Blanc, then turned abruptly into an alley that seemed to take them down the hill again. It was fully dark now but Japrisot was driving with only his parking lights.

'I'm lost,' said Holliday.

'I'm not,' said Japrisot.

'We're going around in circles.'

'It's the one-way streets,' said Japrisot, cocking one bushy eyebrow. 'They're everywhere.'

The policeman slowed and they watched Valador turn right and disappear from view.

'He's getting away,' said Rafi.

'No, he's not,' answered Japrisot, his voice calm. He cracked his window, flipped out his cigarette butt and lit another. Holliday had long ago lost track of how many the burly man had smoked, but strangely enough he found himself enjoying the rich earthy scent of the *tabac noir*. They waited in the alley for almost ten minutes. Holliday could hear Rafi fidgeting in the backseat. The French cop smoked. Finally Japrisot glanced at the illuminated dial of his wristwatch.

'Bien,' he said and nodded. *'On y va.'* Let's go. He eased the shift back and they rolled slowly out of the alley. According to the sign they were now on the rue Felix Faure, another one-way street, this one lined with small shops. Japrisot slid the Peugeot into a parking space on the far side of the street. At the end of the block Valador was unloading the van. He was parked in front of a narrow shuttered storefront, unloading the last of the fish boxes. Beside the store,

taking up the entire corner, was the awning-covered façade of a restaurant with a brightly lit green and yellow sign that read *Huitres Astoux & Brun*.

'An oyster bar,' said Holliday, realizing that they hadn't eaten since lunch in Marseille.

There were a dozen or so plastic tables under the white fabric awning, all empty. A fat man in a long white apron was chaining plastic stacking chairs. The restaurant was closing.

'What now?' Rafi asked.

Japrisot shrugged.

'We wait. We smoke. Perhaps we talk about women.' He paused and smiled. 'Who knows? The night is long.'

Valador finished his unloading, locked up the van and disappeared inside the store. A few seconds later a light could be seen behind the shutters. Almost half an hour passed. Then the light in the shop went out, and after a few moments another light went on, this time in the apartment above the store.

'He's gone to bed,' said Rafi, a note of anger in his voice.

'I think perhaps you are right,' said Japrisot.

Rafi snorted.

'So we spent half the day following a guy all the way along the Riviera delivering fish and this is what it amounts to? Watching him get ready for sleep?'

'Police work is mostly waiting,' answered Japrisot. 'And very boring. I'm afraid you must be patient.'

'Rafi's right,' said Holliday finally. 'My cousin has been taken hostage. We don't have time for staking out some low-level smuggler. We need information. Now.'

'Stakeout?' the French cop said. 'You mean *comme le bifteck? Une barbeque?*' Japrisot lifted his caterpillar eyebrows and winked. Holliday scowled, realizing that he was being teased.

The headlights of an approaching car washed through the rear window of the Peugeot.

'Attendez,' said Japrisot, and hunched down in his seat. Holliday and Rafi did the same. The car went past, then parked between a pair of wrought iron stanchions at the curb in front of the dark, deserted restaurant. There was an old-fashioned streetlight on the corner and Holliday could see the car clearly. It was a dark blue Audi Quattro.

Two people got out: a well-dressed man with a Vandyke beard and a highly attractive woman in a short black cocktail dress.

'That's the couple I saw at the casino,' whispered Holliday. 'What are they doing here?'

'As they say in my country, Colonel Holliday, *Tout vient à point à qui sait attendre*. Good things come to those who wait.'

6

They watched as the couple from the Audi walked back along the sidewalk in front of the restaurant and paused in front of Felix Valador's store. There was an intercom box high on the left-hand side of the doorframe. The man with the Vandyke reached into his jacket and took something out of the pocket.

'What's that?' Holliday asked, squinting.

'*Gants de latex, je pense,*' said Japrisot. 'Surgical gloves, I think.'

The man with the beard deftly snapped the gloves onto his hands, then pressed a button on the plastic intercom box and waited. A few seconds later there was a loud buzzing sound and the bearded man leaned forward to speak. His companion kept her back to the door, looking up and down the street. Without the film festival, night-time in Cannes was relatively quiet. The sidewalks were deserted.

There was a second buzz from the intercom,

and then a heavy clicking sound Holliday could hear from halfway down the block. The door opened and the couple from the blue Audi disappeared inside the store. A moment later the light came on behind the shutters over the front windows.

Japrisot took a small notebook and a gold-plated automatic pencil from his sagging suit coat pocket and climbed out of the Citroën. He walked down the street and wrote down the license number of the Audi. Thirty seconds later he slipped back into the car.

'AHX 37 45,' he said. 'Czech. I think "A" is for Prague.'

'What do the Czechs have to do with any of this?' Rafi asked.

Japrisot turned in his seat.

'Maybe nothing, maybe everything.' The policeman shrugged. 'Prague was once the European end of the old Silk Road. It is still a central point for smugglers. You can find anything you want in Prague from beautiful Russian girls to heroin from Bangkok. Why not stolen artifacts?' He held up a finger. *'Moment.'* He dug a cell phone out of his jacket pocket and let out a burst of rapid-fire French. He snapped the cell phone closed and returned it to his pocket. 'Now we wait again.'

No more than two minutes later the lights in the store went off. Almost immediately the woman from the Audi stepped out and stood by the door, wiping her hands on a tissue. She looked up and down the street, then turned and spoke through the open doorway behind her. The man with the Vandyke stepped out, carefully closing the door behind him, then stripped off the latex gloves and slipped them back into his pocket. He stood for a moment, then reached into his other pocket and brought out a flat gold cigarette case. He took out a cigarette, put the case away, then pulled something from his lapel and began delicately poking at the filter.

'What the hell is he doing?' Holliday asked.

'I know *precisement* what he is doing,' said Japrisot with a grimace. 'He is putting pinholes in the paper of the cigarette. It is something long-time smokers do to convince themselves they are being healthy.'

'That's crazy,' said Rafi from the backseat.

'*Bien sûr,*' replied Japrisot. 'Of course. Smoking is for crazy people, yes?'

They watched as the bearded man brought out a heavy-looking gold lighter and lit his cigarette.

Then the couple walked back up the street to the Audi and got in. The engine started, the headlights came on and they drove off. They turned right on rue Louis Blanc and went up the hill.

'They were in there for less than three minutes,' said Rafi. 'I timed it.'

'Not very long,' said Holliday. 'What kind of business can you do in three minutes?'

'Bad business,' said Japrisot. He stared out the window at the darkened storefront. He slapped the steering wheel with the palm of his hand. *'Je suis une connard! Nique ma mere!'* He swore under his breath. 'Something is wrong.'

The Frenchman sat for a moment, his features grim.

'M-e-r-d-e,' he breathed, drawing out the word. Finally he reached across the console, popped open the glove compartment and took out an ancient and enormous Manhurin-73 revolver with a wooden crosshatched 'blackjack' grip and a huge five-inch barrel.

'Big gun,' commented Holliday, impressed. The revolver was chambered for .357 rounds. It was the French version of the weapon used by Dirty Harry.

'Yes,' said Japrisot. 'And it makes very big

holes in people, which is why I like it.' The grizzled policeman looked at Holliday severely. 'Stay in the car, please.' He got out of the Peugeot and approached Valador's shop, the heavy pistol held at his side.

'We going to stay in the car?' Rafi asked.

'Mais non,' said Holliday. 'Not a chance.'

They got out of the vehicle, keeping their eyes on Japrisot. The policeman turned and saw them. He scowled, gesturing them back, then turned to the door once again and raised the revolver. He spread his fingertips on the door and pushed gently. It opened slightly. He toed it with his foot and it opened wider. Japrisot took a hesitant step forward, arm raised and elbow locked, the long barrel of the big pistol leading the way.

Holliday and Rafi held their breath as Japrisot stepped inside the store. A few moments later the lights went on and a few moments after that Japrisot appeared in the doorway, the revolver by his side again. With his free hand the cop waved them forward.

The interior of the shop looked more like something out of a Dickens novel. There were antiques and collectibles piled everywhere in no kind of order: wooden filing cabinets, a thirties-style leather couch, a sunburst mirror from the fifties, armoires, religious paintings, eighteenth-century gas lamps, a Louis Sixteenth Bergere confessional chair, chandeliers, figurines, an old-fashioned Bakelite wall phone between two plaster columns, lamps, picture frames, a giant clock face, granite garden lions, a pair of Pallisandre armchairs, a dozen faux wax fruit clusters in bell jars, three holy water fonts, seven ornately framed copies of Edgar Degas's *Two Dancers in Blue*, a giant stuffed peacock staring into a long cheval glass beveled mirror in a tilting stand and a Minnie Mouse ventriloquist's dummy laid over the leather saddle of a battered and faded carousel horse. Ten of the fifty-kilo fish boxes were piled up in front of the merry-go-round figure. There was no sign of Felix Valador.

Japrisot was standing in the middle of it all, the big pistol stuffed haphazardly into the sagging pocket of his jacket. He had a handkerchief in one hand and a bemused look on his face.

'Good grief,' said Rafi, looking around at the array of exotic clutter.

'Where is he?' Holliday asked, looking at Japrisot's expression.

The policeman eased his bulky figure down

the central aisle of the little shop and stopped in front of a tall, dark oak armoire with carved bird and floral patterns on the doors. The triple-barrel hinges and the long, turned handles were brass. There was a single sunburst spot of blood on the floor in front of the armoire like a tiny crimson marker. Japrisot used the handkerchief on the door handles and pulled the doors open.

'*Voilà,*' said the policeman.

Valador was crouched inside the armoire, knees drawn up under his chin, head bent forward and twisted to one side, one hand under his buttocks, the other between his upraised knees. One eye was wide open and the other half closed in a grotesque parody of a wink. Bizarrely, an obviously fake ruby the size of a robin's egg was neatly balanced in the dead man's earlobe.

Holliday squatted and took a closer look.

'I don't see any wound,' he said.

'Strangled?' Rafi suggested calmly. As an archaeologist he'd seen hundreds of dead bodies in his time, but generally not so fresh as Valador's. The eyeballs were only just beginning to glaze and shrink in their sockets. 'And what's with the plastic ruby?'

'There's no sign of a struggle,' answered

Japrisot. 'And there wasn't time. Strangulation is a very slow way of murdering someone.' The policeman grimaced. 'Also, his face would have become purple and his tongue would be sticking out.' The Frenchman shook his head. 'It was quick and it was a surprise.'

The blaring first chords of ABBA's 'Mama Mia!' boomed out. It was the ring tone of Japrisot's cell phone. He dragged the cell out of his pocket and held it to his ear.

'*Oui?*'

He listened, staring down at Valador's corpse and plucking a fleck of cigarette tobacco from his fleshy lower lip.

'*D'accord,*' he said after a few moments.

He closed the cell phone and slipped it back into his pocket. He cleared his throat.

'According to my people the couple in the Audi are Antonin Pesek and his Canadian-born wife, Daniella Kay. They live on Geologika Street in the Barrandov district of Prague. They are contract killers. Assassins. They work regularly all over Europe. The Peseks, *en famille*, have worked for everyone from the East German Stasi to the Albanian Sigurimi. Monsieur Pesek's weapon of choice is a short-barreled CZ-75 automatic pistol. His wife prefers ornamental plastic hatpins. They go right past the metal detectors at airports. Apparently she is quite the artist. In her file it uses the phrase "surgically precise."'

Japrisot crouched down on his haunches beside Holliday and, still using the handkerchief, he gripped the ruby in Valador's ear between his thumb and forefinger. He tugged. The ruby slid out along with six inches or so of clear Lucite plastic. The hatpin made a slight grating sound as it was withdrawn from Valador's head, like someone chewing on a mouthful of sand. He held it up to the light. It was lightly greased with brain matter. A trickle of pink, watery blood drained out of Valador's ear.

'Surgically precise, indeed,' murmured Japrisot, squinting at the needle-like murder weapon. 'Into the middle ear and then through the temporal bone to the brain via the internal auditory nerve canal.' The policeman nodded thoughtfully to himself. 'It would take a great deal of skill.'

'You sound as though you know your anatomy,' commented Holliday.

Japrisot lifted his shoulders and sighed.

'I spent three years in medical school. My father, God rest his soul, was an otologist.' The policeman shook his head sadly. 'Unfortunately it was not to be. I could not face a lifetime of oozing pus and wax. Japrisot *Pere* was very disappointed, I am afraid.'

He stood up, grunting with the effort. He turned and gently laid the ruby-ended stickpin down on a convenient stack of Blue Willow polychrome dinner plates. The dinnerware was stacked up on a dusty chunk of architectural marble that had once been part of a fluted column on an old building.

'*C'est ca,*' said Japrisot. 'Now we shall see what this is all about.' He went down the crowded aisle to the pile of fish boxes. Holliday and Rafi followed. The cop looked at the boxes for a moment, made a little grunting sound in the back of his throat and used one of his meaty hands to pry the close-fitting lid off the top of the box.

'*Viens m'enculer!*' Japrisot whispered, his eyes widening.

'What is it?' Holliday said, stepping closer and looking over the policeman's shoulder. He stared, gaping.

Carefully fitted into custom-made Styrofoam slots was a row of five gold bars, each one approximately five inches long and two inches wide. Japrisot reached into the box and pried one of the bars out of its nest. It looked about half an inch thick. Holliday reached into the box and took another one out. It was heavy in his hands, almost unnaturally so, and it had an odd, greasy feel to it that was unaccountably repellant.

The bar was rudely made, the edges rounded and the surface slightly pitted. 'I KILO' was stamped into the upper quadrant, the letters *E.T.* in the middle and an instantly recognizable impression in the lower end of the bar: the palm tree and swastika insignia of the German Afrika Korps of the Third Reich. There was no serial number or any other coding on the bar.

'Fifty kilos a box, ten boxes, five hundred kilos,' said Japrisot quietly.

'One thousand one hundred and three pounds,' murmured Rafi. 'A little more than half a ton.'

'Dear God,' whispered Holliday, 'what have we stumbled onto?'

'Clearly our Czech friends Pesek and his wife didn't know, either,' said Japrisot. He put the bar back in its niche. 'If they'd known what was in the boxes they wouldn't have been so quick to leave.'

'At eight hundred an ounce that's about thirteen million dollars,' calculated Rafi.

'Motive for any number of murders,' said Japrisot.

'It's got the Afrika Korps *Palmenstempel*,' said Holliday. 'I doubt that the E.T. means extraterrestrial.'

'Walter Rauff again,' said Japrisot. 'E.T. would be the Einsatzkommando Tunis, his unit.'

Holliday stared at the buttery slab of bullion, horribly aware of its origins. He put it back into the fish box, a chill running down his spine. Suddenly he felt as though he was going to be sick. Rafi stepped forward and took a close-up shot of the gold with his cell phone. Japrisot did not look pleased.

'I am about to call in my people from Marseille. By helicopter it will take them no more than thirty-five minutes from the time I call. I have done the service required by my relationship with my friend M. Ducos. That obligation has been attended to. Unless you wish to become involved with a great deal of French police bureaucracy I suggest that you leave here immediately. *Comprenez?*'

'Of course,' Holliday said and nodded. 'One question.'

'One only.'

'Was Valador's boat capable of making the North African coast?'

'*Certainement.* Tunis is five hundred miles from Marseille. A boat such as his could make the trip in thirty hours or perhaps less in good weather. The ferry gets you there overnight.'

'Thank you,' said Holliday. 'You've helped us a lot. Please extend my thanks to Monsieur Ducos as well.'

'*C'est rien,*' said Japrisot. It's nothing. 'Now leave.'

They did so, walking quickly down the hill from the corner.

'Now I see what must have happened,' said Rafi. 'Peggy and her expedition must have tripped over a cache of old Nazi gold lost in the desert somewhere. That's why no one's asking for ransom.'

'The Vichy French and the Germans controlled

most of North Africa for the first three years of the war,' said Holliday, 'and the Italians even before that.'

'What's your point?' Rafi asked.

'If Rauff collected all that gold from North African Jews, you would have thought he'd have sent it back to Germany. So what was it doing out in the desert?'

They reached the bottom of the hill and flagged a silver Mercedes taxi cruising the harbor front, trolling for business from the restaurants overlooking the water. Twenty minutes later they'd booked themselves into a garish pink suite overlooking the crescent of beach in front of the Royal Casino Hotel in Mandelieu-la-Napoule.

'I guess the next stop is Tunisia,' said Holliday, crouching in front of the minibar and getting out the fixings for a stiff drink. Both the sight of Felix Valador's grisly corpse in the cupboard and the nasty feel of the Holocaust gold in his hands had shaken him badly.

'Not necessarily,' said Rafi, sitting on the edge of one of the beds and flicking through the channels on the big flat-screen TV. He dug into his pocket and pulled out his cell phone.

He tossed it to Holliday. 'Check out the shots I took.'

Holliday put the phone in picture mode and scrolled through the photos. There were two or three general views of the antique store interior, one of Valador, dead in the armoire, the phony ruby in his ear, three pictures of the gold bar and two more of the old Bakelite wall phone between the Grecian columns. The first of the two was a wide shot of the phone's relative position between the columns and the last shot was a close-up of the phone itself.

'What do you see?' Rafi asked.

'A bad picture of an old dial telephone.'

'What's on the wall above the phone?'

Holliday squinted, then zoomed in.

'A number.' He read it off. '01120320875 82.'

'Zero-one-one is the international dialing prefix. The next two digits are a country code and the single digit after that is the city code.'

'What country? What city?'

'Let's find out,' said Rafi. He went to the phone on the night table between the beds and dialed the concierge in the lobby. Holliday mixed his Jack and soda. '*Parlez-vous anglais?*' Rafi asked.

There was a pause. 'Great. I wonder if you could tell me what telephone country code is twenty . . . two-zero, yes. And the city code three. *Trois, oui,* yes. *Merci bien.'* He hung up the telephone.

'Well?' Holliday asked, sipping the drink.

'Alexandria,' said Rafi.

'Virginia?' Holliday asked, not entirely surprised. Alexandria, Virginia, wasn't too far from MacLean and Langley, home of the CIA. It figured that they'd be involved.

'No,' said Rafi. 'Egypt.'

7

They flew out of the Nice-Côte d'Azur Airport
the following morning on a rattletrap Boeing 737
in faded blue Royal Air Maroc livery. The aircraft
was ancient, some of the ceiling panels held up
with duct tape. Rafi's seat table kept collapsing,
almost spilling a suspicious-smelling breakfast
of something yellow in his lap, and throughout
the trip small children ran up and down the aisle
screaming at the top of their tiny lungs. There
was no drink service and the toilets were overflowing after the first hour. Holliday was sure he
smelled cigarette smoke coming from behind the
ill-fitting cockpit door.

Their journey was a convoluted one, going
first to Paris-Orly and then to Casablanca, where
they waited to be refueled for three hours. From
Casablanca they hopped north again to Tangier,
then east to Oran in Algeria for a brief stop
before flying on to Algiers.

In Algiers there was another unexplained

layover on the tarmac, where they were served a lunch of flatbread and something called *tagine*, which was generally brown and looked like it might have begun life as a stew. It tasted of mutton and cardamom and had a large dollop of runny yogurt on top. By this point in the journey Holliday began to understand that he was no longer in Kansas anymore, or anywhere else in the regular world. It was beginning to feel like an episode of *The Twilight Zone*. Beside him Rafi didn't seem to mind at all. Holliday presumed it took a Mediterranean mind to appreciate the nuances of travel in North Africa.

After an eternity staring out the grimy window of the plane at the barren expanse of Houari Boumedienne Airport and the burnt-out, skeletal and overgrown remains of an Air Afrique 737 from a crash decades old, they took off once again, landing in Tunis for what the pilot referred to as a 'Mechanicals techniques problem.' With the mechanicals techniques apparently fixed the plane took off two and a half hours later, ceiling panels drooping, toilets reeking and overflowing and the central aisle awash in garbage and small children.

Three hours after that the old plane dropped

through the dense brown fog of fumes over Cairo. A long frustrating hour and a folded fifty-dollar bill got them through customs and immigration into the cat-litter atmosphere of the ancient city. Another forty minutes in a taxi got them to the ornate palace of the nineteenth-century Ramses Railway Station.

Half an hour after that, utterly exhausted, they squeezed on board the early-morning train to Alexandria. They rolled out of the dreary broken suburbs of a Soviet-era Cairo into the ghostly mists of the Nile Delta marshes and finally arrived at the great arc of the city by the sea, which the English expatriate novelist Lawrence Durrell had once described as the White Metropolis – Alexandria.

By the time they reached the Regency Hotel on Corniche Street, facing the beach and the ocean less than a hundred feet away, they had been traveling for almost exactly twenty-four hours on a trip that should have been barely half that long. Within five minutes of arriving both men were asleep.

The following morning after a room service breakfast of two eggs over easy, Holliday phoned the telephone number Rafi had photographed in

Felix Valador's store and discovered that it belonged to a gift shop on Masjed el Attarine Street.

'What do we do?' Rafi asked. 'Just walk into the place and say: Hi, we're pals with Felix Valador so tell us everything you know?' He pushed back from the breakfast table.

'All I know is we're going to stand out like a pair of sore thumbs on any back street in Alexandria,' said Holliday.

'So we need some protective cover,' responded Rafi.

'Phone the concierge and see what he can rustle up for us.'

What the concierge rustled up was his taxi driver cousin, a young man in his early twenties named Faraj. Ten minutes after the concierge called, Faraj was at the front door in a black and yellow Lada taxi that looked as though it had been used in a war. Faraj himself was a beanpole in a spotless white galabia and a matching skullcap. He wore Coke-bottle glasses, smiled a lot and was trying to grow a desperate little beard. According to the concierge, young Faraj was a university student who only drove a taxi part-time and spoke excellent English.

'You speak English, Faraj?' Rafi asked.

'Certainly. Very excellent. Lindsay Lohan.'

'Lindsay Lohan?' Holliday asked, a little startled.

'Certainly,' Faraj said and nodded. 'Black hole. Certainly excellent.' He began to sing. His voice was surprisingly good, low and mellow; an Egyptian Barry Manilow.

'Enough,' said Holliday, holding up one hand in surrender. 'How much for the day?'

'Please?'

The concierge aimed a burst of angry Egyptian toward his cousin and they held a brief, intense conversation. The concierge finally turned to Holliday and showed a mouthful of gold teeth.

'Four hundred pounds,' said the concierge.

Holliday gave Rafi a quick inquiring look.

'About a hundred U.S. dollars, perhaps a little less,' said the Israeli.

'Deal,' said Holliday.

Everybody shook hands. The concierge kept his hand extended.

'He wants his money in advance,' said Rafi.

'His money?'

'He's Faraj's agent. He'll take his cut and pay him at the end of the day if everything goes all right.'

'American dollars?' Holliday asked the concierge.

'Certainly. Excellent.' The phrase seemed to run in the family. Holliday counted out a handful of bills and passed them over. The concierge gave Faraj his orders and the young man leapt forward to open the rear door of the wretched little car.

'Run into the automobile certainly,' said Faraj, beaming. Holliday and Rafi clambered into the taxi. They tore away from the Corniche with its canyons of brand-new high-rise buildings by the beach and into the twisting, dusty, packed-earth streets of the Old City. After a tooth-jarring ten-minute ride Faraj dropped them off at their destination and parked. Faraj began to croon to himself. Holliday and Rafi went to a makeshift street-side coffee shop and *sheesha* bar and sat down at a tiny plastic table.

The coffee shop had a faded old sign translated into both English and Cyrillic Russian that showed a hand-painted, steaming cup of Turkish coffee and a *sheesha* hookah pipe. Directly across the narrow traffic-clogged street was the open front of the Abu Ibrahim Gift Shop. Rafi ordered two cups of thick sweet coffee in passable Arabic and waved off a waiter bearing an ornate brass and glass pipe. Around them at half a dozen other tables Egyptian men were smoking, drinking coffee and chatting amiably. In any other circumstances Holliday would have been enjoying himself.

A donkey cart rolled by loaded down with a huge pile of old bald automobile tires. The crumbling sidewalks were busy with pedestrian traffic moving back and forth. Beneath everything was a never-ending primal roar of four million people going about their business. The air was thick with dust, smelling of hot brick and a heady mixture of spices and a tang of salt, reminding Holliday of how close to the ocean they were. The odor was certainly better than the urinal stink of Cairo.

'Not very promising, is it?' Rafi said, looking across at the gift shop.

'No,' agreed Holliday.

The shop was a dizzying glut of tourist junk arrayed on scores of narrow shelves. The souvenirs were brightly painted, garish 'reproductions' of Egyptian artifacts that ranged between quarter-sized plaster imitations of the famous King Tut mask and plastic mummy key chains.

There was even a shelf full of Brendan Fraser action figures. A short dark man in a short-sleeved white shirt, black trousers and sandals sat on a high stool, smoking a cigarette and looking lazily out at the street. He was presumably the owner, Abu Ibrahim. Chained to the uprights of the rolled-up metal shutter that closed off the shop at night was an old motor scooter.

'When I was at Oxford getting my postgraduate degree I saw an old black-and-white Alec Guinness comedy called *The Lavender Hill Mob*. A bunch of idiot crooks steal a bullion shipment, melt it down into miniature Eiffel Towers and smuggle them out of England as cheap souvenirs. Maybe that's what our friend over there is doing.'

'I doubt it,' said Holliday. 'All that stuff over there is made in China, I'll bet. Besides, the gold we saw in Valador's place was intact, not melted down.'

'Then what's the scam?' Rafi asked. 'Valador didn't have that number written down for nothing.'

Holliday thought for a long moment. Across the dusty street the man in the white shirt pinched out his cigarette and dropped the butt into his pocket. Their coffee arrived. Holliday added a couple of sugar cubes from the bowl in the middle of the table, then took a first sip of the thick bittersweet brew. They'd been sitting at their table for ten minutes and not a single customer had entered the gift shop, but the man in the white shirt didn't seem at all concerned.

'Japrisot was a smart cop,' said Holliday at last. 'If you saw that number on the wall, then so did he.'

'What are you saying?' Rafi asked.

'Japrisot knows that Valador was smuggling stuff, antiquities and now gold bars. He also knows that the Egyptian Antiquities Police aren't immune from corruption. He'd get bogged down in bureaucracy if he tried to track down this guy on his home turf. We don't have that problem.'

'So we do his work for him?' Rafi said.

'Why not?' Holliday answered. 'What does he have to lose?'

'So what do we do now?'

'We sit, drink coffee and talk about zee women, *oui*?' Holliday grinned, doing an awful imitation of Japrisot.

'You sound like Inspector Clouseau in the *Pink Panther*,' Rafi said and laughed.

'Shut up and drink your coffee.'

After two and a half hours Holliday was beginning to feel sympathy for cops on stakeouts. His guts were in an uproar from too much coffee. His eyes burned from the insistent glare of the sun and itched from the dust. To top it all off he had to pee.

'Something's happening,' said Rafi urgently.

Holliday blinked, suddenly aware that he'd been dozing, a full cup of coffee cooling in front of him. He blinked again and looked across at the gift shop. The man in the white shirt was hauling down the steel mesh screen in front of his store. Holliday dropped a handful of bills on the table and stood up.

'Back to the cab,' he said. They walked up the street to where Faraj was dozing, a newspaper spread over his face. Holliday woke him up while Rafi watched through the rear window of the Lada.

'He's getting onto his scooter,' said Rafi.

'Which way is he going?'

'This way, I think. He'll go right by us.'

'Follow the scooter,' ordered Holliday. Behind them he heard the sewing machine whine of a two-cycle engine starting up.

'Scooter?' Faraj asked.

Holliday made a gesture with his hands like someone twisting the throttle on a motorcycle.

'Vroom, vroom. Scooter.'

'Ah,' said Faraj. 'Vroom. Scooter, yes. Excellent, certainly.'

The man from the gift shop rattled past them.

'Follow!' Holliday yelled and pointed toward their quarry. Faraj finally got it. He switched on the engine, ground the gears and went after the scooter.

'Following, excellent!' Faraj laughed, racing through the traffic, careening side to side like a wildman surfer riding a wave, pedestrians leaping out of the way, cart drivers screaming oaths in Arabic, other drivers honking. Ahead of them, barely in sight, the scooter chattered through the twisting back streets without a backward glance. They kept up the chase for twenty hectic minutes, threading their way towards the ocean.

'Where in hell is he going?' Rafi muttered, craning his neck, hoping for some recognizable landmark. They came out onto a broad avenue and he glimpsed a street sign telling him they were now on Gamal Abdel Nasser Road and heading west. Then the scooter turned right into another maze of streets.

Faraj turned around in his seat, beaming, completely ignoring the crush of traffic directly ahead. 'Winston Churchill!'

Holliday leaned forward and physically turned the young man's head forward. 'Watch the road!'

'Winston Churchill!' Faraj crowed a second time. 'Al Capone! MI-6! Bond, James Bond! Pussy Galore! Excellent, certainly!'

'He's gone mad,' said Rafi.

'Maybe not,' said Holliday as they swung around a bright yellow three-car tram that looked like it belonged in the 1950s. Half a dozen half-naked boys were getting a free ride on the back bumper. A minute or so later the taxi came out onto a palm-filled square. Across the street, almost on the beach, was a small ornate hotel with a *Sofitel* sign on the roof. They watched as the scooter roared across the square and pulled to a stop in front of the hotel. Faraj parked the taxi on the far side of the street and pointed at the building. He turned around in his seat.

'Winston Churchill. Somerset Maugham,' he said proudly.

'It's the Hotel Cecil,' said Holliday, laughing. 'Faraj is right. Churchill stayed here during the war and so did Maugham. MI-6 had a bunch of suites permanently rented.'

'What's our friend on the scooter up to?' Rafi asked.

The man in the white shirt finished parking the scooter, wheeling it up into the shade offered by the hotel, then walked around the corner. He approached the hotel doorman, an older gentleman in a brown and gold uniform complete with a fez. He handed the doorman something and the old gentleman disappeared into the hotel. The man in the white shirt lit a cigarette and waited under the entrance awning, looking out into the square.

A few moments later a brand-new cobalt blue Citroën C6 luxury sedan pulled up in front of the hotel and a valet parker leapt out and opened the driver's-side door for the man from the gift shop. More money changed hands and the man got behind the wheel.

'Interesting,' said Holliday. 'It would appear that Mr Abu Ibrahim leads a double life.'

'He didn't buy that selling knickknacks,' said Rafi as the valet closed the door.

Faraj began to sing to himself.

'Stor-y, for-me? I never realized just how much I loathed Lindsay Lohan,' muttered Rafi.

The Citroën moved off.

Holliday tapped Faraj on the shoulder.

'Follow!'

Faraj, still singing, followed.

8

They followed the big Citroën east on the Shari 26 July to the Corniche Road along the long shallow crescent of crowded white sand beaches. On the city side of the road there were rows of bright white high-rise hotels built like a protective wall hiding the crumbling eighteenth- and nineteenth-century buildings of Old Alexandria.

At first Holliday worried that the gift shop owner would spot them in his rearview mirror but he quickly realized just how many of the bumblebee taxis were on the road, all perfectly interchangeable, all black and yellow, all the same Soviet-era vintage Ladas, all dirty, one as banged up and battered as another.

Eventually the Corniche and the ramparts of resort hotels ran out and they continued west on the Shari al-Gaysh, a ten-lane divided highway that continued along the water, then veered south as they reached the oddly named Miami Beach district. The road dropped down to two lanes and the beaches weren't quite as white or quite as crowded, with stacks of green plastic lounge chairs piled up and waiting to be rented. There was another crop of slightly less sumptuous hotels along Montaza Beach, and finally a welcome swatch of empty green marshland opposite the beach at El Maamora.

'Where's our man going?' Rafi asked, looking out the grimy side window of the car. Farther out on the water they could see pleasure boats and the occasional brightly painted fishing trawler riding easily over the moderate waves. The sea was benign as a postcard photo, rolling calmly onto the beach in peaceful tumbling waves.

'Who knows?' Holliday said. 'We keep on going the way we're going, we'll wind up at the Suez Canal.'

'Suez?' Faraj said, turning around in his seat with his ever-present smile. 'No. No. No Suez! Abu Qir, Abu Qir!'

'Abu Qir?' Rafi said. 'I seem to remember there's some sort of Roman ruins underwater there. Not much in the way of smuggling opportunities.'

'Horatio Nelson. Kiss me Hardy! Boom, boom, Napoleon!' Faraj said enthusiastically.

'What's he going on about now?' Rafi said.

'This kid knows his history,' said Holliday, impressed. 'Aboukir was where Nelson fought the Battle of the Nile and destroyed the French fleet, August first, 1798. Abu Qir is why the Rosetta Stone is in the British Museum, not the Louvre.'

'I'm an archaeologist, not a historian,' said Rafi.

'You're just embarrassed because old Faraj here showed you up.'

'Yes, well,' said Rafi primly, 'I can actually *read* the Rosetta Stone. Can you?'

'Touché,' Holliday said and laughed.

'Nelson was at Abu Qir two hundred years ago. What's there now?' Rafi asked.

'As I recall it's the home of the Egyptian navy, or a big part of it at least. A few frigates and a lot of fast patrol boats, Russian and Chinese mostly.' Holliday shrugged. 'I think the Alexandria fishing fleet docks there as well.'

'Why would this Abu Ibrahim fellow want to be around the Egyptian navy?' Rafi asked. 'The Israeli navy spends half its time chasing smugglers. You'd think Ibrahim would want to be anywhere else but where the navy hung out.'

'Who knows?' Holliday shrugged. 'Maybe he's enlisted sailors to smuggle for him.'

Abu Qir was effectively the eastern suburbs of Alexandria, a 'village' of old Soviet-style apartment blocks, newer hotels along the water and the original, cramped town of tumbledown stucco-sided buildings crammed in between the old and the new. On the other side of the railway lines that split Abu Qir down the middle were the relatively modern naval base on the peninsula, the old fishing harbor beside it and at the south-eastern end of town the huge, ultramodern campus of the Arab Academy for Science, Technology and Maritime Transport.

Behind the fishing harbor was a large barren area of waste ground known as Lord's Land. A single broad roadway, lined with more deteriorating slab concrete apartment blocks and old rusting sheet-metal warehouses, led down to the fishing harbor and the sea.

To the left a crumbling concrete quay ran past a yard filled with piles of steel pipe and stacks of oil drums. To the right was a line of rusting warehouses and a haphazard clustered school of small trawlers and other workboats at anchor or drawn up on the mudflats at the east side of the harbor. The air was thick with the stink of the tidal ooze and rotting fish. It was almost midday and the waterfront had a bleak, abandoned look.

The Citroën drove directly to the docks and parked on the quay opposite an ancient wooden-hulled tugboat moored with heavy lines fore and aft. Once upon a time the ship had been black and red with a white superstructure. Now it was simply filthy, dark with accumulated grime. Faraj parked the taxi behind a screening skip loaded with what looked like bags of fertilizer. The wooden nameplate above the wheelhouse door of the tug was in Arabic script.

'*Khamsin,*' said Faraj. He pursed his lips and made a whooshing noise.

'A *Khamsin* is a wind from the Sahara,' offered Rafi. 'I think that's the boat's name.'

'Wind, yes,' Faraj said, nodding happily.

The trunk of the Citroën popped open and the man in the white shirt got out of the car. He went to the trunk of the big sedan and lifted out an old-fashioned briefcase. He crossed the quay to a gangplank leading to the tug and stepped across it quickly. He dropped down onto the deck, walked aft to the companionway ladder and climbed up to the wheelhouse. It didn't look as though there was anyone else on board. The man opened the wheelhouse door and disappeared inside. Two minutes later he reappeared without the briefcase, climbed down the companionway ladder and went back across the gangplank to the Citroën. He got in, started the engine and drove off, heading farther along the quay.

'Follow?' Faraj asked.

Holliday turned to Rafi.

'Well?'

'I'd love to see what's in that briefcase,' said Rafi.

'Me too,' Holliday said.

'Follow?' Faraj asked again.

Holliday shook his head.

'Wait,' he instructed.

'I wait. Certainly, excellent,' their young driver said as he nodded. He picked up the newspaper from the seat beside him, leaned back and dropped the paper across his face. Holliday and Rafi climbed out of the taxi and crossed the pier to the tugboat gangplank.

'What if there's somebody else on board?' Rafi asked.

'We'll cross that bridge when we come to it,'

answered Holliday. 'But first we cross the gang-plank.'

They crossed the gap between the pier and the tugboat, oily water lapping sluggishly below them. They reached the main deck and paused, listening for any sounds from behind the bulk-head doors directly in front of them. There were three doors and three portholes, the portholes covered by so much grime that they were almost opaque. There was a companionway stair leading to the deck below and the steps leading up to the wheelhouse. Both the deckhouse and the wheel-house-bridge above it were made of wood, probably mahogany or teak, covered by so many coats of white paint the planking was almost invisible. The filth laid over the paint had turned everything a greasy gray color. A heavily over-painted cast iron builder's medallion read *Neafie, Levy & Co. Philadelphia – 1906*.

'This thing is more than a hundred years old,' said Rafi, staring at the oval plate bolted to the deckhouse.

'They built to last back then,' said Holliday. 'A thousand storms, a couple of world wars. The British were still occupying Egypt when she was built.'

Rafi was peering through one of the grimy portholes.

'Looks like the galley,' he said. 'Nobody there.'

Holliday nodded and turned towards the companionway leading up to the wheelhouse. Rafi followed close behind him. They both turned and looked towards the dock. Still deserted. A noontime siesta in the heat of the day. The sun blazed down and Holliday felt sweat running down in itchy streams under his shirt. The man in the Citroën had looked cool. The Citroën, unlike Faraj's taxi, was almost undoubtedly air-conditioned.

They reached the wheelhouse and stepped inside. The interior was almost primitive. There were slatted wooden scuppers on the floor to let water drain, an amateurish welded aluminum dashboard with a few engine controls and a six-spoked mahogany and brass wheel that looked as though it might have been the original. There was a simple engine room telegraph attached to the right-hand bulkhead marked *Full*, *Half*, *Slow* and *Stop*. A tall iron braking handle came up from the floor to the right of the ship's wheel. There was a marine radio bolted to a bracket in the roof above the front windscreen, a black plastic compass in a glycerin float, a modern GPS unit and an echo sounder. For a hundred-foot-long vessel it was definitely seat-of-the-pants navigation.

'Whoever drives this bus is either very good at his job or he's insane,' said Holliday.

'Or both,' commented Rafi. There was a single bulkhead door at the rear of the wheelhouse. It was unlocked. Holliday and Rafi stepped through into a combination chart room and captain's cabin. The briefcase was sitting on a small table beside a porthole. Holliday snapped the latch and pulled it open. It was filled with nautical charts and nothing else.

'Looks like he's getting ready to go somewhere,' said Holliday.

'Where?' Rafi asked.

Holliday opened one of the folded charts and laid it out on the table.

'As-Sallum to Al-Iskandariyah,' he said, reading the chart legend. 'The scale is one to three hundred thousand. About a hundred and forty miles from Alexandria. Looks like some sort of harbor.'

'As-Sallum is also the last place anybody heard

from Peggy and the expedition,' said Rafi. 'It was their last staging point before crossing into Libya. It's right on the border.'

'It can't be a coincidence,' said Holliday. He folded the chart again and put it back in the briefcase. He closed and latched the briefcase and put it back exactly where he'd found it. 'Let's see if we can find out why our knickknack salesman is going to this As-Sallum,' he said.

They left the wheelhouse through the harborside door, screening themselves from anyone on the pier. They went forward on the main deck and then carefully down a lower companionway to the foc'sle, listening as they descended. The only sound was the clicking hum of an automatic bilge pump somewhere below and the faint lapping echo of small waves against the hull.

The foc'sle consisted of two small cabins, six pipe berths against the port and starboard bulkheads, a small galley and a zinc-topped mess table with benches bolted to the floor. Dim pan lights dangled above them, throwing shadows everywhere. The ceiling was low, a forest of cables and conduits hanging on metal brackets. The stuffy little area had obviously been in recent use; there were photographs and pinups above the narrow berths and the unmistakable smell of fried onions in the air.

'No one home,' said Rafi.

'Let's not stretch our luck,' answered Holliday, a nervous edge in his voice. Being below decks and blind to possible attack went against all his military experience, not to mention his basic survival instincts. 'Five minutes more and then we're out of here.'

They made their way aft down a narrow corridor and then stepped through a bulkhead door into a cargo area between the foc'sle and the engine room farther back. The cargo area was stacked with seventy or eighty long wooden crates. The crates were each secured with lead customs seals and stenciled with arcane numbers and letters. The only clue to their contents was a stenciled logo of a rearing horse and the word DIEMACO.

'All of a sudden I'm getting a bad feeling about this,' said Holliday.

'What's DIEMACO?' Rafi asked.

'Die Manufacturing Corporation of Canada. They make machine guns.'

'Canada?' Rafi asked with a look of surprise.

'Sixth-largest exporter of small arms in the world. Bigger than Israel.'

'You're kidding.'

'A billion dollars a year. Don't let the maple leaves and maple syrup fool you. The Green Berets can trace their history back to the Devil's Brigade, a Canada-U.S. commando unit. Nobody mentions it much these days, but it was Canadians from the Second Parachute Battalion who trained the Americans, not the other way around.'

'One history lesson after another,' Rafi said with a grin.

'Let's open one of these up,' said Holliday.

There was a short pry bar on a shelf against the portside bulkhead. Holliday used it to twist off the wire customs seal, then slipped it between the crate and its stapled wooden lid. Inside the crate were half a dozen flat, neutral-colored hard cases. Holliday undid the clasps on the top case and opened it.

'Our man's not smuggling stuff out of Egypt – he's smuggling stuff in,' said Holliday, peering into the case. Inside, seated in custom-cut foam niches, was an entire weapons system. The weapon was sand-colored with an odd, flat surface texture.

'What is it?' Rafi asked.

'A Timberwolf sniper rifle. Dead accurate at four thousand yards. And I mean "dead" accurate.'

'That's more than two miles.'

'That's right,' said Holliday flatly.

There were a dozen much smaller cases fitted into the ends of the crates. He took one of the small cases out and dug even deeper, coming up with a dozen or so parcels wrapped in heavy paper. He opened up one of the small cases. Inside was a squat, dead black handgun with a beavertail grip and a snub barrel shorter than his index finger. The entire gun fit into the palm of his hand.

'A Para-Ordnance Nite Hawg,' murmured Holliday. 'Another Canadian company. Forty-five automatic.' He ripped the paper off one of the smaller packages. Boxes of ammunition. He slipped the handgun into the right-hand pocket of his jacket and stuffed half a dozen boxes of ammunition into the left.

'You get caught with a handgun in Egypt and we'll both go to jail for a very long time.'

'We get caught by the bad guys without one and we could wind up dead,' responded Holliday. He stuffed the empty gun case and the torn paper from the ammunition package back into the wooden crate.

Suddenly there was an echoing metallic clang

as the bulkhead door leading aft crashed open. A thin beardless man wearing a grease-stained light blue boiler suit stepped into the cargo hold, frowning and looking as though he'd just awakened from a nap. He blinked, surprised to find two strange men aboard the tug. He said something in a high, almost girlish voice.

'*Maa fee shay jadeed?*' Holliday couldn't understand a word but the intent of the question was clear: Who the hell are you and what are you doing on my ship? The man reached into the deep front pocket of the boiler suit and tried to pull something out of his pocket. It looked to Holliday like an enormous Webley service revolver that was standard issue for the British Armed Forces from the Boer War onward. As the thin man hauled the heavy pistol up the front sight got hooked on a tear in the pocket and snagged.

Holliday barely hesitated. Heart beating wildly, adrenaline pumping frantically into his bloodstream, he swept up the steel pry bar from the top of the crate, took two steps forward and ripped a vicious curving swipe at the man's head. The hooked end connected with the left temple with a wet crunching sound, stopping him in his tracks. The man shrieked, eyes bulging, and crumpled to the ground, his arm flung out, his hand still gripping the heavy revolver. He didn't move.

Rafi stared down at the man in the boiler suit, horrified.

'Is he dead?'

Holliday bent down and took the Webley, just in case. He felt for a pulse in the man's neck. There was none. There was no visible blood but the side of the man's head looked like a deflated balloon, the bones crushed like a soft-boiled egg.

'Yeah, he's dead,' said Holliday with a sigh. He'd seen enough combat to know a corpse when he saw one.

'We've got to go. *Now*,' said Rafi urgently.

'We can't,' answered Holliday, shaking his head. 'Not yet.'

'What are you talking about!?' Rafi asked. 'The longer we stay here, the more chance there is of our gift shop guy coming back!'

'That's the point,' explained Holliday. 'Up to now these people didn't know we were onto them. We leave a dead body lying here it's a whole new ball game.'

'What are you saying?'

'We get rid of the body.'

It took them almost half an hour and it was an object lesson in the concept of deadweight. They manhandled the limp, dragging corpse up the companionway stairs, arms and legs flopping, head lolling and banging gruesomely up each step. They brought him up on the windward side, the deckhouse shielding them from the pier. Out in the harbor brightly painted fishing trawlers bobbed easily in the shining water like a rustic postcard from the Mediterranean: *'Arrived Abu Qir. Hotel not quite five-star, harbor wonderful, wish you could be with us. Love, Alice.'*

Panting from their exertions, chests heaving, they reached the deck and stopped to catch their breath, the body hidden below the sight line of the gunwales of the old tug. Rafi peered over the side. Thick oily water banged listlessly against the scarred black hull. A rime of harbor muck covered the surface, a mixture of floating garbage, dead fish, plastic, and long dark mats of seaweed.

'Do bodies float or sink?' Rafi asked.

'They sink for a while but gasses bring them up eventually,' said Holliday.

'How long?'

'I don't have the faintest idea.'

'Then we need something to weigh him down,' said Rafi.

At the stern of the tug they found an old skiff turned bottom up and half covered by a rubberized canvas tarpaulin. The little boat didn't look like it had been used in decades. Originally it must have served as a lifeboat or to inspect the hull, something that clearly hadn't been done for a very long time. Hidden underneath the dinghy was a very old British Seagull 1.5-horsepower engine that looked as though it had been designed by a mad prewar inventor in his shed at the end of the garden. Along with the spindly little outboard they found a half-rotted coil of rope that had once been the skiff's painter.

They hauled the engine back to the foredeck and used the rope to bind it as securely as they could to the body of the man in the boiler suit. When they were done they checked to make sure no one was watching from one of the fishing boats in the harbor, then heaved their unwieldy burden over the side. He landed on the surface with a huge splash. The surface muck parted, then swallowed the body whole. Ten seconds later the muck was a single undulating layer of flotsam, the body having vanished without a trace.

'The engineer wasn't being paid enough and he deserted,' said Rafi.

Holliday looked down at the placid surface of the water.

'Sounds reasonable enough,' he said and nodded.

'Now what?' Rafi asked.

Holliday thought about Peggy and the task that lay ahead.

'We get to As-Sallum before the good ship *Khamsin* does.'

9

After discharging Faraj, they took the midnight train from Alexandria to Mersa Matruh by way of El Alamein, the small Egyptian seaside town where Montgomery held the line against Rommel's tanks and began the drive to the west that eventually pushed the German general out of Africa altogether.

The terrain, what little they saw of it, was a mixture of dreary, splintered desert, raw, low dunes and scrubby patches of dusty green farmland trying to survive in an arid ocean of sand. In the distance, on the right-hand side of the train, with the dawn light creeping up behind them, the ocean appeared like an enormous mirage of the water the desert could see but never vanquish.

By the time they'd boarded the train in Alexandria there were no sleeping compartments available so they'd spent the night in the surprisingly elegant wood-paneled bar car, drinking from fat silver cans of Luxor Beer and discussing their situation. By dawn, still awake, they were alone in the car except for the bartender, asleep on his stool in the far corner. The cold fury of the sunrise turned the sky around them a thousand shades of pink and gold and the wheels chattered monotonously over the endless track beneath their feet.

'Tell me everything you know about this German, Walter Rauff. There must be some clue in his history in North Africa that could help us track down the gold.'

'Find out where the gold came from and we find Peggy?' Rafi said.

'Something like that.'

Rafi thought about it for a long moment, assembling his thoughts. At the far end of the car the bartender woke up briefly, saw that he wasn't needed and instantly was asleep again.

'I don't know if this is completely accurate, but as I recall he was in the navy and got thrown out over some sex scandal – sleeping with an admiral's wife, or daughter or maybe both. Anyway, he managed to get into the SS, the death's-head battalion in charge of the camps. He figured out a scheme of gassing people using mobile extermination units and on the basis of that he was sent to North Africa with Rommel. His job was to come in behind Rommel's units exterminating North African Jews from Morocco to Palestine. He was also in charge of sweeping up their assets – the source of all the gold. In 1942 and 1943 Rommel got stopped in El Alamein, right around here actually.' Rafi glanced out the window at the barren landscape.

'Anyway, he fell back to Tunisia to round up the Jews with his Einsatzkommando Tunis for a while, then beat it out of Africa altogether. Italy, I think. That was 1944. After the war he was captured by the Americans, escaped and used Bishop Hudal's "ratline" to escape via the Vatican, first to Syria for a while, then to Chile.' Rafi shrugged. 'He ran a crab-packing plant for several years, then started working in intelligence for the Chilean government. He used to travel back to Germany all the time but he was never caught.'

'Did this Rauff have any contingency plan for escaping if Rommel was killed or captured?' Holliday asked.

'Most of the SS units had secret plans for escape if they started losing the war. The Vatican had their whole ratline system set up as far back as 1942, taking SS men first to Syria, then to South America.'

'Any alternate routes?' Holliday asked.

Rafi nodded, then took a last swig from his warm can of beer.

'Down through Libya by air to a desert air base in Vichy-controlled Niger, then across the ocean to Brazil or Chile.'

'This is beginning to make a little sense now,' said Holliday. He took a large-scale folded map of Egypt and Libya from the little overnight bag on the seat beside him. He spread the map out on the table. 'Any idea where the air base in Libya was?'

'The name Al-Jaghbub sticks in my head, but I'm not positive.'

Holliday found it on the map.

'There's an oasis town called Al-Jaghbub half-way down the map.'

'Wait a minute,' said Rafi, excited now. 'Didn't Ducos mention it when we were talking to him?'

'I can't remember,' said Holliday, 'but it fits. It would make a perfect staging base for a long-distance flight to Niger.'

'So the Nazis get freaked out by Rommel losing and put the gold on a plane for Brazil?'

'And it gets lost somewhere between point A and point B,' Holliday said, nodding.

'And that fits, too,' said Rafi. 'Hudal was a bishop with connections and insiders both in the SS and at the Vatican.'

Holliday sat back in his seat.

'Now I see,' he said. 'The monk from Biblical Archaeology School in Jerusalem, this Brother Brasseur or whatever his name is, he wasn't searching for Templar texts in the Archives; he was trying to find Hudal's records. They were looking for the SS gold right from the beginning.'

They arrived in Mersa Matruh at six thirty in the morning. It was a city of two hundred thousand or so, a miniature Alexandria, the sea masked by a line of hotels and resorts along the Corniche, all new and all modern, with the old city of its real Berber inhabitants behind the high-rise façade, selling the produce grown on the little desert farms they'd seen from the train. They booked into the Beausite, a moderately priced five-story hotel with its own sand beach. A single phone call to the concierge presented them with an insurmountable problem. They took their complimentary continental breakfast out onto the balcony of their narrow room to discuss the situation.

'We're screwed,' said Rafi abjectly, looking out over the ultramarine ocean in front of the hotel. He tore off a corner of his croissant and buttered it. 'It'll take you weeks to get a visa for Libya with an American passport and I probably couldn't get one at all.'

'So then we do it without visas,' said Holliday, sipping his strong coffee.

'How do we manage that?' Rafi asked.

'Look on the map,' said Holliday. 'The closest place on the Egyptian side is Siwa Oasis. That's only a couple of hundred miles from here. Siwa is less than fifty miles from Jaghbub.'

'Across an impenetrable border,' grunted Rafi. 'They've got something like two million land mines planted. Fences, cameras, the whole deal. Egypt and Libya were at war back in the seventies.'

'That's LRDG territory,' said Holliday. 'I guarantee it's like a sieve.'

'LRDG?'

'Long Range Desert Group,' explained Holliday. 'The Brits and the Germans chased each other back and forth across the border for years.

There has to be dozens of caravan trails through there.'

'Not any that I know about,' said Rafi.

'Then we'll find someone who does,' answered Holliday. 'I'm not about to give up on Peggy now.'

Later that day they purchased a high-wheeled military surplus Czech-made UAZ-469 tin-can jeep from a defunct safari tour company. They spent the afternoon stocking the knockoff, tin-roofed Land Cruiser with supplies, including as many maps of the area as they could find. The following morning they left for Siwa Oasis, traveling due south through the desert. The bare-bones vehicle drove like a tank and had virtually no suspension but the simple Peugeot-Citroën diesel engine ticked over nicely, and even though the dashboard and its instruments were primitively built, everything seemed to work well enough. The top end of the speedometer read 120 kph, but the reality was more like 90, or about fifty-five miles an hour.

'I wonder what "*pri vjezdu voziola do terenu zapni predni nahon*" means,' said Rafi, reading a riveted notice on the dashboard behind the plain, three-spoked wheel of the truck. 'Sounds a little ominous.'

'Let's hope we never find out,' said Holliday, sitting forward, trying to peel his perspiration-soaked shirt away from the sticky vinyl seats. No wonder the safari tour company had gone under. He tried to imagine some cheesesteak-overweight tourist from Winnetka enduring a sweltering day in the un-air-conditioned Soviet truck. It wasn't pretty.

They drove for five hours, switching drivers every fifty miles and stopping only four times, once to eat their prepared lunches, twice for bathroom duties at one of three government rest stops and once to fill the gas tank from the jerry cans of diesel fuel lined up in the cargo area of the truck. Other than dunes the only changes in the landscape were occasional radio transmission towers, half a dozen roadside oil rigs, a few sand drifts across the two-lane blacktop and the remains of an ancient fort. Here and there they saw signs in Arabic and English telling them they were either entering or leaving a military zone. There wasn't a single gas station, hotel, motel or refreshment stand to be seen.

'There was a sixth-century B.C. king of Persia named Cambyses who once sent an army here,' said Rafi, looking out at the bleak, monotonous landscape. 'They were on a mission to destroy the Oracle at Siwa.'

'What happened?' Holliday asked.

'There was a sandstorm. The whole army vanished, all fifty thousand of them. They were never seen again.'

Finally after more than a hundred and sixty miles the landscape began to change, dunes becoming hills, hills becoming stony, stunted mountains, palms and patches of green beginning to appear. Abruptly the lands fell away and a palm-filled depression appeared, saltwater lakes twinkling in the brilliant sun, fields of alfalfa bending in the desert wind. Siwa lay below them.

Siwa is not the oasis most people visualize from the movies. Instead of a single pool of water surrounded by a grove of palm trees, Siwa is a fifty-mile-long depression, twenty miles across, once the bed of a fast-flowing mountain river, perhaps even the Egyptian version of the Grand Canyon. In this long, relatively narrow depression there are large groves of date palm, olive groves, wheat fields, saltwater lakes and freshwater streams and springs that turn the desert into a blossoming verdant sanctuary.

The oasis at Siwa is known to have been

occupied by man for at least ten thousand years. When Alexander the Great came to Siwa to consult the oracle of Amon Ra the town was already dominated by the enormous clay and mud fortress known as the Shali, a complex construction of fortified buildings as much as five stories tall built up the slopes of an artificial mountain. The huge fort lasted for thousands of years until the 1920s, when three days of successive torrential rains 'melted' the mud-brick structure like a child's sand castle ruined by the encroaching tide. Even now the Shali is an impressive creation and still looms over the town.

The town of Siwa contains about ten thousand inhabitants, mostly involved with the marketing and sale of Siwa grapes and olives as well as tourism. Most of the townspeople as well as the farmers and grove owners are ethnic Berbers. There are half a dozen small hotels in Siwa and Holliday and Rafi chose what appeared to be the best of them, the Safari Paradise, a lodge surrounded by a cluster of individual bungalows and all facing a bubbling springwater pool. After booking into one of the little cottages, they freshened up, then headed for the main dining room in the lodge.

The dining room of the Safari Paradise was surprisingly elegant considering that it was located in a place that, along with Timbuktu, may well have inspired the phrase 'the middle of nowhere.' The white plaster walls were hung with colonial oils of Egypt and Siwa in particular, and the ceiling was crisscrossed with coffered wooden beams. The tables were covered with white linen, starched napkins fanned elaborately at each sterling silver place setting. The maître d', whose name was Omar, wore evening clothes. There was a variety of entrées on the enormous tasseled menu, from New York strip loin and prime rib to chicken *kishk* and *kofta kebabs*. Appetizers ranged from French fries or zucchini strips to pita and *baba ghanouj* with *zabadi*-mint yogurt dip and *wara'enab*-stuffed grape leaves. They ordered from a pleasant waiter who spoke perfect English. Holliday, being the more adventurous eater, chose the chicken *kishk* and the stuffed grape leaf appetizer. Rafi ordered a cheeseburger and fries. They both ordered tea.

They were just finishing up their meal and thinking about coffee when a man materialized at their table. He was tall, broad-chested and wearing long shorts and an old-fashioned fatigue jacket with a collarless white shirt beneath it. His face was square with a full gray beard, shaggy gray hair down to his shoulders and heavy dark eyebrows over large, intelligent, pitch-black eyes. The nose was long and aquiline and would have suited a Caesar. His skin was dark as iced tea. When he spoke he showed a line of small white teeth, bright against the dark tan. He had the rich baritone voice of an actor or a politician. The accent was not quite British, Mid-Atlantic. Canadian maybe, thought Holliday, but he wasn't absolutely sure.

'My name is Emil Abdul Tidyman,' said the man, sitting down without being asked. 'I hear you're looking for a guide.'

10

'What makes you think we need a guide, Mr Tidyman?'

'Simple enough,' said the tall man with a smile. 'You drive into Siwa in an old Czech Goat, which means you must have bought it outright, because nobody rents them, and if you bought a Goat you must be thinking of going somewhere the usual safari treks won't take you. You also clearly have a military background; you walk like a soldier, and you have a soldier's haircut and bearing. I expect at least a major, but probably a colonel.'

Tidyman shook his shaggy, gray-haired head, then continued.

'And certainly no one but an experienced officer, probably with time in Afghanistan, would know that despite its point of origin, a Czech-made Ulyanovsky Avtomobilny Zavod-469, even well used, is a far superior vehicle for desert use than either the Land Rover or the Toyota Land Cruiser. Which, in my experience, means you probably want to go somewhere you have no business going.' Tidyman sat back in his chair. 'Am I close . . . Colonel?'

Holliday ignored the question.

'Just what experience of yours would that be, Mr Tidyman?'

'Much the same as yours, I expect,' answered the man. 'But mostly confined to Africa. The Congo, specifically Katanga Province, Biafra, Angola, Sierra Leone, Equatorial Guinea . . . there are others.'

'A mercenary?'

'Soldier of fortune.'

'Macho crap for idiots who drive around with rifles in their pickup trucks. Most mercenaries I've run into are section eight discharges and goofs who couldn't get through Marine basic training. Losers.'

Tidyman shrugged and smiled, showing off his pearly little teeth.

'Whatever gets you through the night, Dr Holliday.'

'You know my name.'

'I'm an old friend of the desk clerk here.'

'You live in Siwa?'

'I summer here, you might say, I winter in cooler climes.'

'Odd choice,' said Rafi.

'One of the perks of multiple citizenship,' said Tidyman. 'And one of the drawbacks. My Canadian citizenship gets me free health care, but I have to live there for several months a year. The same is true of the free dental care I get in England. My Egyptian citizenship provides me with my livelihood.'

'Neat trick,' said Holliday, laughing. 'Three passports.' He was beginning to like the smooth-talking man across from him despite himself. He was very charming in a slightly devilish way. And clearly he was extremely intelligent. 'How did you work that?'

'I'm the perfect expatriate,' answered Tidyman. 'Never at home wherever I go. My father was a Brit, my mother was Egyptian. I was born in Cairo shortly after World War Two but raised in Canada, where I became a naturalized citizen. Unlike you hyper-patriots in the States, Canadians are quite tolerant of people with various passports. You have your melting pot, the Canadians have their mosaic. All depends on your point of view.' He smiled. 'And despite propaganda to the contrary, Canadian health care really is quite excellent.'

'What's this livelihood you mentioned?' Rafi asked.

Tidyman smiled again, showing his teeth.

'People come to me with their fondest wishes and I provide them with their heart's desire.'

'Very poetic,' said Holliday. 'If a bit enigmatic.'

'What was it Churchill said about enigmas?' Tidyman said, smiling broadly, the black eyes twinkling.

'It was a radio speech in 1939,' said Holliday. 'He was talking about Russia: *It is a riddle wrapped in a mystery inside an enigma.* In other words, it's complicated.'

'A historian,' added Tidyman. 'Interesting.'

'I thought it was Jim Carrey who said that as the Riddler in *Batman Forever*,' said Rafi, smiling himself now.

Tidyman laughed.

'Ah, yes, Mr Carrey, another expatriate Canadian. You can bet your bottom dollar he gets his annual checkups back in Canada.'

'What are you getting at, Mr Tidyman?' Holliday asked.

'What I'm getting at is that my livelihood is like Churchill's quotation: complicated.'

'And how does that involve us?'

'I suspect that your heart's desire is complicated, too,' answered Tidyman.

'And why would you suspect that?'

'Come, come, Doctor, we're going around in circles. We're both being a little circumspect, feeling each other out as the saying goes, but we wouldn't be doing even that if you were an innocent tourist, would we?' The man hooked a thumb in the direction of the maître d'. 'You would have called old Omar over and had me ejected if that were the case.'

'I gather you and Omar have an understanding,' said Holliday.

'You know the word *bakshish*?' Tidyman said, his smile at full wattage.

'A bribe,' said Rafi.

'Quite so,' said Tidyman. 'It is the way business is done in my country.'

'Which country would that be?' Holliday said.

'Touché, Dr Holliday,' said the gray-haired man. 'Since we are fencing again.'

'Why don't we cut the bull twaddle and get to the point, Mr Tidyman. Right now you're between me, a cup of coffee and something called *Ohm Ali* that the waiter says is terrific.'

'The Egyptian version of a cherry Danish, but considerably better,' said Tidyman. 'I might join you.'

'The point,' insisted Holliday.

The waiter shimmied up to the table with a little bow, summoned by some invisible clue from Tidyman. The three-way expatriate ordered something in rapid Egyptian, presumably a portion of *Ohm Ali* and a cup of coffee. The waiter nodded and slipped away.

'The point is this, Dr Holliday,' said Tidyman, leaning over the table and keeping his voice low. 'You are someone who knows his history and you certainly are not a wide-eyed tourist. I trust that you aren't one of those bizarre Internet fanatics who thinks the lost army of Cambyses the Second actually existed and is out there somewhere wearing diamond-studded armor or the like.'

'Not guilty on both counts,' answered Holliday.

'Then there is only one other answer. You and your friend here are on some sort of mission. Add one Czech Goat, a vehicle designed for off-road uses in deserts both hot and cold, and the conclusion is inescapable. For whatever reason, you need someone to take you across the border into Libya, presumably with a certain amount of discretion. Hence my initial assertion that you needed a guide.' Tidyman sat back in his chair and stroked the chin of his beard, watching Holliday carefully.

'And if your assumption is correct?' Holliday asked. 'What would we do then? You could just as easily be a policeman setting us up.'

'That would be entrapment,' said Tidyman.

'This is Egypt,' answered Holliday. 'We could be in some nightmare of a prison in Cairo for ten years before the case came to court.'

'Yes, this is Egypt, where you could also be rotting away in Borg al-Arab prison for ten years because you had this in your possession,' responded Tidyman. He casually reached into the pocket of his old faded fatigue jacket and took something out. It was the palm-sized Nite Hawg automatic Holliday had taken from the hold of the tugboat.

'Where the hell did you get that?' Rafi hissed, eyes wide.

Tidyman slipped the pistol back into his pocket.

'I went through the luggage in your room while you were down here eating dinner.' He smiled broadly. 'You could have been a cop just as easily as I could have.' Tidyman paused. 'The point is, I didn't turn you in, and believe me, catching a tourist with a gun would certainly have been worth my while.' He shrugged. 'But I'm betting I can make a better deal with the two of you than I could with the local donut huskers.'

Dessert arrived. It was delicious, a sweet bread pudding smothered in crème fraiche, tasting richly of walnuts and cherries. They ate in silence for a few minutes. Finally Holliday put down his fork. He glanced over at Rafi and caught the young archaeologist's eye. Rafi raised an expressive eyebrow and then shrugged. Holliday turned back to Emil Abdul Tidyman.

'Okay,' said Holliday at last. 'Let's talk.'

In the end they didn't tell Tidyman anything about the gold or the involvement of the Vatican and their intelligence apparatus, Sodalitium Pianum, preferring to keep that to themselves, at least for the moment. Holliday still wasn't sure how much the Holy See itself knew, or whether it was just the French arm of the spy organization La Sapinière that had gone rogue and was acting on its own behalf. Nor did they mention their past confrontation at West Point, and even before that while they were on the trail of the secret of the Templar sword that had once belonged to Holliday's uncle.

'I'm still not sure we should trust him,' said Rafi later, back in their little bungalow.

'Neither am I,' said Holliday. On parting in the hotel lobby Tidyman had slipped him the automatic, which he was now loading, pressing the ten copper-tipped shells into the magazine. 'But that doesn't mean we can't use him. I was never crazy about trying to get into Libya on our own. He's right – we need a guide.'

'I don't think Mr Tidyman cares about anyone but himself. He's what the English call a "main chancer." If he gets himself into trouble or sees the chance to make a buck, he'll turn us over to the authorities in a minute.'

'Maybe,' said Holliday. 'But if he's making money with Siwa as his base of operations, it's by smuggling. People and drugs most likely, maybe guns as well. If he's the main chance type you feel he is, then he'd do pretty much anything to protect his supply routes.' Holliday shook his head. 'I don't think we have anything much to worry about on that score.'

'I hope you're right,' said Rafi. 'We won't do Peggy much good if we're lounging around in one of those Cairo prisons you mentioned.'

11

It took Tidyman a day to collect what he thought they'd need, and another day to plan the trip and spread the rumor that he was taking his two new 'pigeons' on a tourist visit to Bahariya Oasis to the east, getting the requisite permits to bolster the story. It was a reasonable objective: lots of tourists who came to Siwa went to Bahariya, some for the folk music the oasis was famous for and others because it was an alternate route back to Cairo. After the crazy people who came for the total eclipse a few years before, the people of Siwa were ready to believe just about anything was possible where their foreign visitors were concerned. As long as they left some of their money in Siwa they could do anything they liked.

They drove east along an almost arrow-straight two-lane paved highway, heading directly away from Siwa and in the opposite direction from the Libyan border. Tidyman was at the wheel. Empty plastic jerry cans for water had been stored in bolt-on racks on the sides and roof that Tidyman had purchased the day before. Extra fuel was stored in the cargo compartment in the rear along with their other supplies. The three men were crowded into the bench seat up front.

Tidyman had explained their jog to the east. According to him the Siwans were an inquisitive, curious bunch and the ride toward Bahariya Oasis was a ruse for their benefit. There was also the slim chance that they would be spotted by a National Border Police overflight, although Tidyman thought it was unlikely; the light-plane pilots they used were terrified of being shot down by Libyan fighter jets and even their own air force.

After half an hour Tidyman slowed the vehicle, then reached over and dragged down a black-knobbed stick beside the shift lever.

'What's that?' Rafi asked as there was an odd lurch. The engine note changed as well.

'Just like it says on the sign,' answered Tidyman. ' "*Pri vjezdu voziola do terenu zapni predni nahon*" – "When going off-road engage four-wheel drive." '

'You speak Czech?' Holliday asked, impressed.

'Just enough to drive a Goat,' their companion

said and laughed. 'A necessity in some of the places I've fought. A colleague who called himself Švejka taught me. A good soldier, Švejka.'

'What happened to him, or shouldn't I ask?' Holliday said.

'You shouldn't ask,' answered Tidyman. Abruptly the Egyptian hauled around the big wheel and they thumped off the road and into the hard-packed sand, the oversized mud tires gripping easily. They swung high to the right, arcing away from the highway until it was lost behind them in the rolling dunes. He dug into his pocket and tossed a Garmin Rino GPS unit across to Holliday. 'Know how to use that?' Tidyman asked.

'Sure,' said Holliday. He'd first used the technology during combat missions in Desert Storm, the first brief war with Iraq. The theory was as old as navigation, but instead of using a sextant to take a bearing on the sun and stars you used a radio beam to triangulate your position by pinging off a series of geosynchronous satellites.

'It's already been set with our base coordinates,' said Tidyman. 'Now you just follow the bouncing ball.'

Twenty-five minutes later they reached the Siwa-Mersa Matruh highway and crossed it at right angles, running along the northern edge of the long east-west depression that held the oasis. After another hour, the town well behind them, Tidyman guided the Goat down a barely visible track that led into the depression. In the distance to the south one of the huge saltwater lakes that dotted the oasis glittered in the brilliant sun. To Holliday the shimmering lake looked like a heat mirage on the highway.

The desert here was rocky, interspersed with small pockets of vegetation. Ahead of them dark, bare hills with windswept crags and plateaus rose before them. So far they hadn't seen another vehicle. Every few minutes Tidyman would ask if they'd reached the next flagged location on the GPS and Holliday would call out the coordinates.

'Do you have some sort of plan?' Rafi asked. 'Or are we just playing this by ear?'

'First we get across the border. Then we head for Jaghbub.' Tidyman eased the Goat around an outcropping of sandstone, then found the track again. 'I have friends there,' the gray-haired Egyptian continued. 'If they've heard anything about your friend, they'll tell me.'

'Where exactly are we?' Holliday asked, looking down at the GPS unit in his hand and then at the barren landscape ahead of them.

'This is the Masrab al-Ikhwan,' answered Tidyman. 'What they once called the Thieves Road.'

'Appropriate,' muttered Rafi.

'Once upon a time it was the only southern passage between Egypt and Libya. It was used mostly by smugglers and slave traders going to and fro.'

'You seem to know your way around even without this thing,' said Holliday, indicating the GPS unit in his hand.

'My father was a captain in the Long Range Desert Group, based at Siwa during the war. His maps were just about my only inheritance. I've put them to good use over the years. They used to rattle back and forth through here all the time.'

'When we find the people who took Peggy, *if* we find them, then what are we supposed to do?' Rafi asked, a skeptical tone in his voice.

Tidyman glanced over at him and smiled blandly.

'I would have thought that was obvious, my young Israeli friend.' The smile broadened. 'We kill them.'

At the next GPS waypoint Tidyman hauled the wheel around, turning the old truck north, navigating carefully along the base of the ranging lines of dunes following the now invisible pathway through the sand. There were no landmarks now, only the burning sky above their heads and the relentless sun.

'We're traveling parallel to the border now,' commented Tidyman. He waved a hand. 'The old Italian fence is a couple of miles to the west. Long since buried by the dunes, of course. Mussolini was really an arrogant fool, thinking that he could tame the desert with a string of wire.'

They traveled for another twenty minutes, then pulled into the meager shade offered by a wind-sculpted pinnacle of rock. The sandstone looked vaguely like a truncated version of the Sphinx.

'Why are we stopping?' asked Rafi, suspicion clear in his voice.

'A bit of a recce, as my father would say,' Tidyman said and smiled. 'And a little bit of protective coloration.' He half turned in his seat and dragged a small knapsack from the back of the Goat. 'Get out and stretch your legs,' the Egyptian offered. 'It will take a minute or two.'

Tidyman climbed out from behind the driver's seat with the knapsack and Holliday joined him.

'Your Israeli friend doesn't seem to like me very much,' said Tidyman.

'He's worried abut Peggy.'

'He is romantically involved with your cousin?'

'Yes.'

'Don't worry. We'll find her,' said Tidyman. He put his hand on Holliday's shoulder. 'Tell him I am sorry for his pain.'

'I will.'

Tidyman nodded, then followed a steep pathway that ran up the tall pale outcropping of stone. Holliday turned and saw Rafi approaching.

'What was that all about?' he asked.

'Extending the hand of friendship.' Holliday shrugged. 'He thinks you don't like him.'

'He's right,' grunted Rafi. 'I don't like him and I don't trust him.'

'He's all we've got at the moment,' said Holliday. 'So make nice.'

Rafi nodded and walked a little way into the shadows off the rocky outcropping. Joining him, Holliday saw it wasn't rock at all; the outcropping was made up of aggregated fossil oyster shells and dense chalk.

'Miocene,' said Rafi. 'Twenty million years old, give or take a millennia or two, despite what your so-called Creationists think.'

Holliday's shoe stubbed itself on something buried in the hard-packed sand at his feet. He squatted down and swept some of the sand away. It looked like a blackened tin. He dug away more sand and tugged at the can. He held it up. The can had oxidized over the years but the label was still readable.

'Campbell's Cream of Tomato,' said Holliday.

Rafi had discovered another tin.

'Vacuum Oil Company.' Like the soup tin, this one was blackened with oxidation.

'The original name of Socony Mobil,' said Holliday. 'This must have been a Long Range Desert Group camp back in the war.'

'So what do we call this place?' pondered Rafi. 'A garbage pit or an archaeological site?'

'That would depend on your point of view, I suppose,' said Tidyman, coming down from the rock. 'On my father's maps it is referred to as the Mushroom, I suppose because of its shape.'

Rafi turned away without comment. Tidyman shrugged and smiled thinly at Holliday.

'As I said, your friend does not like me.'

'He doesn't have to,' answered Holliday, a little curtly. 'Did you see anything up there?'

'A great deal of nothing,' said Tidyman. He nodded politely to Holliday, then went to the truck. He squatted down and took a screwdriver out of his knapsack, then removed the blue-and-white Egyptian license plate and replaced it with an oblong Libyan plate, black on reflective green. That done, he put on a rear plate and then a magnetic stick-on symbol on the door, much like the one Felix Valador used on his truck in Cannes.

'The license plate I understand,' commented Holliday. 'But what exactly is that?' The stick-on symbol showed four lengths of open pipeline in forced perspective with a line of cursive Arabic below it.

'It's the insignia of the Great Man-Made River Authority, Qaddafi's big irrigation project. Jaghbub Oasis is the wellhead for the pipeline that goes to Tobruk.' He stood back and examined his handiwork. 'Luckily they use a Chinese knockoff of the Goat called a BJ-212 to get around in.' He shrugged. 'It won't stand close inspection but it would pass a quick surveillance from the air.'

'Is that likely to happen?'

'It's happened to me before. But Colonel

Qaddafi is rather stingy with fuel for those Mil-24 Hind helicopters of his and they have to come all the way from the air base at Kufra; that's almost four hundred miles south.'

'How far is Jaghbub from here?'

'About twenty miles. But we'll wait here until it's dark. The actual border is only about two miles west of us.'

They waited for nightfall, Tidyman dozing, his back against the Mushroom, Rafi pacing, listening for sounds that weren't there and worrying, Holliday looking idly at the debris left behind by the Long Range Desert Group more than half a century before. Not for the first time in his life Holliday found himself thinking about the borders between countries and why men fought over such artificial boundaries. Once a holocaust had been birthed for one man's need for *Lebensraum*, but Hitler was by no means the first to fight for more territory, nor would he likely be the last.

When night came it came quickly, the sun burning down among the windswept dunes and flat-topped sandstone buttes, leaving nothing behind but a dark pink curtain against the darkness. Tidyman roused himself and they climbed back into the Goat. There was a chill in the air and Holliday shivered as Tidyman started the engine and went around the base of the tall mushroom-shaped rock.

'Ten minutes to the border now. If there is any trouble I will handle it,' the Egyptian said quietly. They drove on, the desert more rough stones and gravel now rather than sifting sand. The darkness was almost absolute and Tidyman piloted the truck along the trail more by instinct than sight. When they crossed the border there was no indication other than a brief pinging sound from the GPS unit in Holliday's hand.

'That's it,' he said. 'We're in Libya now.'

12

Tidyman drove the old vehicle carefully, guiding it slowly, picking his way forward.

'At this rate we'll never get there,' said Rafi.

'Speed is not of the essence,' said Tidyman, keeping his eyes rigidly facing ahead. 'Care is. This part of the journey can be very treacherous. Drive off the track and we could easily get mired in the sand. And then we *really* won't get there.' The Egyptian said something briefly in Arabic. 'Dying of thirst is not just an expression in this country – it is something to seriously be avoided.'

They drove on through the night, the only sense of the terrain around them coming from looming areas of blackness where the stars were blotted out. They seemed to be hugging the base of a large uneven mound on their left. On the right another mound rose about a hundred yards away. The ground below them was rough, the suspension rattling, jarring Holliday and his companions.

Suddenly it was bright as day. A bright white flare rose above them and lit up the Goat. In the sudden burst of illumination Holliday could see another vehicle less than a hundred feet away, directly in front of them, blocking the track ahead. Tidyman jammed on the brakes. The other vehicle was almost identical to theirs in configuration, but with the back half of the cab removed and a long-barreled Russian-made KPV heavy machine gun mounted. A uniformed soldier stood behind the gun. If Holliday remembered correctly the weapon fired about five hundred rounds a minute and was capable of shooting down airplanes, or in this case turning the Goat into scrap metal along with its passengers. The flare faded out and the other vehicle's headlights flashed on, pinning the Goat down.

'Now what?' Rafi said.

'Don't move,' ordered Tidyman.

'Wouldn't think of it,' said Holliday.

'When I lower my arms switch on the headlights,' instructed the Egyptian quietly, pointing to a black knob on the dashboard.

'Roger that,' said Holliday.

Tidyman cracked open his door and climbed out of the truck, raising his hands in the air.

'Do you think he knows what he's doing?' Rafi asked as Tidyman walked forward into the light.

'He'd better,' said Holliday. 'If he doesn't we're dead.'

Tidyman walked forward, keeping himself in the center of the twin pools of light thrown by the other vehicle, his silhouette casting long twisting shadows behind him.

'What the hell is he doing?' Rafi said urgently, his voice tense.

Holliday didn't bother responding. His hand hovered over the knob. He panicked for a moment, wondering if the knob pulled out or pressed in. He finally decided it pulled out and prayed that he was right. A wrong decision and he and Rafi would be blown to kingdom come.

Tidyman reached the other truck. Above the sound of the idling engine Holliday could hear the Egyptian's voice speaking in deliberately loud Arabic, his hands still high above his head. Someone in the truck responded. Tidyman did a slow pirouette.

'Checking him for weapons,' said Holliday.

Tidyman completed his turn, then stopped, hands still high. There was a curt order from inside the other truck. Tidyman walked over to the driver's side and bent down slightly, talking with whoever was inside.

Holliday tensed, sensing something in Tidyman's movement.

The Egyptian's hands dropped abruptly, something glinting as it slid out of the sleeve of his jacket.

Holliday hit the lights.

The blinding beams lit up the other truck and Holliday had a brief impression of Tidyman's hand sweeping in the side window of the vehicle. A split second later a gun appeared in his other hand and there was the barking sound of a single shot being fired. The man at the machine gun didn't even have an instant to respond; he simply crumpled into the bed of the truck as Tidyman's other hand withdrew through the driver's-side window, the dripping blood on the long blade of the knife he held black in the headlights. The whole thing was over in the blink of an eye.

'Dear God!' Rafi whispered, horrified.

Tidyman walked away from the truck, wiping the blade on the leg of his pants. He came back to the Goat and leaned through Rafi's open window. The young archaeologist recoiled in horror.

'You killed them!'

'Of course I killed them,' snapped Tidyman, sounding angry for the first time since they'd met. 'As they would have killed you. This is the real world, my friend, not some theoretical position argued in a debate. There is no morality in this business. They were the enemy.' He looked across at Holliday. 'I'm going to drive their vehicle off the track and behind that group of rocks on the left. I'll need some help with the bodies. If they're not buried the birds will come and lead anyone to them. If we are lucky the search parties won't find them for a while.'

'I'll come,' said Holliday.

Tidyman opened up the back of the Goat and took out his pack as well as something that looked like a paint roller and a mop handle. He screwed the handle onto the roller.

'What's that for?' Holliday asked.

'Cleaning up tire tracks,' answered Tidyman. 'Got the idea from stories my father used to tell me.'

'Is that really necessary?' Holliday said. 'Won't the wind do it for us?'

'In 1927 a man named Ralph Bagnold crossed

the Libyan desert by automobile. He was the first commandant of the LRDG. You can still see the tire tracks from his expedition if you know where to look.' He shook his head. 'The sand crust has a great deal of salt mixed with it and is quite friable. Some parts of the desert are very unforgiving.' The Egyptian put the roller device over his shoulder and headed off into the darkness. Holliday followed.

It was almost midnight by the time they finished. When they were done they trudged back to the Goat, where Rafi awaited them. Before re-entering the truck Tidyman took a flashlight from his pack and turned it on. He swept the beam around the area. The tracks were gone; there was no sign that the other truck had even existed.

'Not perfect; they'll tumble to it eventually,' said Tidyman. 'But it will do for now.' He tucked the flashlight into his pack and got behind the wheel again. This time Rafi sat by the door rather than rub shoulders with the Egyptian. Tidyman started up the truck and headed onward again. They drove on in silence, the steep sloping walls of the sand hills gathering around them. The moon began to rise.

'How soon?' Holliday asked finally.

'Not long,' said Tidyman. 'Almost there.'

And suddenly they were there. Coming through a narrow passage between two rearing slabs of wind-carved sandstone they saw the town of Al-Jaghbub in the distance far below them, looking like a child's clay model, the bleached houses and walls smoothed by time, some crumbling and some no more than ancient foundation stones. In the middle of the town, like a jewel in the center of a crown, the dome of a mosque and its accompanying minaret rose above the buildings around it. Holliday was astounded to see that kind of sophisticated architecture in such an out-of-the-way location.

'The mosque of Muhammad bin Ali As Sanusi. He is buried there,' said Tidyman, reading Holliday's thoughts. 'This was the capital of the Sanusi movement and he was its founder. It is little known now but some scholars mark it as the birthplace of Radical Islam, precursor to the creatures who brought us 9/11.'

To the north they could see the oasis itself, a dense green shadow of date palm trees and small fields of grain. On the south side of the old walled town, separated by a distinct end to any vegetation at all, was the Great Sand Sea, an endless vista of elegant waves, frozen by some celestial wizard, never breaking on the shore, creeping forward inch by inexorable inch through the millennia. The moon stood high in the late-night sky, turning everything to shades of cold black shadow and golden sand.

'It's beautiful,' said Rafi, speaking for the first time since the death of the two men in the other truck.

'And to us it's very dangerous,' warned Tidyman.

'Then why are we here?' Rafi asked belligerently.

'We're not,' answered Tidyman.

'Then where the hell are we going?'

'Nowhere,' answered Tidyman obscurely. He put the Goat in gear again and turned southeast, heading out into the sea of dunes following the snaking line of troughs, working directly away from the town.

'Where exactly are we going?' Holliday asked.

'Exactly?' Tidyman answered. 'We're going to twenty-eight degrees forty-eight minutes and fifty-five seconds north by twenty-three degrees forty-six minutes and ten seconds east.' He paused. 'Exactly.'

'And what, *exactly*, are we going to find there?' Rafi asked.

'I told you,' answered Tidyman with a secretive smile. 'Your heart's desire.'

They drove on through the night, stopping every now and again for toilet duty and once to gas up. They ate on the run, chewing their way through cheese and pita sandwiches wrapped in foil, made up for them by the hotel in Siwa. Holliday kept an eye on the GPS unit in his hand and finally, with the sun rising on their right, they reached the coordinates the Egyptian had described.

'We're here, give or take a hundred yards or so,' said Holliday. There was nothing to see but the undulating sand and a single spine of sandstone directly in front of them. Tidyman drove ahead, then turned around the base of the stone obstruction.

'Holy crap,' said Holliday, borrowing one of Peggy's favorite expressions.

There in front of them, like a giant's favorite toy that had been cast aside, was the broken remains of an airplane, the tail section at right angles to the fuselage. It had a bubble nose, the Plexiglas clouded by the passage of time, and a second turret just behind the cockpit. Holliday knew there would be a bottom ball turret in the sand below. It was a World War II B-17 bomber, the star and bar of the United States Air Force still just barely visible on the portside wing. There was a unit identification number on the tail section: a boxed letter *G*, a line of numbers and then an open letter *E* below. The numbers were still clearly visible: 230336.

As they neared the wreckage of the old aircraft the sun climbed above it and they could make out the faded nose art on the fuselage just beneath the cockpit: a finned bomb shaped like a valentine heart with the italicized name curved below the design – *Your Heart's Desire*.

'Very funny,' said Holliday.

'I thought you'd appreciate the irony,' said Tidyman. He pulled the truck to a stop a dozen yards from the wreckage. 'The crew must have bailed out somewhere to the north; there was no sign of any bodies in the aircraft itself. The plane flew on until it ran out of gas and bellied into the sand.'

'What does this have to do with anything?' Rafi asked, the anger clear in his voice. 'We didn't pay you to take us on a nostalgic tour.'

'I think I know,' said Holliday calmly, looking out the windshield at the remains of the old bomber.

'There were maps dated 1945 for Libya and what they once called French Equatorial Africa, part of which they now call Niger. A place called Madama was circled along with the words *"Festung"* and *"Benzin"* written in grease pencil.

'The map was in German. *Festung* is German for fortress and *Benzin* means fuel. They were going to refuel there.'

'I don't get it,' said Rafi. 'The plane has American markings.'

'It was called KG200,' explained Holliday. 'Battle Group 200. They flew captured aircraft, English and American. This plane was probably part of their First Squadron; they were completely run by the SS. This is the plane that was used to ferry out Walter Rauff's booty.'

'Quite right,' said Tidyman. 'Four thousand kilograms of gold; almost five tons.' He turned to Holliday and Rafi. 'Come and take a closer look.' Without waiting for a reply the Egyptian climbed out of the Goat and walked toward the wreckage.

'He knows about the gold,' whispered Rafi.

'Apparently,' said Holliday.

'But how?'

'I think we'd better find out.' Holliday opened his door and followed Tidyman toward *Your Heart's Desire*.

The tailplane had torn off the rest of the fuselage just behind the waist gun positions, offering the only easy access into the aircraft. Sand had drifted into the opening but the interior was clearly visible.

'Interesting,' commented Holliday, coming up beside Tidyman. Holliday had once toured an intact B-17 named *Fuddy Duddy* on a visit to the National Warplane Museum in Elmira, New York, and he could see that *Your Heart's Desire* had been completely stripped. The waist gun positions had been removed, as had the bulkheads between the gun positions and the bomb bay. There was an odd collection of empty wooden pigeonholes retrofitted against the fuselage walls and it took Holliday a minute to figure it out.

'Storage for the gold bars arranged so that the

weight would be equalized,' he said finally. 'Hell to fly, I'd guess.'

'I suspect so,' Tidyman said and nodded. 'When it was discovered, there was a set of auxiliary fuel tanks in the bomb bay made from fifty-gallon drums. An extra five hundred gallons, which must have stretched their weight to the limit.'

Rafi appeared beside them.

'You seem to know a great deal about it,' said Holliday to the Egyptian.

'Indeed I do,' answered Tidyman. 'Not surprising since I was the one who discovered her.'

'So you removed the gold, hid it away,' said Holliday. As casually as he could he slipped his right hand into the pocket of his jacket.

'Oh, dear me, no.' Tidyman laughed. 'I'm nothing more than a toiler in the fields, a journeyman smuggling cigarettes and a few guns from time to time. A billion and a half dollars in gold would be a death sentence for a man like me. That sort of greed gets your throat cut in a Cairo back alley or the Bouhadema slums in Benghazi. No, no, Colonel Holliday, I put the bullion in much safer hands.'

'You knew who we were right from the start, didn't you?' Holliday said.

'Of course, just as I know that you have a small pistol in the right-hand pocket of your jacket. Be so good as to remove it with your thumb and forefinger. Then drop it on the ground.' Tidyman's own weapon, an old Helwan 9mm, appeared in his left hand and he put the muzzle up to Rafi's temple. 'You have until the count of three before I blow your young friend's brains all over the nice clean sand.'

'You traitorous son of a bitch,' breathed Rafi hotly, his voice shaking with anger. 'I never trusted you, not from the very beginning.'

'The wise man doesn't insult he who has a gun to his head,' said Tidyman. His eyes on Rafi, the Egyptian began to count aloud. 'One . . . two . . .'

Holliday brought the palm-sized Hawg .45 out of his pocket and dropped it at his feet.

'Now kick it away,' instructed Tidyman.

Holliday did as he was told. Tidyman stepped back three paces, well out of range of any foolish attack, the pistol in his hand still raised.

'So whose safe hands did you put the gold into?' Holliday asked.

Tidyman tilted his head to the left.

'Theirs,' he said.

Holliday and Rafi turned to look.

A hundred feet away half a dozen men sat perched on camels. They were dressed in full Tuareg costume, long indigo robes, almost black robes, indigo turbans and veils worn like masks over the bottom half of their faces. Five of the men carried Chinese Norinco Type 86S automatic rifles, a Bullpup variant of the Russian AK-47. The sixth man carried a Norinco rocket-propelled grenade launcher strapped across his back. A long tether made from braided leather was snubbed around the high horn of his saddle, leading back to three pack camels behind them. Chain bridles were threaded through their wide nostrils to keep them in check. The camels had a uniformly sour expression on their faces, as though they were all chewing something foul-tasting.

'My brothers from the Brotherhood of the Temple of Isis, the men who kidnapped your friend.'

13

Tidyman drove the Goat into the lee of the spine of rock, pulling it in as close to the sandstone wall as he could. It was easy enough to see why. The rock promontory ran almost exactly north-south. Left where it was, the sun rising over the length of rock in the morning would cast an enormous shadow running away from the truck and easily visible from an air patrol passing overhead.

The men in Tuareg dress spoke briefly to Tidyman, then gave him a bundle of robes from one of the pack camels. Fifteen minutes later the Egyptian, Holliday and Rafi, now dressed exactly like the six armed men, were aboard the trailing camels and moving west, away from the wreckage of the B-17. Ten minutes after that *Your Heart's Desire* had been swallowed up by the endless sand. To a distant observer on the ground or in the air, they would look no more ominous than a plodding caravan of nomads.

They rode for twelve long days, heading deeper and deeper into the Great Sand Sea. At night the camels would be rope hobbled and tied to simple picket lines to keep them from wandering off and the men would set up simple leather tents over bent 'withies', skeletal supports of thin twigs. Tea was boiled on simple stoves made out of galvanized bowls placed over tin cans filled with dried camel dung. Meals usually consisted of goat meat jerky or nocturnal desert rat, fennec fox, and even surprisingly succulent sand vipers the men sometimes hunted in the late evenings.

At night Holliday and Rafi were inevitably bound with ropes and guarded by at least one of the men with automatic rifles. From the moment they had been captured, Tidyman kept well away from the two men, sleeping in his own tent. During the long, tedious days Tidyman rode the last pack animal, while Holliday rode the first. An armed guard rode in the rear.

Holliday had no idea where they were going. All he knew was that they were traveling southwest, the sun setting ahead of them and well away to his right-hand side. They were headed roughly in the direction of the Niger border, the same route that *Your Heart's Desire* had been taking when some long-ago disaster struck; perhaps a multiple engine failure, a control malfunction, or maybe a fuel leak. It didn't matter; whatever the problem, it had been enough to precipitate the desperate act of bailing out over the desert.

He tried to imagine what it would have been like for the bomber crew, most likely only four men since there would have been no need for gunners: pilot, co-pilot, engineer and navigator.

They would have hit the silk low because the aircraft would have been flying that way to conserve fuel. They would have hit the desert hard but close together, and then they would have taken stock of their situation. It couldn't have been good.

The men would almost certainly have had neither water nor food, and if by some chance they did, it wouldn't have been much – sandwiches perhaps, or a thermos or two of coffee. Four men, probably relatively small in stature, as most airmen were at the time, would last seventy-two hours at most and probably much less if they traveled in the heat of the day. They would have known that, but they would have tried anyway. But how far can a person walk in the shifting sands of a desert in the three or four days they had before they collapsed and died? Sixty miles, seventy, a hundred at most. Not enough.

Somewhere along the way they would have started stripping off their clothes, the worst thing they could do since it would only accelerate the evaporation of their sweat, hastening their dehydration. Their tongues would thicken, their lips would crack and their noses would begin to bleed.

Eventually they'd stop perspiring and fever would set in. As the cells in their brains dried out convulsions and hallucinations would begin. Trapped within the skull the cerebral fluid would actually begin to boil. Soon after that the kidneys and other major organs would begin to fail one after the other, leading quickly to toxemia, plasma loss, coma and eventually death.

It would be an inexorable, inevitable, excruciating way to die. Somewhere in the rolling sands around him, probably mummified, were the remains of those four men, anonymous and long forgotten, their mission lost to eternity.

Somehow, as Holliday plodded on hour after hour, it became terribly important that he find out the names of the crew of *Your Heart's Desire*, and he vowed to do just that if he somehow managed to get out of his own predicament. Failed or not, the mission and the men who flew it deserved their small place in history.

On the thirteenth day of their journey the landscape began to change; the rolling dunes gave way to smaller, more sculpted waves of sand, broken with hard crust desert and stretches of barren, hard, rocky plateaus with very little sand. They traveled faster on the plains and traveled longer, sometimes far into the numbingly cold nights. There was a tension in the air; Holliday had seen it often enough on forced marches – they were nearing their destination. It couldn't be soon enough for him; Peggy had been missing for more than three weeks now and Holliday was beginning to fear terribly for her safety. Rafi was almost frantic with worry.

On the fourteenth day the landscape changed again. The broken plain gave way to a massive escarpment rising above the flatland at least two thousand feet, a huge, apparently impenetrable wall directly in front of them. As they approached it throughout that day Holliday began to pick out sandy scars in the face of the escarpment, the mouths of wadis, or ancient riverbeds forming sloping approaches to the high wall.

Towards the end of the day they reached one of these and barely slowed as they climbed up the escarpment along the winding trail of sand. Holliday tried to imagine what this place would have looked like when man first walked here a hundred thousand years ago. Probably paradise; in huge areas of Libya and Egypt the weather ran in cycles, drying and wetting, the desert expanding and contracting like a gigantic lung. As recently as the time of the pharaohs much of the landscape they were traveling through had been home to waving fields of grain, tumbling rivers and streams and forests and veldts alive with herds of wandering animals and their predators. The riverbed they were working their way along was easily as wide as the Mississippi and had probably been much faster. It was all very hard to imagine.

They reached the top of the escarpment and left the sand-filled riverbed as darkness fell, and by the time they pitched camp for the night they had traveled a good distance along it. The next day was spent moving across the top of the plateau, traveling more west than south now. Every now and again they passed the abandoned ruins of mud- and salt-brick villages and once something that had to have been an old colonial fort, Italian or French. At noon they actually crossed a road lined with electrical transmission towers and in late afternoon they crossed another.

By Holliday's rough calculations they had traveled at least six hundred miles from the wreckage of *Your Heart's Desire.* That put them closer to the border of Algeria, Niger, and Chad than anywhere else. *From one frying pan into another,* he thought. Algeria was a corrupt semidictatorship and a hotbed of ethnic Berber al-Qaeda terrorists, Niger was in the midst of a Tuareg insurrection and Chad had their UFDD rebel alliance. Who was it who said that God had forgotten Africa? A very bad place for an American to be, worse for a woman and suicide for an Israeli. Getting out of this was going to be some piece of work.

The sixteenth day turned out to be the last. Late in the morning they reached another, much narrower wadi and instead of crossing it they turned abruptly, following it almost due north. By midafternoon the wadi petered out and they climbed up out of the ancient watercourse. They were at the edge of the escarpment, two thousand feet above a giant tract of rolling desert that reached the horizon. The small caravan came to a momentary stop.

To their left, along a precipitous goat track that angled down the face of the cliff, there was a sand rift between the main escarpment and a long extrusion of sandstone. It looked like the space between a person's thumb and forefinger. From where Holliday sat perched on his camel the sandy rift looked to be ten or twelve miles long. Big enough to hide an entire army if you wanted. To the right, in the far distance, was a large blot of green shimmering like a mirage in the light of the burning sun. Something that looked suspiciously like a paved road ran directly through it, angling along at the foot of the escarpment.

Civilization.

Holliday felt a single small surge of hope and exhilaration. He saw what the men from *Your Heart's Desire* had not: a way out of their predicament. He yelled to the man on the camel in front of him.

'Hey!'

The man in the Tuareg robes turned in his saddle, the lethal automatic rifle clutched in his hands. When he spoke his muffled voice was harsh and dry; he was a man who had spent his life in the parched desert.

'*Matha tureed?*' the Tuareg said, dark eyes peering out over the masklike veil over the lower half of his face. Holliday pointed towards the oasis in the distance. The turbaned man looked.

'Where are we?' Holliday said, his arm extended, finger still pointing. The man called to his companion on the camel ahead of him and the other Tuareg turned in his own saddle and replied in a long string of guttural Tamasheq. The man in front of Holliday nodded, then turned again.

'*Wadi el Agial, sadiqi. Zinchechra. Germa.*'

Whatever the hell that meant.

They edged down the goat path for several hours, the unprotected drop only a gut-clenching foot or so away from their camels' slapping hooves, every lurching, swaying step threatening to be their last. Holliday had never had a problem with heights, but after twenty minutes or so he was forced to look the other way and finally simply shut his eyes against the nauseating vertigo.

They reached the bottom at about four o'clock and spent another hour crossing the flat hardpan of the little valley, heading for the fingerlike extension of the escarpment that separated them from the expanse of desert beyond.

The surroundings included scrub bushes, thornbushes, the occasional desert beetle, and a great deal of hard, crusted white sand. Then they began to see small herds of goats being herded by Tuareg men in their traditional turban, and some children playing. Eventually they saw what appeared to be a permanent camp of some kind in the distance.

The closer they got, the larger the encampment became. The goat-and-camel-skin tents were much larger than the pup-sized ones they and their captors used and there were thornbush enclosures of goats and picket lines of camels everywhere. Taking a quick count as they passed, Holliday estimated that there were at least five hundred men in the camp. Interestingly the location of the tents and corrals was such that except at high noon it would be perpetually in the shadow of either the escarpment or its extension, making it next to invisible from the air. Up-to-date tactics for an ancient people against a modern enemy: the airplane and the satellite.

At the far side of the camp the group stopped in front of a moderate-sized tent and gestured for Holliday and Rafi to dismount. One of the armed men gave a harsh command and rapped the camels on the nose with a little stick. The animals obediently dropped down on the knees of their front legs and Rafi and Holliday climbed down. The guard gestured to the tent opening and they went into the stifling interior.

It was luxurious in comparison to what they'd seen in the last two weeks. The walls were set out with heavy pillows and the floors were covered with woven rugs in a dozen different vivid patterns. A small cast iron grill stood in the middle of the tent and there was a ventilation hole in the ceiling to let out the smoke. Their guard turned and spoke.

'*Sa arje'o halan,*' he said.

Holliday nodded even though he didn't know what had been said. So did Rafi. The man in the turban and robe turned on his sandaled heel and walked out of the tent. Outside they heard an exchange and then the sound of the camels moving off. Both Holliday and Rafi dropped down onto the pillows.

'He said he'd be right back, I think,' muttered Rafi. Holliday nodded, exhausted.

'Two weeks on a camel. My fanny's turned to stone,' he grunted.

'I'd hate to tell you what mine feels like,' said Rafi, sighing, then leaning back and closing his eyes. 'What did our blue friend tell you when we were up on the plateau?'

'Something like: *Wadi el Agial, sadiqi. Zinchechra. Germa,*' answered Holliday, trying to remember. 'Any idea what it means?'

'I know exactly what it means,' said Rafi, opening his eyes and sitting up. There was excitement in his voice. '*Wadi el Agial* means Valley of Life, *sadiqi* means my friend, Zinchechra is the name of an ancient mythical castle and Germa is the capital of an almost forgotten kingdom. I know precisely where we are: this is Virgil's Garamanthia, the warrior kingdom of the Garamathes. This is one of the most important archaeological sites in the world.'

'It feels like the ends of the earth,' said Holliday.

'You don't get it, do you?' Rafi said, almost laughing.

''Fraid not,' said Holliday, unmoving on his pillows. His voice was filled with sleep.

'This explains a lot,' said the young archaeologist. 'Draw a straight line a thousand miles east of here and you reach the Nile River at Karnak, where the historical Imhotep appears, "Out of the setting sun," as the ancient texts say. That's usually taken to mean he came from the land of death, from Anubis, god of the underworld. Some other stories have him as one of the sons of Ra, the sun itself. It's a variation on all the religious mumbo-jumbo about the birth of Christ. On top of that, Imhotep's mythological mother is said to have been Hathor, the Warrior Queen.

'The point is there was no desert in those days, at least not here. Imhotep, or certainly his real father, could have made the trip easily. It fits! Imhotep, the real one, isn't buried somewhere in Egypt. He came home to die. He came here. This is the location of Imhotep's tomb, or at least someone thinks so!'

There was the slow sound of applause from the entrance to the tent. Startled, both Holliday and Rafi looked up. A man stood beside the tent flap, clapping. He was in his early forties, good-looking, fit and tanned with thick, black, very curly hair. He was clean shaven. He wore slightly tinted glasses and was dressed in a white *Archaeologists Like It Dirty* T-shirt, faded blue jeans and a pair of black Nike Air Hiking Boots.

'An excellent theory, Dr Wanounou, and you're

quite right; someone does think that this is the location of Imhotep's tomb. Me. Not only do I think it – I know it for a fact. You and Colonel Holliday arrived at an exciting time.' The man's accent in English was vaguely British, maybe an affectation.

'You seem to know quite a bit about us,' said Holliday coldly. There was something not quite right about the man in the T-shirt.

'Of course.' The man smiled pleasantly. 'For instance, I know you teach history at West Point Military Academy, lost your eye in a freak accident in Afghanistan and have recently rather annoyed the intelligence arm of the Holy See. I know that Dr Wanounou's Ph.D. thesis was entitled *The Development, Significance and Function of Tool-Making and the Evolution of the Blacksmith's Craft in the Land of Israel during the Iron Age I Period*, because I both read and enjoyed it. I also know that he was involved with your last contretemps in Jerusalem and suffered a terrible beating because of it.'

He hadn't got all that from a quick conversation with Emil Abdul Tidyman, thought Holliday.

'Who the hell *are* you?' Rafi asked.

'Forgive me,' said the man in the T-shirt.

'Where are my manners? The press knows me as Mustafa Ahmed Ben Halim. My real name is Dr Rafik Alhazred. I am an archaeologist like yourself, among other things.' Alhazred smiled. 'I am also the leader of the Brotherhood of Isis and the man responsible for kidnapping the delightful Miss Peggy Blackstock.'

14

'Why did you take Peggy?' Rafi demanded. 'She's no part of your agenda.'

'She was there, her bad luck. She could have been killed,' answered Rafik Alhazred. 'And what do you know about my agenda?'

'You're a terrorist. What's there to know?' Holliday shrugged.

'Most terrorists are lunatics of one stripe or another,' said Alhazred. 'They generally have issues about the size of their genitalia. Scratch a terrorist and you'll find a small penis. Any graduate student in psychology can tell you that. Hitler, Stalin, bin Laden; why do you think he blew up the World Trade Center, America's phallic symbol? He had weenie issues. Even George Bush was in a pissing contest with his father.'

'George Bush wasn't a terrorist. He was the president of the United States,' answered Holliday.

'Your patriotism is exemplary, Colonel, but

Bush the younger terrorized his own people and used Homeland Security to do it, much like Hitler used the Gestapo. The Fuhrer had Himmler. Bush Jr had Dick Cheney.

'A little simplistic, don't you think?' Holliday asked. Come on now; a philosophical argument about what constitutes a terrorist while sitting in a camel-skin tent in the middle of the Sahara Desert? It was insane.

'We could go on with this argument forever,' said Rafi. 'But it's got nothing to do with Peggy.'

'Miss Blackstock went on at length about her relationship with you and yours with her. It was touching. I'm sorry to have caused undue anxiety.'

'What have you done with her?' Holliday asked.

'She's quite safe, at least for the moment,' said Alhazred. 'Unlike her companions, all of whom have gone to meet their maker, I'm afraid.'

'You murdered a bunch of priests?' Holliday said.

'I defended myself,' answered Alhazred. 'And they were no more priests than I am a colonel.'

'Then who were they?'

'Brother Charles-Étienne Brasseur, the leader

of the expedition, was a longtime operative for La Sapinière, French Vatican Intelligence. He was the only real archaeologist in the group. Even Miss Blackstock was suspicious of that; there wasn't even a graduate student on the so-called team.'

'Then who were they and what were they doing with Brasseur?' Rafi said.

'They were mercenaries hired from the ranks of true believers, like the men of Propaganda Due or Opus Dei. They all had previous military experience.'

'How do you know that?' Holliday asked.

'Well, in the first place they were armed,' responded Alhazred. 'When we eventually made contact they opened fire on us with automatic weapons, mostly Beretta AR-70s. They killed three of my men before they had a chance to return fire.' He paused. 'Hardly the pious behavior of priests.' Alhazred pulled a crumpled package of Marlboros out of his back pocket, tapped one out and lit it with a paper match. He blew a plume of smoke up at the roof of the tent. 'Later we found out that they had all been in the Département protection sécurité, the storm trooper arm of the National Front Party in

France and the First "Draghi" desert unit of the Italian R.A.O., the Reggimento Ricognizione e Acquisizione Obiettivi – in other words, commandos.'

'You're saying they were on a military mission?' Holliday asked.

'Thieves in the night, Colonel. They came for *Your Heart's Desire* and the gold it contained; Imhotep's tomb was just an excuse for the expedition.'

'What about Brasseur's theory?'

'Bogus; Brasseur was a medievalist. He was interested in the Templars' role at Damietta certainly, but the Imhotep theory was an invention of Centro d'informazione pro Deo, Vatican Intelligence in Rome. Brasseur discovered the wartime journals of a man named Father Andrew Felix Morion. He was the one who set up the removal of the gold for Rauff in 1944.'

'You seem to know a lot about the Catholic Church,' said Rafi.

'Why shouldn't I?' Alhazred said, smiling coldly. 'I was raised in it.'

'You're not a Muslim?' Rafi asked, surprised.

'I've never heard of a Catholic terrorist, either,' said Holliday.

'A terrorist is as a terrorist does. I was born in Beirut, Lebanon. My father was native Lebanese, my mother was French Canadian of Lebanese descent. They were both doctors. They were working at Nabatieh, a Palestinian refugee camp, in July of 1974 when the Israelis bombed it to rubble.' He looked across the tent at Rafi. 'Your people, Dr Wanounou. They murdered my parents for no reason. I was two years old at the time. I have no memory of my parents. I know them only from a few photos and the stories my uncle told me. They were stolen from me the way Walter Rauff stole the Jewish gold on that plane, the way they would have stolen it from me if they'd had the opportunity. As I said, a terrorist is as a terrorist does. I'm no terrorist, gentlemen. I'm just a man taking his revenge.'

'No political motivation at all?' Holliday asked.

'Only the politics of thievery, other people taking other people's things. My Tuareg friends here having their land stolen away for lunatic projects, their cultural history stolen just as surely. Did you know that the Germa site has never been excavated by Libyan archaeologists? French, American, British, yes, colonial powers all. But Libyans? Not on your life.'

Alhazred finished his cigarette, then turned and stepped out of the tent for a second, grinding out the butt into the sand at his feet. He stepped back inside the tent.

'So my companions in the Brotherhood decided that we would make money out of it all at least, which is how things started. I was toiling as a field-worker at the Zinchechra site, stealing small artifacts and selling them to smugglers. That's how I met the estimable Mr Tidyman. We had much in common. He was an expatriate and so was I; we had a shared, partial Canadian heritage. Blood brothers if you will. That led to a whole chain of connections up the smugglers' network, to Cairo, Alexandria, Tripoli, Tobruk, Tunis, Marseille, a lot of places.'

'Valador and his fishing boat. The tugboat in Alexandria,' said Holliday.

'That's right, the *Khamsin*.' The handsome Lebanese man smiled. 'Then I found the tomb and everything changed.'

'Imhotep?' Rafi asked.

'Himself,' confirmed Alhazred. 'I was looking for a place to cache artifacts I'd taken from the main dig when I stumbled on it. The site at Zinchechra is enormous. As well as the old town ruins and the Garamathes' fortress there are also hundreds of beehive tombs from the earlier group who occupied the oasis. I shouldn't have been surprised; the tombs look like miniature truncated pyramids, much like the step pyramid at Saqqara built by Imhotep for King Djoser in 2600 B.C. It's clear now that's where the design came from; Imhotep simply enlarged the scale.'

'He was buried in one?' Rafi asked.

'Hidden would be a better description. Like Edgar Allan Poe's "The Purloined Letter". I believe the term is "hidden in plain sight",' said Alhazred. 'In most of the tombs the occupant was buried upright; that's what I expected to find in the one I opened. A tiny space but big enough for what I had in mind. Instead there was a shaft and a passage leading to quite a large underground chamber.'

'The tomb,' offered Holliday.

'Yes,' said Alhazred.

'Sealed?' Rafi said.

'Sealed and with Imhotep's cartouche pressed into the plaster when it was still wet.'

'What did you see when you opened it?' Rafi's eyes were like saucers. Alhazred was describing every archaeologist's fondest dream; their heart's desire, in fact.

'Wonderful things,' said Alhazred wistfully, remembering. 'Not the tomb of a king, like Tutankhamen, but the tomb of a thinking man, an architect, an engineer, an inventor, a doctor and a mathematician. Architectural models, intact clay and wax tablets, wall paintings, small sculptures, a great deal of jewelry. All authentic Third Dynasty. Worth millions.'

'If you'd gone public with the find it would have made your reputation,' said Rafi.

'Who discovered King Tut's tomb?' Alhazred sneered.

'Howard Carter,' said Rafi promptly.

'Not so,' said Alhazred. 'It was his foreman, Ahmed Rais, an illiterate Egyptian. Carter could have kept digging for the rest of his life and never found it.'

'You're saying you wouldn't have gotten credit for the find?' Holliday said.

'Not in a million years. I got my doctorate at the American University in Beirut. The head of the Germa dig was a postdoctoral Fellow at Oxford. Do you know anything about the politics of academia in the archaeology field, Colonel Holliday?'

'Nothing,' admitted Holliday.

'I do,' said Rafi.

'What luck would I have had getting credit for an enormous find like that?'

'Not a chance in hell,' agreed Rafi with a sigh.

'Exactly.' Alhazred nodded and lit another cigarette. 'So I kept it quiet.'

'You and your friends started smuggling artifacts from the tomb,' said Holliday. Rafi winced, knowing the historical loss that came from that kind of destructive, unscientific looting. Movies like Clive Cussler's *Sahara*, the modern *Mummy* series, and worst of all the *Lara Croft: Tomb Raider* films extolled the worst kind of archaeology. At least Indiana Jones wasn't in it for the money.

'That's precisely what we did, and we were getting rich doing it, Emil and I. Then Emil tripped over *Your Heart's Desire* while he was taking a load of booty from the tomb back to Siwa. We knew we were in trouble right from the start.'

'I'd hardly call finding a billion dollars in bullion trouble,' said Rafi.

'Really?' Alhazred gave a mocking laugh. 'A billion dollars that isn't yours in a country ruled by a lunatic dictator crazier than Saddam Hussein? It was trouble, believe me. As soon as we started trickling the gold out a few bars at a time the people at the far end of the smugglers' chain of command started asking questions. Bad people. So we invented the Brotherhood of Isis and became political. It made us more dangerous to the big-time criminals we had to deal with. It also got us friends and a few accommodations about traveling in the revolutionary zones in Niger and Chad. My Tuaregs loved it. Calling themselves the Brotherhood reminded them of their warrior past and gave them status among the other tribes. Problems still exist. We are well hidden here, and remote, but far too many people know about the gold now. Eventually the trouble will come to a head. I would like to act before that happens.'

'How did you find out we were coming for Peggy?' Rafi asked.

'She said you would,' explained Alhazred. 'Both of you. I thought it was bluff and bluster, but then Fusani's body floated up and I knew you were coming.' He smiled. 'I guess neither of you was a Boy Scout; your knots weren't tight enough.'

'Fusani?' Rafi frowned.

'The engineer on the *Khamsin*,' suggested Holliday.

'Quite so,' said Alhazred.

'At which point you set us up with Tidyman,' Holliday said.

Again Alhazred nodded.

'Yes. It was logical that without papers to cross the border at Sollum you would find your way to Siwa. After that it was easy.'

'It's a great story,' said Holliday. 'But it doesn't get us any closer to Peggy.'

'Nor will it, not for the moment.'

'Not for the moment?' Holliday said.

'How do we know she's even alive?' Rafi asked bluntly.

'You don't,' said Alhazred. 'But I can assure you that she is.'

'What do you want from us?' Holliday asked.

'I'd like your opinion about something,' said Alhazred. 'Yours from a military perspective, Colonel Holliday, and yours from an archaeologist's point of view, Dr Wanounou. Do that for me tomorrow and I'll be happy to tell you where Peggy is.' He gave a curt little nod. 'We'll head for the tomb tomorrow evening, less chance of being seen. Until then feel free to wander about the camp. Try to escape and Miss Blackstock will be killed within the hour. Understand?'

'Yes,' said Holliday. Rafi was silent.

'Good,' said Alhazred. He turned on his heel and threw back the tent flap, then disappeared outside.

'Illuminating,' said Holliday, leaning back on the pillows, staring thoughtfully at the entrance to the tent.

'How much of that do you believe?' Rafi asked.

'All of it. None of it. Who knows?' Holliday shrugged. 'All I *do* know is that guy talks too much and there's something creepy about him. Something missing.'

'Is Peggy alive?' Rafi asked, his voice cracking.

'If she's not I guarantee you *sayyed* Alhazred is a dead man,' vowed Holliday grimly.

15

They awakened with the rest of the camp at dawn the following day. Holliday knew there was a guard outside the tent throughout the night because he heard him singing softly to himself. The songs were all quiet dirges, like memories of the enormous desert they had just crossed. Sleep didn't come easily and his thoughts inevitably turned to Peggy and her whereabouts. He'd told Rafi that Alhazred would die if he'd harmed her in any way, but privately on his own restless voyage through the night, Holliday also promised himself that the man's death would not come either quickly or easily.

Breakfast was strong black coffee and *taguella*, a thick crepelike bread made from millet flour and goat's milk but without sugar. A Tuareg brought them the overnight bags they'd brought with them from Siwa and they changed into fresh clothes. After that, just as Alhazred had promised, they were given the run of the camp. Holliday was the first to decipher the site's design.

'It's a Roman castra,' he said after a few minutes of walking through the camp. 'A square inside a sand rampart and a dry ditch. About three hundred by three hundred and all the tents laid out in rows. That big tent in the middle is probably Alhazred's. It's a military formation. The first real attempt at urban planning.' They climbed up the sandy hill at the south side of the camp. A Tuareg guard patrolling the top of the rampart with a rifle slung across his back eyed them speculatively. Like targets. Or prey.

'New weapon from the looks of it,' said Rafi as they reached the summit of the sandy wall. 'Alhazred equips his people well.'

'It's a C7 assault rifle,' said Holliday. 'Knockoff of the U.S. Army M-18. Canadian again.'

'Tidyman was raised in Canada and Alhazred's mother was Canadian as well; they must have lots of connections there. I know they have a big Lebanese immigrant population; it's been that way for a long time.'

'Canada, the terrorist's Switzerland,' replied Holliday, looking down at the camp. 'Easy to get into on a visitor's visa and the border is a four-thousand-mile sieve. You can walk through a wheat field in Saskatchewan and not even know you'd crossed into Montana.' He shook his head wearily. Holliday knew a few Homeland Security types who'd told him that between terrorists and high-grade marijuana, the Canadian border needed a fence even more than Mexico. 'During the Vietnam War they said more Russian spies crossed into New York State at Niagara Falls than anywhere else. Couldn't go on a tour bus without running into some guy in a Hawaiian shirt named Vladimir.'

'Funny place,' said Rafi, a slightly wistful tone in his voice. 'There was a beautiful girl in one of my classes at university named Joy Schlesinger. She had the greatest . . . Anyway, she came from some place called Medicine Hat. What *is* a medicine hat?'

'I don't have the slightest idea,' said Holliday, distracted. He turned around and looked out across the open stretch of sand between them and the ragged promontory of rock that separated the camp from the main desert beyond. The camp had been situated about two miles from the foot of the dark, stony crags. Far enough away so that the steep cliffs offered no strategic high ground. An enemy could be seen coming from miles away. He turned again and looked at the Tuareg guard. As well as the rifle he had a pair of Leupold 10×50 binoculars. Holliday turned toward the distant hills. He squinted and shaded his eyes.

'What are you looking at?' Rafi asked.

'Look out here,' Holliday instructed. 'What do you see about five hundred yards out?'

'Sand,' Rafi answered. 'Blindingly white sand.'

'Look closer.'

Rafi thought he could make out a slightly darker strip in the bright hot sunlight.

'A road?'

'Except it doesn't go anywhere,' murmured Holliday. 'Look.'

Rafi stared. The 'road' looked like a line of hard-packed sand about half a mile long, parallel to the camp.

'What kind of road doesn't go anywhere?' The archaeologist frowned.

In the distance, overhead, there was a faint mosquito whine that grew louder with every passing second.

'A runway,' said Holliday, glancing up. 'These guys have got a plane.'

A minute or so later, coming from the west and dropping down from the high plateau to the south, the aircraft appeared, an old design with two booms creating twin tailplane assemblies. As it began its approach to the runway the guard on the parapet grew very agitated, unlimbering the rifle from his back and rushing toward them, brandishing the weapon.

'*Edh'hab! Edh'hab!*' the man screamed.

'I think we're supposed to get off the rampart,' said Rafi.

The plane's wheels touched down and the propeller sounds deepened as the pilot backed the engines. The guard stopped, lowering the weapon and aiming it at them.

'I think you're right,' agreed Holliday. They scrambled down the sandy hill. Above them the guard seemed to relax. Holliday and Rafi made their way between two rows of igloo-shaped tents and walked towards the big camel enclosure close to the center of the camp.

'What was that all about?' Rafi asked. He turned his head and looked up at the guard. The Tuareg had gone back to patrolling the rampart.

'I don't think we were supposed to see the plane,' said Holliday.

'Why not?' Rafi said. 'It's not like either one of us can fly.'

'I flew in planes like that all the time in Vietnam,' said Holliday. 'It was a Cessna Skymaster. They called them O2s in-country. They bird-dogged downed pilots and worked as forward artillery spotters. They used to take me and my men into Cambodia and Laos. They even made a movie with one in it. *Bat* 21, I think it was called. Danny Glover and Gene Hackman, our French cop's favorite actor.

'*Popeye-goddamn-bloody-Doyle*,' said Holliday, doing a fair imitation of Louis Japrisot, the police captain in Marseille. '*Gene 'ackman this, Gene 'ackman that!*'

'Could it get us out of here?' Rafi said.

'I think it had a range of about twelve hundred miles. It would get us across the border back into Egypt, probably Tunisia. If either one of us could fly, that is.'

'We can't,' said Rafi thoughtfully. 'But Peggy could; she's got her pilot's license, doesn't she?'

'I don't know if she's rated for twins though; the Skymaster's a push-pull.'

'Better a single-engine pilot than none at all.'

'We'd have to find her first,' said Holliday.

'Isn't that why we're here?' Rafi said, the words a challenge.

By four thirty in the afternoon they were no farther along in their search for the elusive Peggy. The only thing they'd accomplished was a slightly more accurate count of the number of people in the camp – 220 – and the fact that a mixed herd of goats and sheep smelled even worse than an equal number of camels. It amazed Holliday that goats and camels both gave sweet milk but smelled so nauseatingly foul, like a combination of raw sewage and a kid's wet wool mittens roasting on an old-fashioned radiator.

Rafik Alhazred caught up with them just as they were heading back to their assigned tent. Wearing an outfit much like the one he'd had on the day before, he was at the wheel of a brand-new dusty white 200 Series Toyota Land Cruiser without a nick or a ding on it. The big truck looked as though it belonged in a suburban drive-way. The sign on the door read:

Fezzan Project – Libyan Dep't of Antiquities
British Academy
King's College, London
Society for Libyan Studies

There was Arabic text below that was presumably a translation of the English above.

'The truck is mine but the sign's authentic enough,' said Alhazred. 'Change into the robes you arrived in, a little protective coloration. Hurry, please,' he added. 'I'll wait here.'

Holliday and Rafi did as they were told and piled into the truck, robed from head to toe, including the muslin veil across the bottom part of their faces. A real Tuareg crouched in the rear cargo compartment. He wasn't visibly armed but Holliday was sure there was some kind of weapon hidden in the indigo folds of his native costume.

'If we get stopped you say nothing. Speak, and my friend Elhadji back there will slit your throats, quick as a wink. Don't worry – my site identification is perfect. The dig has been in operation for more than a decade; field-workers come and go all the time; no one knows anyone anymore, which is to our benefit.'

Alhazred drove out of an opening in the north rampart that boxed the camp, then immediately turned east, heading towards the neck of the fifteen-mile-long valley, the dark, ominous basalt crags quickly closing in.

'So, Colonel, what do you think of my little pied-à-terre back there?'

'It bears a strong resemblance to a Roman military camp,' said Holliday. 'I'm sure it was no accident.'

'Quite right, quite right,' said Alhazred, clearly pleased. 'I spent a great deal of time at Baalbeck, in the Bekaa Valley, as a student. Very impressive to a young man.'

'Very impressive to the Emperor Vespasian as well,' commented Holliday. Rafi threw him a sudden perplexed glance then looked away. Holliday kept talking. 'Although I doubt his son Trajan appreciated the oracle's prophecy of his death in the Parthian Wars.'

'No, indeed not,' said Alhazred. They drove on. At the head of the valley Alhazred turned the Land Cruiser north and suddenly they thumped onto a paved road. Abruptly and jarringly they were confronted with reality in the form of an old faded billboard offering *Koka Kola* in Russian.

'The good old days,' Alhazred said and laughed.

Gee, we're just the best of pals, aren't we? Holliday thought. *First you threaten to slit our throats. Then you crack jokes.* Alhazred was definitely a few nuts short of his bolts.

They continued eastward along the modern highway for ten or twelve miles, passing huge transport trucks, rattletrap old Lada vans and a few donkey carts heading to market, loaded down with produce. The buildings on either side of the road were mostly mud brick, but there were a couple of quite modern Tamoil gas stations with big blue and white plastic signs over the pumps. The few people they saw were dressed in the ubiquitous indigo robes. No one paid the slightest bit of attention as they passed; the sign on the side of the truck was obviously an open sesame for them.

Without warning Alhazred engaged the four-wheel drive and swung the big Toyota due north again, off the road and onto the crusted desert sand. They headed across the plains, the gigantic dunes of the Erg Murzuq rearing up like wind-scooped mountains on the far side of the wide valley, the sun lowering towards them, casting long shadows trailing behind the truck.

'We're coming in the back door,' commented Alhazred. 'Discretion being the better part of valor and all that.'

Holliday and Rafi were mute, staring out the windows. They saw a few isolated stands of palms and a narrow lake that wouldn't have rated much beyond a pond back in the United States.

In the distance, ruins began to appear, the roofless mud-brick walls of what must have once been a good-sized town. The ruins were so densely packed together they looked like a rat's maze.

'This is the town from the Roman era, first and second century A.D.'

'This isn't where we're going?' Rafi asked.

'No. The beehive tombs are much older than that.' They drove past the old ruins, veering steadily to the right. They hadn't seen a soul since leaving the highway. Suddenly a Russian Gaz Tiger appeared from behind a flat outcropping of rock. It was the Eastern Bloc version of an armored Hummer. There was a soldier in brown Libyan army fatigues who stood poking his upper body through the angular vehicle's top hatch, his hands gripping the firing handles of a big .50-caliber machine gun.

'Trouble?' Holliday asked, tensing as the big truck rumbled toward them.

'Doubtful,' said Alhazred without turning his head. 'They're lazy. Stop us and they'll have to fill out an incident report; they're like soldiers everywhere, they hate paperwork.'

'Is there a military base around here?' Holliday asked, surprised that they'd never stumbled on Alhazred's band of terrorist Tuaregs.

'Just a small squad for constabulary duties,' said Alhazred. 'They must have come out here to drink wine or smoke, or just for something to do. They won't be a bother, I assure you.'

He was right. The armored vehicle roared to within a dozen yards of the Toyota and then the driver saw the sign on the door and waved at Alhazred. He waved back, smiling, and the Tiger sheered away. Within a few seconds it had disappeared behind them. Holliday exhaled.

'You see?' Alhazred said pleasantly. 'Not a problem.'

Good thing, too, thought Holliday. After two weeks in the desert he was burned as much as he was tanned. He looked a bit like an overcooked lobster. Perhaps Rafi could pass as a Tuareg, but even in his indigo robes Holliday knew perfectly well he stood out like a stop sign.

Ten minutes later they reached the field of tombs and Alhazred slowed, weaving his way through the maze of salt-brick structures. Each one was made of rough brick a shade or two darker than the desert around it. They looked like sawed-off pyramids about twelve or fourteen feet high, some pierced with square windows on one or two sides, some solid.

Each of the squared pyramids was separated from its neighbor by what appeared to be a measured fifty feet on every side. The older tombs, the ones farthest to the north, were worn by the wind, blurred and almost shapeless mounds like the beehives that gave the tombs their name.

'One mummy per tomb, usually buried upright,' said Alhazred, pulling to a stop in front of one of the older structures. They'd put the mummy and his or her possessions in the tomb then fill it up with sand.

'Mummy, as in "curse of" and all that?' Holliday asked.

'Yes,' replied Alhazred. 'There are natron lakes all around here, so the process was quite simple. The general consensus among experts is that Fezzan was the place where mummification was invented.'

'Natron?'

'It's a naturally occurring form of soda ash,' put in Rafi. 'Sodium carbonate decahydrate to be precise,' he added. 'It cured human flesh like beef jerky and it was a natural insecticide so it kept the bugs away. The dry heat of the desert did the rest.'

'Forty days in a natron bath and you lasted forever,' said Alhazred, grabbing a big Husky spotlight on the seat beside him and cracking his door open. He turned in his seat, smiling at Holliday and Rafi. 'Come along, gentlemen, we have arrived; the tomb of Imhotep awaits.'

16

'So how exactly do we get inside?' Holliday asked, looking at the smooth mound of ancient mud brick. There was no obvious door or entrance of any kind. As he stood there he was amazed that anything made of mud could last for that long. If Alhazred was right the tomb was at least four thousand years old.

'Follow me,' said Alhazred. He headed around to the far side of the tomb, Holliday and Rafi behind him and the Tuareg guard, Elhadji, bringing up the rear. At the back of the structure Elhadji handed Alhazred a corkscrew-shaped device from beneath his robes. Alhazred squatted down and squinted, eventually locating an almost invisible hole in the sloping mud-brick wall. He pushed the 'worm' of the corkscrew device into the little hole, twisted and then pulled.

'Hey presto!' Alhazred said theatrically. A crack appeared in the mud brick that became a square two feet on a side. He dragged on the corkscrew and the entire square came loose. With Elhadji helping him they lifted the trapdoor aside and set it down.

On closer examination Holliday saw just how ingenious the trapdoor was. The mud brick on the exterior was a cleverly made veneer no more than an inch thick, the phony brick epoxied to a thick slab of Styrofoam underneath. The whole thing probably didn't weigh more than five pounds. From the outside the illusion had been perfect.

Alhazred spoke in a brief incomprehensible torrent to Elhadji and the Tuareg nodded in silent reply.

'You'll have to duck down,' instructed Alhazred. He got onto his hands and knees, then scuttled through the small opening and disappeared inside the tomb.

'Age before beauty,' offered Holliday. Rafi gave him a nasty look, then followed on the heels of Alhazred. Then Holliday ducked through the secret doorway. Elhadji stayed outside.

The inside of the tomb was stifling hot and dark, lit only by the wash of sun coming through the hole in the tomb wall. Rafi and Alhazred were only vague blobs of gray in the center of the tiny chamber. The trapdoor was reinserted and Alhazred switched on the powerful spotlight. Holliday looked around; for the tomb of one of the most important figures in not just Egypt's history but in the rise of Western civilization, the chamber was almost depressingly austere.

The chamber was small, reflecting the outside dimensions, about twelve feet on a side, just a bit larger than the average prison cell. The interior walls were plain undecorated brick left unplastered and the floor was smooth flat slabs of dark basalt, obviously quarried. The paving stones of the floor were slightly larger than the trapdoor, a little less than three feet square. The roof overhead was made of basalt beams each about two feet across.

There was one paving stone missing in the exact center of the floor. In its place was a square dark opening with a wooden ladder steeply canted down into the shaft below. On the far side of the room were the remains of something that looked like a broken wooden box about six feet long, the top splintered into several pieces.

There were a number of faded symbols on the side of the box, including a large pair of ornamental eyes. Grotesquely, inside the box Holliday could see something that looked like two leathery legs bound together with lengths of tobacco-colored bandage. There was no torso, arms or head. It was the ruins of a human mummy.

'His name was Ahmose Pen-nekhbet,' said Alhazred. 'From what I can tell he was some sort of high official. When I found the tomb it was empty. Someone had already broken in, excavated the sand the tomb was filled with, then stolen everything of value. When they were done they resealed the tomb exactly where I placed the trapdoor. The sarcophagus had been in a vertical position in the center of the room, disguising the floor stone that hid the shaft. The grave robbers tipped the coffin over to get at whatever jewelry the mummy had been decorated with.'

'Where's the rest of the body?' Holliday asked.

Rafi supplied the answer.

'The grave robbers took it. Sometimes mummies had gems and valuables inserted into the stomach cavity. The robbers were probably in a hurry, so they simply tore the remains of the corpse in half.'

'That was my opinion as well,' Alhazred said and nodded. 'It was all fate of course, *inshallah* — as God wills it. If the robbers hadn't knocked over the sarcophagus I wouldn't have seen what the robbers missed – the cracks around the center paving stone revealing the shaft beneath.'

'When do you think it happened?' Holliday asked.

'There's really no way to tell,' answered Alhazred.

'Probably not long after the original burial,' said Rafi, ignoring the Lebanese man's look of irritation. 'There are hundreds of these tombs; whoever broke into this one knew there was someone important buried in it. It's like the grave robbers in Victorian England. They read death notices for wealthy people and attended the funerals to see if they were being buried with their best jewelry.'

'Ghoulish,' grunted Holliday.

Rafi shrugged.

'Practical, if that's the business you're in,' he said.

'We going down the hole?' Holliday asked.

'Claustrophobic, are we?' Alhazred asked, smiling.

'No, *we* are not claustrophobic in the least,' answered Holliday. '*We* just want to get on with it, if you don't mind.'

'Of course, Colonel,' answered Alhazred a little stiffly. 'Your wish is my command.'

'If that was true,' snapped Holliday, 'you'd tell us where Peggy is.'

'Patience, Colonel, all in good time.'

'Then like I said, let's get on with it.'

'You and Dr Wanounou first,' said Alhazred, handing Holliday the spotlight. 'I don't think I'm quite ready to turn my back on you.'

'The feeling's mutual, believe me,' said Holliday. He gave the spotlight to Rafi, who pointed it towards the shaft. Holliday eased himself onto the ladder and went down the hole. He found himself in a small, low-ceilinged chamber lined with mud brick and barely large enough to turn around in.

It was at least ten degrees colder in the chamber than it had been within the tomb. A few moments later Rafi joined him and finally Alhazred appeared, carrying the light in one hand. He pointed the spotlight to the left. Holliday saw a set of stairs carved directly into the limestone bedrock.

'After you, gentlemen,' murmured Alhazred. Holliday went down first, the stone on either side brushing his shoulders. At the bottom of the shallow flight of steps there was an extremely narrow corridor.

It was colder here than the chamber behind them – the dry sterile cold of death and the passage of time. They were deep enough so that the tunnel-like corridor was in bedrock, the walls still bearing the chisel marks of the quarrymen who had excavated it thousands of years before.

The spotlight beam threw long, bobbing shadows in front of Holliday as he walked. At the end of the passage, about a hundred feet or so from the limestone stairs, was a second antechamber, empty once again, the walls decorated with carved hieroglyphics. As Alhazred appeared with the light, Holliday saw that the same set of symbols was repeated over and over again.

'The owl means beloved,' explained Alhazred. 'The seated man is a scribe. Surrounded by a cartouche, a royal border, those are the symbols that form Imhotep's name. I almost fainted when I first saw them. I knew the name immediately, of course,' the man added, obvious pride in his voice.

'Was there a door from the antechamber into the room beyond?' Rafi asked, playing the beam of the big flashlight around. 'A seal?'

The walls of the antechamber were alive with brightly colored paintings, mostly scenes of every-day life: gathering water from irrigation channels, milling wheat, fishing in lily-covered ponds and marshes.

The figures in the paintings all seemed to be women and children, all richly dressed. The floor of the room looked freshly swept. A doorway yawned emptily at the far end of the living-room-sized chamber hewn out of solid rock. As the beam swept over the open doorway Holliday could see a hodgepodge clutter of what looked like furniture. Alhazred spoke.

'There was a plaster seal and a hemp line wrapped around the two handles of double doors. The doors were cedar, sheathed in gold.'

'Whose seal was pressed into the plaster?'

'The same as the glyphs. Imhotep's; there is no doubt.'

'I wonder who buried him,' Rafi said quietly. He went to the wall on his left, peering at the repeated name of Imhotep. In some repetitions there was another set of glyphs within the cartouche, repeated each time as well. Rafi pointed it out and commented on it. 'A woman's name,' he said, looking carefully. 'Het-shep-sit.'

'Do you know what it means?' Holliday asked.

'Glory of her Father,' translated Rafi.

'Imhotep's daughter, then,' responded Holliday.

'Almost certainly,' said Alhazred.

'I didn't even know he was married,' said Holliday.

'The daughter could well have been illegitimate,' said Rafi. 'There's a four-glyph word after her name: *H'mt-a*. It's the word for a female slave.'

'My thoughts as well,' added Alhazred. 'We should move on. The next rooms are the most important.'

Rafi obviously wanted to linger for a moment, peering at the walls of the large room, but he turned towards the open doorway.

'What happened to the doors?' Rafi asked.

'Unfortunately they were destroyed when we opened the tomb rooms. The sheathing was removed and has been stored for safekeeping,' answered Alhazred.

The next room was a clutter of jumbled furniture and artifacts, tumbled together like junk in an attic. Holliday could see small statues and models of chariots and houses, several small ship models, piles of ornately decorated boxes, tables, chairs, stools, and dozens of alabaster jars. It looked as though everything in the room had been looted then pushed to the side, allowing egress into the next room.

'I'm afraid Elhadji and his colleagues aren't the most careful of workers. In fact it was Elhadji who destroyed the gold doors opening up the burial chamber.'

You were the boss, thought Holliday. *Why didn't you stop him?*

They stepped into the burial chamber. Holliday and Rafi stopped in their tracks as Alhazred shone the beam of the spotlight around the room. In the center of the chamber was an enormous stone sarcophagus, obviously quarried from the living rock. The lid of the giant coffin leaned against its side.

The sides of the ossuary were carved with images of the old gods: crocodile-headed Ammit; cat-headed Bast and Khefy, the Scarab King, god of the Dawn. There was winged Isis, keeper of the Dead; Maahes, the Lion Prince, son of Bast and Selket, the Scorpion Queen. Wepwawet, the Jackal god. Munevis, the Sacred Bull. Horus, son of Isis, the falcon-headed god, and finally Ra, the Sun and the Creator of life, the greatest god of all. Each of them was there, carved in stone or drawn in vivid colors on the walls, looking as though they had been painted only yesterday.

The entire wall at the head of the sarcophagus was given over to a single large fresco of a ship, double-ended with high prow and stern, powered by three huge sails and a hundred oars of gold. A single figure, much larger than the others, carrying a clay tablet in one hand and an odd-looking crossed stick in the other, stood at the bow of the ship, hands upraised like an ancient priest giving blessings to his flock.

The ship had been depicted at the mouth of some great river, perhaps the Nile, the banks thick with tall evergreens, the shoreline populated with people wearing light kilts, their upper bodies bare, their hair long, their arms and chests tattooed, all seeming to worship the man in the ship. Above the scene a stylized sun with a single beam of light looked down, the beam piercing the raised right hand of the priest figure.

'It is my opinion that the painting depicts Imhotep's mystical voyage to the land of Punt. The evergreen trees suggest that Punt was actually in Lebanon, the source of much of the cedar used by the ancient Egyptians.'

Alhazred swung the spotlight beam towards the foot of the massive coffin and suddenly everything exploded in a soft buttery yellow glow. Holliday and Rafi found themselves staring at a two-and-a-half-foot-thick and ten-foot-long wall of solid gold, gleaming like the greedy dream of some long-ago King Midas.

'Four tons of gold,' said Alhazred. 'It took us three months to get it here.' Again there was pride in his voice. He walked across the room to the enormous pile of bullion. He stared at it in the light from the lantern, the reflected light glittering in his eyes. Holliday was more interested in the sarcophagus. He crossed to it and looked, then stared up at the painting of the ship on the wall.

'I thought you wanted to ask me a question,' said Rafi, moving partway across the burial chamber.

Alhazred looked at his wristwatch.

'Perhaps some other time,' said the Lebanese man. 'It's getting late.'

'Where's his body?' Holliday asked.

Alhazred turned.

'Removed for safekeeping,' he said.

'I would have thought it would be safe enough here,' answered Holliday.

'Not once the sarcophagus was opened,' answered Alhazred.

'Did the mummy have a gold death mask like Tutankhamen's?' Holliday asked.

'Yes, as a matter of fact he did,' said Alhazred. Holliday saw that his face was flushing, either from embarrassment or anger. 'In point of fact the entire inner coffin was sheathed in gold.'

'Like the doors,' said Holliday, smiling.

'Yes,' answered Alhazred tersely. 'Like the doors.'

'Presumably the inner coffin was removed for safekeeping,' said Holliday, his voice bland.

'Yes,' said Alhazred, his teeth gritted. 'I think we should be on our way,' he added.

'Whatever you say,' said Holliday brightly. 'Come on, Rafi, our captor the archaeologist thinks it's time to go.'

Rafi nodded, although it was clear from the look on his face that he could have stayed in the ancient tomb for hours more. They went back the way they'd come, Alhazred behind them, going back through the antechamber to the burial room and along the narrow corridor, their footsteps ringing on the rough-quarried stone at their feet. They climbed the shallow steps to the bottom of the shaft, then went up the creaking ladder to the interior of the beehive enclosure.

Holliday and Rafi scuttled out of the tomb under Alhazred's watchful eye and stood up in the dying light of the sun. It was dusk, and getting cooler, although the heat was still enough to make them gasp after the chill of the stone below ground. Alhazred appeared and he and Elhadji carefully replaced the trapdoor, rubbing a final layer of sand into the cracks around the edges to disguise the hidden entrance.

They drove back to the camp in silence. Holliday couldn't believe what he'd discovered. If anything the implications were even more important and shattering than his discovery of the Templar treasure the year before, but this was certainly no time to discuss it with Rafi.

They arrived back at the camp just as darkness fell. Alhazred let them out of the 4×4 in front of their tent.

'I thought perhaps that I would have you to my quarters for dinner tonight so we could discuss what you saw today, but I have changed my mind.' He nodded curtly to the two men. 'Perhaps we will see each other sometime tomorrow and talk about your friend Peggy.'

Alhazred put the truck in gear and drove off. Holliday and Rafi ducked into the tent.

'He's a phony, isn't he?' Rafi said.

'Absolutely,' Holliday said and nodded. 'A total fraud.'

Then they heard the helicopters.

17

They made a sound like the hesitant whispering of giant metronomes, a double chattering roar dropping out of the darkening sky like a flight of monstrous steel locusts. From the multiple rotor sounds there were at least four of them. Even without seeing the choppers Holliday knew they were big, most likely Sikorsky S-92s or Italian-made Augusta Merlins.

'What the hell is going on?' Rafi yelled, raising his voice above the screaming thunder.

'The camp is under attack!' answered Holliday. Four helicopters that size could transport almost a hundred men in total, more than enough to take on the Tuaregs.

Holliday headed for the entrance to the tent. Before he could reach it, a man appeared in black combat BDUs, a black balaclava covering his face and a short-barreled MP5 machine gun in his hand. He had an automatic pistol in a quick-release holster on his right thigh, a gigantic combat knife in a Velcro sheath on his left leg and light-weight body armor on his chest. As he burst through the tent flap he raised the MP5. Holliday pretended it was the Army-Navy game and drop-kicked the commando between the legs.

The man screamed and staggered, the machine gun stitching a line of bullet holes across the camel-skin ceiling. Holliday kicked the commando a second time, just as hard, and the man toppled backward. Barely pausing, Holliday dropped with one leg bent, smashing the fallen man with his knee, crushing his nose. Holliday then reached down, swept the commando knife from its breakaway sheath and plunged it between the commando's chin and the top edge of his body armor, bringing the serrated blade across both carotid arteries and the windpipe. Blood foun-tained, splashing the front of Holliday's shirt. The commando made a sound like air being let out of a bicycle tire and died.

Rafi stared at the carnage, mouth gaping open, eyes wide. Holliday grabbed the MP5, then ripped open the quick-release holster on the dead man's thigh. A brand-new Beretta M9, the military ver-sion of their standard 9mm automatic. He pulled back the slide and tossed it to Rafi. The young Israeli looked as though he had a poisonous snake in his hand.

'Point and shoot,' said Holliday. 'Safety's on the left. You know it's on when you see the little red button, just like now. Flip it down and shoot anyone who looks at you wrong. Understand?'

Rafi nodded mutely.

There was a ripping sound behind them. Holliday and Rafi both turned. Like something out of an old Western film a blade appeared in the side of the tent and ripped downward. Unbidden, Rafi raised the big black automatic pistol and Holliday saw his thumb flip down the safety. A face appeared. Holliday expected to see another balaclava-wearing commando. Instead the face was that of Emil Abdul Tidyman, the traitorous smuggler.

'This way!' he ordered urgently. The knife ripped down to the base of the tent. 'Come! Now! The camp is being attacked!'

'Why should we come with you?' Rafi asked, the gun still pointing straight at the man. From where he stood Holliday could see that Rafi's grip on the weapon was firm and unwavering.

The gun wasn't shaking. Holliday smiled bleakly. The lesson had been learned. It seemed that Rafi had overcome his squeamishness.

'There are five big helicopters out there. More than a hundred heavily armed men.' Tidyman said. 'Unless you come with me, you will die.'

'With you we'll live?' Holliday asked.

'I know a way out of here,' said Tidyman.

'Why should we trust you?' Rafi asked.

'Because I'm the only chance you've got.'

Rafi turned and glanced quickly at Holliday, the weapon in his hand still immobile. Holliday gave him a quick nod. He knew Tidyman was right. With nowhere to go a hundred enemies was too many; they'd be slaughtered along with the rest of the Tuaregs. For a moment he considered who the attackers might be and then put the thought out of his mind. There would be time for that kind of analysis later. If they managed to survive, that is.

'Lead the way,' he said to Tidyman.

Rafi lowered the M9. Tidyman's face withdrew from the floor-to-ceiling slit in the wall. Rafi and Holliday followed the Egyptian out into the cloaking darkness.

Tidyman was dressed in military attire, all

black like the commandos but with a beret instead of a balaclava. He carried a holstered pistol but no other arms. Leading the way he crept between the hutlike tents, working his way towards the sheep and goat enclosure on the western side of the camp.

Behind them there were bursts of sporadic gunfire and the choked screams of dying men. Camels shrieked, panicking and tearing at their picket lines, unable to do anything more than stagger into each other with their hobbled legs. Fires sprang up as tracers burst against the tents and rifle grenades found their targets.

Holliday caught a flicker of movement on his left and turned. A figure rose up out of the darkness, an indigo-robed Tuareg – Elhadji. He was carrying a straight sword, four feet long with a simple wooden crosspiece and grip, the nicked blade glinting as it swept down in a deadly arc.

Holliday had a brief flashing memory of a black-turbaned Taliban officer wielding an immense curved pulwar in the ruins of a village just outside Kandahar years before; he did exactly what he'd done then: ducked. He rolled to one side, keeping low to avoid Elhadji's backstroke, then came up on his knees, tearing the commando knife out of its sheath and sweeping it into the fluttering of the Tuareg's robes, cutting through the fabric and slicing into the tendons at the back of his legs, crippling him. As Elhadji fell he managed to slide a lethal-looking dagger from his right sleeve, bringing it up towards Holliday's stomach. Holliday reared back but he knew it was too late; the Tuareg was going to gut him.

A single shot rang out and Elhadji was thrown backward, the right side of his face disintegrating, his turban unraveling in a mess of blood, brains and hair. Holliday looked up. Rafi stood over him, one hand extended, the other holding the smoking pistol.

'Point and shoot, right?' the Israeli archaeologist said, grimacing.

'Point and shoot,' Holliday said, taking Rafi's extended hand and pulling himself up.

'Come on!' Tidyman hissed.

They reached the sand rampart and struggled upward after Tidyman. Reaching the summit, Holliday looked back. Much of the camp was on fire now, and Holliday could see the silhouettes of the Tuaregs etched against the flames. Lines of tracers marked the attacking commando force, and from the spitting spiderweb of light Holliday could see that the attackers were herding the native force against the far eastern wall.

As Holliday watched he saw a new line of fire from the top of the far rampart. The firing came from at least a score of heavy weapons. It was an ambush; a squad had been lying in wait, catching the Tuaregs in a deadly cross fire.

Holliday turned again. They were in exactly the spot they'd been that morning, except now the area between the rampart and the almost invisible runway was blocked by five hulking helicopters in red and white livery. They were Augusta-Westland Merlins, as Holliday had thought. A Merlin variant had just been tested as a replacement for the president's *Flight One*. Holliday knew they had just about the longest range of any medium-sized transport chopper on the market.

Tidyman crouched and Holliday followed suit, pulling Rafi down with him. Standing, they'd be perfect targets, silhouetted against the rising flames behind them.

'What now?' Holliday whispered to Tidyman.

'There,' said the Egyptian, pointing along the parapet. 'Keep low.'

Tidyman began to run along the sand-pile wall, heading for the northeast corner of the structure. Holliday followed, keeping low as he'd been instructed, checking every few seconds to see if anyone left with the helicopters had seen them. Rafi brought up the rear. The only thing obstructing their run was the body of a Tuareg guard, his throat slit by one of the commandos. They stepped over his body and followed after Tidyman.

They reached the corner of the wall and the Egyptian pointed down to the ditch below them. Waiting on the other side of the dry moat was a Russian jeep, an open version of the old UAZ-469 Goat they'd purchased in Mersa Matruh. There was a big machine gun on a pivot mount in the rear. It looked a lot like the Libyan army vehicle they'd seen patrolling that afternoon, but much older.

'Can you work that?' Tidyman asked, pointing at the big machine gun, his whisper hoarse.

'Probably,' said Holliday, peering down. It looked like an American MP-40 but even bigger, probably a Soviet-era Russian Kord. But a machine gun was a machine gun, and the Russians had always had a knack for making their weapons simple, strong and easy to use. That's why the AK-47 was the Coca-Cola of automatic rifles.

'You'd better be able to shoot it,' warned the Egyptian. 'Those helicopters are in our way and they're sure to have left someone back to guard them.'

'Behind you!' Rafi yelled.

Holliday swiveled, bringing up the machine pistol he'd stripped off the dead commando in the tent. A commando was charging up the hill, another man right behind him. As Holliday fired the charging man looked up.

'*Cazzo merda!*' the commando whispered, lifting his own weapon.

Holliday squeezed the trigger on the MP 5 and blew the man back down the hill in a dead tumbling heap. The second man stopped in his tracks, bringing up his own machine pistol, and Holliday turned the weapon on him, firing until the clip was empty. Behind the dead man at the base of the wall a trio of commandos looked up.

'Go!' Holliday bellowed, turning again and throwing himself over the edge of the sloping sand wall as a hail of fire buzzed up from the squad below. He tumbled down the sand, losing his footing and rolling down towards the shallow ditch at the base of the rampart.

He reached the bottom with a heavy thump that knocked the wind out of him. As he climbed to his feet and clambered up the far side of the moat he felt a searing sting of heat as a bullet plucked at the sleeve of his shirt. More slugs twitched into the sand all around him as the commandos high above him tried to pick him off. He reached the truck, threw himself into the back and grabbed the pistol grip below the heavy machine-gun mechanism and swung the weapon around on its pivot.

As Tidyman started the truck and pulled away, Rafi beside him, Holliday dropped the firing lever, locking the belt feed in place, flipped off the safety and angled the gun upward. He checked that the belt feed was running smoothly down into the big ammunition box on the right-hand side of the heavy weapon, took a deep breath and pulled the trigger.

The heavy-barreled weapon came alive under his hands, jumping like a pounding jackhammer and sending out a pulsing rhythmic thump of huge .50-caliber shells that chewed up the crest of the sand rampart like paper through a shredder, instantly turning anyone still on the summit into so much raw meat.

The immediate threat removed, Holliday swiveled the big gun around on its mount and faced the helicopters as the truck roared across the stony plain towards the runway. The commandos had landed in a staggered formation that presented a curved line of defense blocking their way. The fat-bellied transports had sliding doors like a minivan and a rear loading ramp. They weren't usually armed but there were three large windows on each side that could be used as positions for a Gatling Minigun or a .50 caliber like the Kord.

Holliday did a long traverse of the line of choppers moving left to right, aiming for center mass in the middle of the passenger compartments, starting at the cockpit end, firing in short bursts. Even from two hundred yards away Holliday could see the exploding impact of the shells, windshield Plexiglas shattering, metal torn apart, bits of fuselage and chunks of engine flying in all directions. Something flared brightly in one of the center helicopters and then a split second later a huge fireball erupted with an oxygen-eating *whump* of sound. Jet fuel for the big GE turbines.

In the driver's seat of the truck, Tidyman jerked the wheel, veering away from the light cast by the exploding chopper. Holliday saw figures running in front of the blaze. Tidyman yelled a warning.

'RPG!'

One of the running figures had one of the familiar skinny launchers on his shoulder. An RPG-7, capable of stopping an M1 Abrams, not to mention a tin-can Goat. One round from a weapon like that and they'd be vaporized. Holliday swung left, traversing the gun, then twisted in the opposite direction, reverse-tracking and potshotting the running line of men, dropping them like puppets cut from their strings. The man with the RPG dropped along with the rest.

They were through, the line of helicopters behind them, the one in the middle blazing like a torch. At least two of the others had been badly damaged and probably more. Heavily armed or not, if the commando group was stranded without transport they were as good as dead; Qaddafi, father and son, weren't known for their compassion. They'd take a flight of old MiG-23 Floggers out of mothballs and blow whatever commandos survived into eternity.

Tidyman pulled up beside the runway. The Skymaster Holliday had seen that morning was tied down under a Mylar awning beside a line of fifty-gallon drums with hand pumps. Both cockpit doors were wide open.

'Where's the pilot?' Holliday called out as he dropped down from the rear of the truck. The cockpit of the push-pull twin-engined aircraft was empty. He flinched involuntarily as an explosion sounded behind them. He turned. The fire had spread; a second helicopter was burning now. The commandos had almost certainly expected a quick in and out with a minimum of casualties or damage and now it had all turned to crap.

'I'm the pilot,' said Tidyman, climbing out of the truck.

'You've got to be kidding,' said Rafi.

'I got my license in Canada when I was fifteen,' said Tidyman. 'I was flying before I could drive a car.' The Egyptian went around to the pilot's-side door and got in behind the little half wheel. Rafi and Holliday climbed in after him, Holliday taking the copilot's chair.

Tidyman slammed his door shut and latched it, then started flipping switches. Holliday closed and latched the door on his side as well.

'Egypt had compulsory military service back then,' said Tidyman, continuing his explanation. 'I spent two years flying Sadat around in one of these.'

Tidyman set the fuel mixture at Rich, the RPMs at High and held down the ignition switch. The engine coughed and died. He released the ignition and went through the procedures again. This time the engine caught. There was a sharp cracking sound from the tail section of the aircraft and then a second impact.

'Somebody's shooting at us,' said Rafi.

Holliday looked out the window on his right. Except for the flames rising from the burning helicopters the night was black.

The engine roared as Tidyman advanced the throttles. More bullets hammered into the plane.

'Time to go,' said Tidyman. He released the brake and they rolled out from beneath the Mylar cover, turning hard, the front of the aircraft pointing down the dark runway. Tidyman pushed the throttles as far forward as they would go, set his feet on the pedals and set the flaps at one-third down. The twin-engined aircraft leapt down the runway and threw itself up into the enclosing night. They were airborne.

18

'Which way are we headed?' Holliday asked, raising his voice over the steady roar of the engines as they leveled off.

'Northeast, toward Siwa until someone tells me differently,' answered Tidyman as he adjusted the flaps. The only illumination inside the aircraft came from the control panel lights, the little radar screen in the center of the dashboard casting a green, sickly glow over their faces.

'It depends on where the choppers came from,' said Holliday.

'I saw a logo on the side of the nearest one,' offered Rafi. 'A red hummingbird.'

'That's the insignia of the Canadian Helicopter Corporation,' said Tidyman, shaking his head. 'They're the biggest private helicopter company in the world. Mostly servicing oil rigs and air-sea rescue, I think. They've got offices everywhere leasing helicopters to all sorts of third-party users. It doesn't mean anything.'

'The man running up the outer wall said something just before I shot him. *Cazzo merda*. Italian for holy crap,' said Holliday.

'Our friends from the Vatican looking for a little payback?' Rafi suggested.

'Looking for the gold more likely,' scoffed Tidyman. 'Vengeance is mine, sayeth the Lord, but the cash belongs to mother church.'

'Or they were looking for something else,' murmured Holliday, remembering the tomb.

'Like what?' Tidyman asked curiously.

'Nothing,' said Holliday. 'It doesn't matter.'

'Could those helicopters have come from Italy?' Rafi asked.

'The range is about nine hundred miles, as I recall,' said Holliday. 'Would that do it?'

'From Sicily it would,' said Tidyman.

'What's our best landfall closest to Italy?' Holliday queried.

'Tunisia,' said Tidyman.

'Can we make it?'

'Yes. Alhazred kept the plane fully gassed up at all times, in case of unforeseen events.'

'I guess he didn't foresee this particular event,' said Holliday.

'He was a fool; he should have seen this coming or something like it,' grunted Tidyman. 'Gold in such quantities is a magnet for bad luck and death.' The Egyptian adjusted the controls. Holliday watched as the compass needle swerved around the illuminated dial. They were now going sharply north and slightly to the west. 'The old airfield at Matfur is still there, just south of Bizerte on the coast. We can refill there if you wish.'

'Sounds good to me,' said Holliday.

There was a harsh metallic clicking sound from the rear seat. Holliday turned. Rafi had the muzzle of the big Beretta automatic pressed up against the back of Tidyman's skull.

'You're even more of a fool than Alhazred if you think you're frightening me with that,' said the Egyptian. 'You might as well stick the barrel in your own mouth. Shoot me and who flies the plane?'

'Where's Peggy?' Rafi demanded.

'Alhazred shipped her out a week ago.' Tidyman paused. 'Now put down the gun.'

'Do it,' said Holliday.

Rafi ignored them both.

'Shipped her out? What are you talking about?' He pushed the muzzle of the automatic a little harder.

'He has a deal with a man named Antonio Neri.' Tidyman paused. 'He operates a criminal organization called La Santa,' continued the Egyptian.

'Ducos, the Frenchman, mentioned La Santa,' said Holliday, remembering. 'So did Japrisot the cop. He said that Valador, the crook with the fishing boat, had hooked up with them.'

'La Santa trades in pretty girls, among other things. A pretty white girl like Miss Blackstock would be a bonus.'

'Where would he take her?' Rafi asked angrily.

'Put the gun down and I'll tell you,' said Tidyman.

'Do it,' ordered Holliday sharply.

Rafi lowered the weapon.

'Where is she?' Rafi repeated.

'La Santa has its headquarters in Corsica, that's all I know for sure.'

'Is she there or not?' Rafi demanded.

'Neri sends girls everywhere. They travel to Albania and from there they're sent all over Eastern Europe. It's the same with the drugs. There's a network.'

'What about the trade in artifacts?' Holliday asked.

'They go through Corsica to either Marseille or Rome, depending on the final destination,' answered Tidyman. 'Beyond that I have no idea.'

'That son of a bitch,' Rafi said through gritted teeth, 'I'll kill him!'

'Alhazred?' Tidyman said. 'Not if I find him first.'

'What's your beef with him?' Holliday said. 'I thought you two were partners.'

'I had no choice,' explained the Egyptian. 'He kidnapped my wife and daughter in Cairo, held them hostage.' Tidyman shook his head. 'He said I needed an incentive to help him dispose of the gold. When he found out that you were on his trail he threatened to rape and kill Habibah and my Tabia if I didn't bring both of you to him.'

'What changed your mind?' Holliday asked.

In the faint light from the control panel Holliday saw tears forming in the corners of the Egyptian's eyes.

'I flew into Bardai, in Chad, yesterday for

supplies,' said Tidyman, staring dully out through the windscreen at the star-filled night sky, his mind and his heart somewhere else. Far below them the dunes of the desert unrolled like a landscape in an endless dark dream, lit by the rising moon. 'I managed to telephone my neighbor in Cairo. I learned that my wife had been killed trying to escape.'

'And your daughter?'

'*Al'hamdu'li'Allah*, thanks be to God, Tabia managed to get away. My friends have hidden her. She is safe. I was on my way to kill Alhazred in his quarters when the helicopters came. I went to you instead. You did not deserve to die for that man's perfidy.' The Egyptian cleared his throat but made no move to wipe the tears he was shedding for his wife. 'His name is not even Alhazred.'

'What is it?' Holliday asked.

'Bobby Ayoub. He was born in Ottawa.'

'His parents, the doctors?' Rafi asked from the back of the plane.

'He told you that story?' Tidyman laughed coldly. 'His father owned a delicatessen on Elgin Street and his mother was part owner of a bakery. They specialized in pita bread. Both of them died in a traffic accident on New Year's Eve. A drunk driver. Bobby was an only child. He inherited everything, including the insurance. He went to Lebanon with the money and played the big shot; tried to join Hezbollah and the Abu Nidal group but they didn't want him. Tried to go to university there but they wouldn't have him, either.'

'We figured him for a phony,' Holliday said and nodded.

'The bit about Trajan being Vespasian's son was a neat trick,' Rafi said. 'Especially since Trajan wasn't even born until about fifty years after Vespasian died.' Rafi sneered. 'He flubbed a lot of other stuff as well, and he couldn't read hieroglyphics, either. He was no archaeologist.'

'He was crazy. Delusions of grandeur. According to him he was destined for great things. A Mahdi for the twenty-first century, sent by God to free his people from the yoke of tyranny, et cetera, et cetera. In reality he was a baker's child and the son of a man who made smoked meat sandwiches.'

'Hitler's father was a customs inspector,' said Rafi. 'Great oaks from little acorns and all that.'

'He was a wannabe terrorist who nobody

wanted,' said Holliday. 'So he made up the Brotherhood of Isis.'

'Something like that,' Tidyman said and nodded, nudging the yoke a little, watching their course on the compass. 'Crazy, just like I said.' The little pressurized plane was flying at twenty thousand feet now, its optimum altitude for long-distance flight. They were flying so high they couldn't see the flitting batwing moon shadow of their flight across the dunes.

Tidyman lifted his shoulders in a shrug.

'The Tuaregs didn't care; they'd been vandalizing tombs and robbing archaeological sites for years, not to mention raiding the odd caravan. Alhazred, or Ayoub or whatever he calls himself, just made it easier for them to sell their stuff to the smugglers and provided them with better weapons. The lying little bastard brought organized crime to the desert, that's all.' Tidyman sighed and lifted his shoulders wearily again. 'Terrorism isn't about ideals anymore; Gandhi has been dead too long for that. It's just ego and money these days, and that's Bobby Ayoub in a nutshell.'

'You think he'll get away?' Holliday asked.

'Yes,' said Tidyman simply. 'He would have

had some kind of bolt hole arranged, some kind of plan B. He always did.'

'And when he finds his airplane gone?' Holliday said. 'Will he figure it out and come after us?'

'Count on it.' The Egyptian nodded. 'When he doesn't find our bodies he'll know. He had an awful temper when he didn't get his way. This will put him right over the edge. He'll come for us with blood in his eye, believe me.'

Flying at just under one hundred and fifty miles an hour to conserve fuel, the eight-hundred-mile flight over the desert took them until just past midnight to complete. The moon was at its zenith as they crossed the Libyan border, throwing the landscape beneath their wings into sharp relief.

'The only thing I know about modern Tunisia is that George Lucas shot the Tattooine scenes on Luke Skywalker's home planet in a real place called Tattooine,' said Holliday, looking down at the desert landscape below. It didn't look any different from most of Libya.

'That's here, in the south of the country,' replied Tidyman. 'The country's divided in half: the bottom is barren desert, the top is good farmland, Mediterranean, like the south of Spain or Greece, lots of hills and fertile valleys. They do pretty well for such a small country sandwiched between two big ones.'

'*Carthago delenda est,*' said Rafi, half dozing in the seat behind the copilot's spot. '"Carthage must be destroyed"; first thing I ever learned in Latin.'

'The Kasserine Pass,' offered Holliday. 'The first time American soldiers met up with the Germans in World War Two. We got our asses handed to us on a plate. One of the worst defeats in American military history.'

'Good thing you were quick learners,' said Tidyman. He eased the yoke forward and the little airplane went into a shallow dive, the sound of the fore and aft engines deepening.

'Why are we going down?' Holliday asked.

'Trying to get under the radar,' explained Tidyman.

'Will they be looking for us?' Rafi asked.

'Not likely,' said the Egyptian. 'But the commercial airport at Tunis or the smaller one at Bizerte might pick us up accidentally; we're up pretty high for a light plane; they might be a little suspicious if we suddenly pop up on their screens coming out of the desert.'

'Then take us down by all means,' said Holliday.

They dropped steadily until they were flying at less than a thousand feet above the dunes and arid plains of the desert. Ahead, visible now in the far distance, the wall of the jagged Atlas Mountains stood like a blank, black shadow blocking out the star-lit skies. Abruptly the landscape changed. The desert vanished, replaced by small farms, roads and scattered settlements. The plains became more undulating, spotted with wooded hills that climbed straight-walled, like fortresses still waiting for an ancient enemy. Slowly but surely Holliday watched as the needle of the illuminated compass on the control panel swung to the east.

'Where is this airfield?' Holliday asked at the end of their fourth hour in the air.

'Matfur,' replied Tidyman. 'It was a fighter base in a dry lake bed,' he explained. 'Both sides occupied it at one time or another during the war. My father called it Muddy Matfur. Originally German, I think. Nobody uses it anymore, of course, it's just a line in the dirt really.'

'And why exactly are we going there?' Rafi asked.

'If we put down at one of the big airports someone will almost certainly ask questions,' answered Tidyman. 'If Alhazred or Ayoub or whatever his name is does come after us, we'll be harder to find. It's closer to Kelibia than anywhere else.'

'Kelibia?'

'A little coastal town on the Cape Bon peninsula, the other side of the Bay of Tunis,' said Tidyman. 'A dusty little place with hardly any tourists. There's an old fort but that's about it. It's where they ship the women out. It's where the *Khamsin* docks.'

'Get us there,' said Rafi.

An hour's flying brought them to Matfur, a small village at the foot of a bleak, treeless hill surrounded by a pancake-flat plain of smallholdings. In the waning moonlight Tidyman found the lake bed without any difficulty and put the plane down in a perfect three-point landing on the long-abandoned airfield, now little more than a slightly raised track through dry, cracked mud. He taxied the plane around, bringing it into the wind, then switched off the engines. The propellers clattered and whined to a stop and for the first time since they'd taken off from the desert camp in Libya there was silence.

'Now what?' Holliday asked.

'Now we steal a car,' said Tidyman. 'And get ourselves to the coast.'

19

As things turned out, they didn't steal a car. They
bought a truck, a World War II-vintage Austin
Champ left behind in 1943 and pressed into service on a chicken farm owned by a man named
Mahmoud. The truck and five gallons of gas
were purchased for fifty dollars American and
the ignition key for the Cessna Skymaster they'd
left behind on the old airfield. Mahmoud also
threw in an early breakfast of freshly slaughtered, plucked and baked chicken with a side dish
of couscous and several pots of strong coffee.

For a few extra American dollars Mahmoud
also let them have their pick from his meager
wardrobe of Western-style clothes, managing to
outfit Rafi and Holliday in well-worn collarless
shirts and floppy, outsized trousers that seemed
to have been made for someone who had been
both short as well as enormously fat. By day-
break, after a revolting and appetite-suppressing

tour of Mahmoud's farm and directions to the coast, they were on their way.

The trip in the old truck took less than two hours but Holliday was sure the stink of chicken guano would be with him forever.

Tidyman's brief description of the town of Kelibia was entirely accurate. A large fort dating back to the Roman occupation dominated the dusty whitewashed town from a steep hill, and that was about it except for the stink of fish, which immediately began fighting the acid reek of chicken droppings for dominance in their nostrils.

Most of the town seemed to have grown from an intersection of two major roads spreading out in a thoughtless tangle of narrow side streets that had grown over the passing years like a plaster and whitewash virus with no plan or direction. The real focus of the town beyond the obvious power of the vacant fortress was the harbor with its fleet of fishing trawlers and feluccas. According to Tidyman Kelibia was not one of the sanitized *Zones Touristique*, which might have accounted for the litter on the streets and the putrid, filthy water in the harbor. The boats, of all sizes and most needing a coat of paint, were moored four or five deep in a helter-skelter mess that defied any logic or order.

They eventually found the immigration *capitanerie* and harbor master's office in a small building beside an enormous concrete-roofed open-air fish market right on the waterfront. The office was a cupboard with a desk, a chair, a grimy window and stacks of papers on top of ancient green filing cases. The room smelled of stale tobacco and rotting wood.

The harbor master's name was Habib Mokaden, a squat little man who wore his pants up to his armpits and had a magnificent head of silver curly hair topped off with a bright green fez. His pouched face was covered with a sandpapery stubble of gray bristles and he smoked endless Mars brand cigarettes, tapping them out of a bright red package and popping them in the exact center of his fat and wet-lipped mouth. He spoke tolerable English.

'I am aware of this vessel, yes,' he said and nodded when Tidyman asked about the *Khamsin*. Holliday didn't quite believe it considering the mess of shipping in the harbor, most of the boats nameless.

'Why do you remember it?' he asked.

'You do not think this harbor master knows every boat large and small that comes into his port every day and every night?' Mokaden asked, his eyes narrowing. 'Hosni Thabet's green felucca, Akimi's dinghy with the yellow stripe and the rusty portside hole, Fathi Bensilmane's sardine trawler with the holy words from the Qu'ran on his stack. Zoubir Ben Younes and the dinghy that smells so foully? I know each and every one. They are my children, effendi, my friends, my pets.'

'Why do you remember this one in particular?' Holliday insisted.

'This boat arrives here once every month or so. It stays a week, then goes. During that week the captain spends his days drinking coffee and playing chess at the Café de Borj up on the hill. He stays at the Mamounia, where my sister is a cook, which is how I know this. This time he stayed longer than a week because one of his engines had been damaged and he had lost his engineer of long standing. He waited for parts to come but they did not so he only left this morning and still with only one engine and still no engineer. He left very early and in a great hurry, I am sad to say.'

'He left this morning?!' Rafi said.

'This is what I say, effendi. This morning, with the sun. Even before the fishermen.'

'Where was he going?' Tidyman asked.

'I was not there for him to tell me,' Moukaden said with a shrug. He tugged at his belt to bring his pants up a little higher on his great mound of a belly. 'I would expect he was going to his home port.'

'Which is?' Tidyman asked.

'Calvi, in Corsica,' said Moukaden.

'How fast could he go with only one engine?' Holliday asked.

'Five, perhaps six knots,' answered the harbor master.

'So we could catch him,' said Rafi.

'Why would you want to do such a thing?' Moukaden said, startled by the idea, his eyes widening. 'It is an act of piracy.'

'He has something that belongs to us,' said Holliday. 'And we want it back.'

'Then he is a thief,' said Moukaden thoughtfully.

'Yes,' said Tidyman. Rafi was about to add something but a look from Tidyman kept him silent.

'A thief,' said the harbor master again.

'Yes,' said Tidyman a second time.

'Who should be apprehended,' said Moukaden.

'Indeed,' said Tidyman agreeably.

'And to apprehend this thief you would need a boat,' mused the harbor master.

'Quite so,' answered Tidyman.

'A fast boat,' said the harbor master.

'Yes,' put in Holliday, seeing which way this was going. 'A very fast boat.'

'I know of such a boat,' said Moukaden.

'I thought you might,' Tidyman said and smiled.

'It belongs to my cousin Moustafa. He uses it to . . . move things from place to place.'

'Ah.' Tidyman nodded.

'It might be costly,' warned the harbor master. 'The boat is very near to my cousin's heart.'

'Do you take Visa?' Holliday asked.

'Certainly.' Moukaden nodded happily, pulling up his pants again. 'American Express as well.' His smile widened and he reached for the old-fashioned dial telephone on his cluttered desk. 'I will make a call, yes?'

'You do that,' said Holliday.

Moustafa lived a few miles farther up the coast at a tiny beachfront community called Hammam Lekses. His ride turned out to be the marine version of the old Austin Champ they'd bargained for at the chicken farm. In this case it was a seventy-foot Motoscafo Armato Silurante, or MAS boat, the Italian version of the British torpedo boat and the German E-boat.

She sat at the stone pier on the waterfront of Hammam Lekses like a scruffy, battle-scarred old tomcat, her long deck cluttered with old fishnets and crates, her narrow afterdeck piled with roped and rusty fifty-gallon drums to give her range. Even now her hull was painted in old-fashioned Italian dazzle paint, faded with salt and the passage of time. An old tomcat perhaps, but a tomcat nevertheless, her long sleek lines still showing the hidden speed and deadly power lurking just beneath the surface.

The boat had been left behind in 1943 when the Germans and the Italians withdrew from Tunisia, and Moustafa's father had managed to steal the craft from under the noses of the British and Americans, hiding her in a cave along the coast, using it to smuggle everything from olive oil to machine guns from Tunisia to Marseille after the war. Moustafa, it seemed, was following in his father's footsteps.

Moustafa himself was the exact opposite of his cousin Moukaden: rail thin and totally bald. According to Moustafa the seventy-five-year-old boat was good as new and still capable of a tooth-rattling thirty-five knots. By Moustafa's estimation the *Khamsin* would have made less than sixty miles headway by midafternoon, which meant that his boat, the *Fantasma*, the *Ghost*, would catch her in under two hours.

Even better, the Tunisian was also happy to throw in the use of a Russian RPG for an extra fee. As long as cousin Moukaden the harbor master authorized the high-seas boarding of the *Khamsin*, Moustafa had no compunction about getting them to their objective.

He did suggest that they wait for evening before setting out on their expedition. According to him, the Kirogi-class coastal patrols of the Tunisian navy, mostly based in Tunis, didn't like operating in the dark and usually headed home at sunset. Even more important, in Moustafa's experience the boarding of an enemy vessel was usually best accomplished at night. After some discussion and some urgent counterarguments by Rafi, they decided that it was best to follow Moustafa's advice.

The sun was no more than a memory on the western horizon as Moustafa engaged the proud old Isotta Fraschini engines, lovingly maintained first by Moustafa's father and now by Moustafa himself. The sea was utterly flat and the evening air was just beginning to cool as the lights of the houses and villas along the beach faded behind them. Tidyman stayed in the tiny deckhouse with Moustafa while Holliday and Rafi remained below in the big belowdecks wardroom.

Beneath their feet the engines roared loudly as Moustafa brought the boat up to speed, small waves rhythmically banging against the *Fantasma*'s flanks. The entire hull began to vibrate as they accelerated, the bows lifting as the boat began to plane. Within five minutes the *Fantasma* was cutting through the ocean at close to forty miles an hour.

'Are you sure we can trust him?' Rafi asked, seated at the wardroom table.

'Tidyman or Moustafa, or his cousin the harbor master?' Holliday asked with a shrug. 'Who knows? Moukaden, the fat one, could be on the radio right now, talking to the *Khamsin*, warning them that we're on the way. We don't have much choice, do we? This is our only lead, our only path to Peggy.'

'Moustafa and his fat cousin are in it for the money – that's easy enough to understand. It's Tidyman I'm still not sure of.'

'Alhazred had his wife killed. That's reason enough to trust him. Revenge is the best motive of all.'

'And if Peggy's not on board the *Khamsin*?' Rafi asked. 'What then?'

'We cross that bridge when we come to it,' answered Holliday.

They plowed on through the night, the ocean a desert of rolling water as barren as the desert of sand they'd crossed the night before. Holliday went up on deck once or twice to survey the sea and the star-lit sky, but mostly he dozed on one of the narrow V-bunks once used by the ten-man crew of the old Italian torpedo boat. It was well past two in the morning when Tidyman shook him awake.

'Something's wrong,' the Egyptian said without preamble. 'We think we have the *Khamsin* on the radar but she's stationary, dead in the water.'

'Maybe the other engine broke down,' Holliday said, yawning as he stumbled after Tidyman.

They reached the small forward wheelhouse. Moustafa stood at the wheel. Rafi was already there, staring at the sweep of the modern radar unit bolted onto the control panel. From the sound of the engines and the feel of the boat in the water Holliday could easily tell that the *Fantasma* had slowed considerably. He stared down at the radar screen. The sweep illuminated a small bright blip in the upper-right-hand corner of the screen, their own marker an even brighter mark that pulsed kitty-corner to the one in the upper right. The distance between the two markers steadily closed as Holliday watched, but the upper one was stationary.

'What's the distance?' Holliday asked.

Moustafa leaned across the wheel and adjusted a knob on the radar set. The image jumped, then re-formed.

'One mile,' he said. 'Less. A thousand meters.'

'Are we sure it's the *Khamsin*?' Holliday asked. 'Maybe it's a rock or something.'

'No rock. Boat,' said Moustafa, staring out into the darkness, guiding the old gunboat through the smooth swells.

'It's where the *Khamsin* should be,' said Tidy-man.

'All right,' murmured Holliday, thinking hard as they moved slowly forward towards the bright blip on the screen. They had a few weapons, some handguns they'd brought with them from the camp in Germa and Moustafa's RPG. Moustafa also had a World War II-vintage Breda bipod-mounted light machine gun, but as Holliday recalled the weapon had been bad news during the war. He wasn't about to trust it more than sixty years later. Not only was it out of date, but the wooden buttstock was cracked and pale with salt stains after years at sea, and the barrel was thick with grime and spotted with rust. It would almost certainly blow up in your face if you tried to fire it.

'You're the soldier,' said Rafi to Holliday. 'What do we do now?'

Holliday shrugged. 'There's two ways, fast and hard or slow and careful. Personally I favor slow and careful.' He grinned. 'But I'm getting a little old for this kind of thing.'

'I am, too,' said Tidyman.

'Well, I'm not,' Rafi said with a scowl. 'Peggy could be on that boat.'

'Which is why slow and careful might be the best option,' responded Tidyman. 'We have no idea who is aboard the ship. We could easily be outnumbered. Your friend could well forfeit her life for a rash action.'

'The *Khamsin* is old, with a wooden hull,' said Holliday. 'One shot from that RPG is easily capable of sinking her.'

'What are you suggesting?' Tidyman asked quietly. On the radar screen the two blips were getting closer and closer.

'Five hundred meters,' said Moustafa. 'The moon is rising. You will see her at any moment now.'

'We have to make a decision. Now,' demanded Rafi.

'There's a spotlight up in the bow. We come in fast with a lot of light, blind them,' said Holliday. 'We hail them. Act like we're official. Customs or coast guard or something. Mr Tidyman is in the bow with the RPG. We threaten them. Hand over Peggy or we sink her.'

'Sounds good to me,' said Tidyman. He smiled. 'But please, in the future you must call me Emil.'

'Let's go,' said Rafi. 'We're running out of time.'

'Two hundred meters, dead ahead,' said Moustafa.

They came in at flank speed, engines thundering, bow wave foaming up almost to the gunwales. Tidyman was braced against the forward winch, the RPG balanced on his shoulder, the weapon loaded and primed, his finger curled around the forward trigger mechanism.

Holliday and Rafi crouched behind the Egyptian, half hidden by a stinking pile of fishnet, handguns drawn and ready. Standing in the wheelhouse Moustafa waited until the very last second, then snapped on the floodlight in the bow, wrenching the wheel around at the same time, then hauling back the throttle, throwing the old torpedo boat into a sliding turn that left the *Fantasma* broadside to its quarry as it came to a roaring stop in a crashing welter of spray.

'Dear God in heaven,' whispered Tidyman, staring at the terrible vision before him, the horror of it etched by the floodlight in bright and grotesque detail against the night sky. 'What awful thing has happened here?'

20

The weary old tugboat *Khamsin* rolled on the dark sea, broken and adrift. Her entire super-structure, including the main deckhouse and the wheelhouse above, looked as though it had been swallowed up by some hellish piece of machinery that had flailed and chewed the vessel into small pieces. The smokestack had completely torn away from its supports and now sagged down on the starboard side, riddled with holes the size of softballs.

The wheelhouse had almost completely van-ished, windows demolished, bulkheads destroyed, the companionway stairs nothing but twisted wreckage. It was clear that the boat was taking on water; the portside list was so severe that the deck was awash. The deck itself was a splintered ruin, stitched with dozens more of the fist-sized openings that had turned the wheelhouse into a sieve.

There were several bodies, or at least parts of

them, on deck. None was recognizable. There were smears of blood everywhere, great sprays of it against the whitework and more running down in broad streams into the scuppers.

Bizarrely, in the bows, a hand clutched a machine gun, but beyond the shoulder there was no body. Next to the arm a headless corpse hung out of an open hatch, a long ugly tongue of bone scraps and blood and brains spattering back along the decking.

'Peggy!' Rafi moaned, climbing to his feet.

'Wait,' said Holliday, standing and putting a cautioning hand on his friend's shoulder.

'What could have done this?' Tidyman asked, standing beside them and surveying the wreckage as they rocked gently on the night waves.

Holliday knew exactly what had done it. He'd first seen it used from a C-47 Spooky in Vietnam and then the Russian version in the early days back in the eighties as an advisor with the mujahideen in Afghanistan.

The Russians called it a Yak-B12, the U.S. Air Force called it a Minigun – a chain-drive, electrically powered modern-day version of a Gatling gun with a rate of fire somewhere around four thousand rounds a minute. Enough to grind a human body to bloody shreds in the blink of an eye.

'Helicopters,' said Holliday, staring at the nightmare scene. 'Like the ones that attacked Alhazred's camp last night. They hit the boat on the return flight.'

'But why?' Rafi said, stunned and horrified by the awful vision in front of them.

'Revenge?' Tidyman said.

'Or cleaning up after themselves,' said Holliday coldly. 'Silencing their enemies. Maybe our man from the gift shop in Alexandria knew too much.'

'You think the Church did this?' Rafi said, staring.

'I think Sodalitium Pianum, the ones who call themselves La Sapinière, might have done it,' answered Holliday. 'They're cold-blooded enough; look what they did in the desert last night.'

'Terror in the name of God.' Tidyman shrugged. 'Not so hard to believe these days.'

'We have to go aboard,' said Rafi, his voice dull. 'I have to find out if Peggy . . .' He stopped, swallowing hard. 'I have to find out if Peggy was on the boat.'

'Emil and I can go,' said Holliday softly. 'You don't have to come.'

'Better not to,' agreed Tidyman. He reached out tentatively and touched Rafi's arm. 'Some pain should not be endured, or should at least be borne by others, and not alone.'

'No,' said Rafi. 'I have to see.'

A few minutes later Moustafa managed to maneuver the low-hulled torpedo boat close enough to the wreck of the *Khamsin* for the men to simply step off onto the awkwardly tilting deck. Both armed, Holliday and Rafi went below to check the hold while Tidyman made his way up to the ruins of the wheelhouse.

They bypassed the headless watchman in the hatchway and made their way down the steeply canted ladder into the main hold. The ship's interior was silent except for the creaking of the dying hull and empty of life. A ghost ship.

Once upon a time the small area had probably been used to carry supplies or spare equipment, but now it had been subdivided into plywood-partitioned stalls, each one no bigger than a coffin and lined with straw. In each of the subdivided areas a woman was shackled to a large ringbolt welded to the hull. There were thirty stalls and thirty women, or at least what was left of them. Each of the prisoners was naked and filthy.

They were all dead, some torn to ribbons by the rounds from the helicopter chain guns, others flailed by flying shrapnel. Some of them were very young, no more than eleven or twelve. The majority of them appeared to be Berbers, some with traditional tattoos on their hands and faces. There seemed to be no fear in their faces, as though they'd died in their sleep. Holliday was reasonably sure they'd been drugged for their sea voyage to keep them quiet.

'Who are they?' Rafi asked. 'How did they get here? Not by choice surely.'

'Probably from Mauritania,' said Holliday, looking down at the pitiful remains of the women. 'Chattel slavery is big business there. The men work on farms or in the mines, the women and girl children are sold as sex slaves. Alhazred is just a middleman between the slave dealers in Mali and the Sudan and the end users from La Santa.'

'How could any normal human being be involved in something like this? This is madness.'

'No, just business,' said Holliday, his voice

cold with barely contained fury. 'It's not much different from privately run prisons in the U.S. The inhumanity is irrelevant; in the end it's only the bottom line that counts.' He shook his head. 'There's nothing we can do here,' he said at last. 'At least Peggy wasn't on board.'

'Thank God for that,' said Rafi.

'I don't think God is part of the equation here,' muttered Holliday. 'Come on.'

They made their way back up to the deck again. Tidyman was waiting for them.

'Did you find anything?' Holliday asked.

'The only chart still intact at all was for the Tyrrhenian Sea.'

'Naples?' Holliday said. 'Not Corsica?'

'Maybe Naples, maybe somewhere else.' He held up a shattered piece of electronic gear. 'What's left of a Garmin deck unit. If we're lucky I'll be able to figure out what charts they had loaded into it.' He glanced quickly at Rafi and then back to Holliday. 'Any luck?'

'Peggy wasn't on board,' said Holliday. 'At least there's no sign of her. There was a cargo of women belowdecks. Sex slaves. They're all dead. Some of them are just kids.'

'What shall we do?'

Holliday looked up and down the deck. The wreckage hadn't sunk much lower in the water since they'd come aboard. The boat could easily stay afloat for days. He thought about the bodies down below.

'Those women deserve a little dignity,' he said. 'Let's give them a proper burial at sea.'

Ten minutes later Moustafa put off a dozen yards, well away from the remains of the foundering tugboat. This time it was Holliday who carried the familiar weight of the rocket-propelled grenade launcher on his shoulder. He aimed for the open forward hatch, sent up a brief, heartfelt prayer, then pulled the heavy trigger.

There was a sharp cracking sound as the round took off, the recoil throwing him back on his right leg. The high-explosive charge detonated deep in the hull of the old boat and there was a thunderclap of sound as the fuel tank exploded.

A gout of flame tore up out of the hold and there was a ghastly wrenching sound as the ancient tug broke her back, the massive oak keelson twisting, then finally splitting along its length. Almost immediately the *Khamsin* began to sink, rolling once before slipping under the dark swell of the sea, leaving nothing behind but a few flaming pieces of wreckage and a spreading slick of bunker oil. In a little while even that would be gone.

Holliday stood alone on the forward deck of the torpedo boat, staring at the spot where the tug had been only moments before. Briefly he had one of those moments when the past comes back so hard it leaves you breathless, remembering his own father's funeral and seeing his cousin Peggy on the other side of the grave, crying, even though he could not.

Later that day his uncle Henry had taken Holliday aside and reminded him that when he was gone Peggy would be the only family left to him, and that above all else it was Holliday's job to protect her from harm, to keep her safe and see her happy. He'd vowed to do all those things and now he'd failed her. She was somewhere out there, desperate and afraid. It was his job to find her and bring her home.

Rafi appeared beside him on the deck. He held his peace for a moment. Finally Holliday turned to him.

'What?'

'Emil figured out the GPS unit. The *Khamsin* was headed for the island of Ponza, on the Italian coast.'

'How far?'

'Moustafa says he can have us there by sunrise.'

21

The island of Ponza is a five-mile-long and one-mile-wide crescent-shaped spine of volcanic rock rising out of the ocean fifty miles or so southeast of Rome and an almost equal distance northwest of Naples. The closest port offering ferry service is the coastal town of Anzio. The island, named in honor of the infamous Pontius Pilate, was a favorite holiday haunt for Romans in ancient times, a onetime penal colony and a summer resort for the seventeenth-century Bourbon kings of Naples and Sicily. During World War II it was used as an internment camp for troublesome Royalist families and briefly as a place of exile for Mussolini himself. During the twenty-first century, it had reverted to the past and was a summer haven for city-weary Romans during the months of July and August.

Moustafa knew the island well; it had been a haven for pirates and smugglers for the last five thousand years and there wasn't much difference between smuggling wine into Pompeii to avoid customs duty two thousand years ago and smuggling small arms and cigarettes into Anzio and Naples now. There were a thousand caves and hidden beaches where goods could be dropped or transshipped, and there were so many small pleasure boats at anchor in the pretty island's bays and coves to make the job of the maritime Carabinieri and the Guardia Costiera a nightmarish, next to impossible task. According to Moustafa there was as much Lebanese hashish and Marseille heroin in the luggage of people on the return ferry from Porto Ponza as there was dirty laundry.

As easy as it was to smuggle in and out of the volcanic resort island, it also didn't do to flaunt it in the face of officialdom. The Guardia Costiera patrolled the jagged coastline of the little island in half a dozen Defender-class inflatables, so it wouldn't do to have a seventy-two-foot dazzle-camouflaged speedboat rumble into the crowded harbor at Porto Ponza. Instead, Moustafa sold them his own bicycle-patched twelve-foot inflatable, then pointed them in the right direction and dropped them off at extreme radar range in the first gray light of dawn.

The timing was perfect. Using Moustafa's ancient British Anzani 18-horsepower outboard they made it to the clear amethyst waters of Luna Beach on the west side of the island just as the sun began to rise above the crags and cliffs that divided the beach from the town.

They drew the inflatable up onto the dark sand beside a row of rental paddle boats chained in a row, then walked through the quarter-mile-long tunnel dug five hundred years before Christ beneath the cliffs. They came out on the town side of the gloomy walkway just as the first blunt-nosed hydrofoil ferry arrived from Naples.

'Now what?' Rafi asked as they came out through the tunnel's seawall exit.

'Moustafa told us to find a taxi driver named Al,' said Tidyman, blinking in the sudden sun.

'Al?' Holliday said.

'He's from Brooklyn,' answered the Egyptian.

They found Al at an open-air café farther down the promenade. He was drinking coffee from a huge foaming mug, eating a cannoli and smoking a Marlboro. As he ate, smoked and drank he complained about his breakfast.

'You know how difficult it is to find sausages and eggs on an island without chickens or pigs?'

He shook his head. 'Almost impossible, that's how hard. An egg is worth its weight in gold in this town. The only meat they eat here other than fish is rabbits they raise to make their cacciatore.'

Al's full name was Alphonso Fonzaretti but he preferred Al to Alphonso and Fonz to Fonzaretti. He was thirty-two years old and favored *I Love New York* T-shirts in red and yellow. Al's people were originally from Ponza and immigrated to Dover Plains, New York, with half the population of the town just after the war. Al came over to drive a cab during the summers while his cousin Mario switched places and visited relatives in Dover Plains. It seemed to be an equitable arrangement for both of them. Mario made hard currency in the States working in the Fonzaretti garbage business and Al got an Italian vacation and a chance to pick up nice girls and practice the mother tongue. After all, what was family for, *capisce*?

'So what can I do for Moustafa's friends today?' Al asked when the preliminaries were over.

'Girls,' said Holliday bluntly as Al popped the last piece of gooey pastry into his mouth.

'You don't seem the type of guys who'd be looking for girls,' said Al, speculatively. 'You don't have that collegiate look, *capisce*? None of that Brotherhood of the Traveling Panty Hound look you sometimes get here, know what I mean?'

'We're looking for the people who might deal in girls as a commodity,' said Holliday.

'Business,' said Al, nodding, getting the idea.

'Business,' agreed Holliday.

'Not my thing,' Al said with a shrug. 'I'm strictly small-time. Bit of booze, bit of weed, maybe even some blow if you get really hard-core, but that's as far as I go. Like to keep a low profile, right? Flying under the radar, yeah? The Fonz has a good thing going here.' Al gave them a hard look. 'Got the family reputation to protect as well, right?'

'But you know what I'm talking about,' said Holliday.

'Sure.'

'And you *are* connected,' added Holliday.

'But you're not,' answered Al flatly.

'No,' agreed Holliday. 'But believe me, Al, my friends and I can be dangerous.'

'That some kind of threat?' asked the young man, bristling slightly. He stubbed out his Marlboro and lit another.

'More like a warning,' said Holliday. 'We're going to find out what we need to know one way or the other; you can either help us or hinder. It's up to you. These people kidnapped my cousin, my *family*, Al. We're going to get her back even if other people get hurt in the process. *Capisce?*'

Al took a long drag on his cigarette and stared at Holliday.

'How'd you lose the eye?'

'Afghanistan,' said Holliday curtly.

'Army?'

'Rangers.'

'You saying it's Axis or Allies?'

'Something like that.'

'Italians could have saved themselves a lot of trouble, they'd gotten rid of Mussolini in the first place.'

'Agreed.'

'Guy you're looking for has a place in Le Forna, up the road. Runs a dive shop. Goodlooking, forty, forty-five. Gray hair, expensive sunglasses.'

'What's his name?'

'Conti. Massimo Conti.'

Le Forna was a sleepy little village on the upper horn of the island's crescent, and like Ponza Town it clung to a series of stone terraces carved out of the tuffa cliffs millennia before. Al drove them in his Fiat Idea Minivan, following the twisting narrow road along the spine of the island, heading north.

'Conti's not a local,' said Al, from behind the wheel. 'I think he's from Naples. There was a hotel for sale in Le Forna and he bought it. Just appeared one day and started spending money in the town. Hotel one summer, then the dive shop, then an air charter service. Turbo Otters from Rome for the glitterati. Seems to be paying off.'

'Naples,' said Holliday. 'Camorra?'

'Who knows from Camorra?' Al shrugged. 'Mario Puzo time. Everyone wants to be a Soprano.' The young man made an unpronounceable sound like a badger clearing its throat. 'It's all bull.' The young man paused. 'He does have some kind of juice though, that's for sure. Two years and half the town is his.'

'How does he handle the women?'

'It's a way station. Any talent that actually works here are imports from Rome. Classy stuff, not the raw meat you're talking about. Word is he parks the goods in the old abandoned prison on Santo Stefano, then brings them to the mainland when he's ready. Doesn't crap in his own nest so to speak. Uses his dive boats as cover and transportation.'

'Where's Santo Stefano, and what is it?'

'An island twenty-five miles east, closer to the coast. It's a rock, maybe half a mile across. The prison's about four hundred years old. They used it right up to the sixties.'

'What else is there?'

'Nothing. There's another island, Ventotene, about a mile and a half away with a few hundred people on it, but that's it.'

They arrived in Le Forna. Al found them another café high on the cliffs above the harbor. He ordered coffee and rolls for everyone, then pointed out Conti's dive shop far below them. It was no more than a shack on an old seawall that looked as though it was part of a Roman ruin. As they watched, a big cabin-decked inflatable was being hauled down a long stone ramp into the clear, sparkling water. The aluminum boat's inflatable collar was bright orange and the upper deck and cabin were red and white.

'Two hundred grand a pop with a pair of Honda 225s,' commented Al. 'And he's got six of them.' The young man snorted. 'Like I said, juice from somewhere.'

'Color scheme's interesting,' commented Holliday. 'I saw one just like it back in the harbor at Ponza.'

'Noticed, did you?' Al laughed. 'Same as the Guardia Costiera. You can bet he's got some sticky signs around that say just that.'

'I take it he's bringing in more than women,' said Holliday, watching as the inflatable was rolled into the water. There were half a dozen tourist types watching from the pier as scuba tanks were loaded on board.

'There's places on the island you could unload a small freighter, no problem,' Al said and nodded. 'I've seen it for myself. Bales of dope, crates of weapons. He's got a whole black market going. Anything people buy, Massimo Conti and his people sell.' The Brooklyn taxi driver nodded toward the shack on the ancient pier below them. 'Speak of the devil,' he said quietly.

A middle-aged very fit-looking man in Gucci sunglasses and an eighty-dollar haircut appeared. He stood by the small group of tourists on the pier, chatting as their dive boat was prepared. He clapped one of them on the back and they headed down the old stone ramp. He watched for a second, then stepped back into the shack.

'That was him?' Holliday asked.

'Yup.' Al nodded.

'You know anything about his schedule?'

'Wednesdays he goes out on his boat. Big Dalla Pieta 48 he keeps in Ponza. Comes back Fridays. Says he's diving on an old destroyer that was sunk off Anzio, the HMS *Inglefield*.'

'You don't believe it?'

'Not his kind of thing. Look at him. George Hamilton with pecs. Mr Adventure. He'd go for a Roman wreck maybe, something with class, but not a rusty old piece of tin from the Second World War.' Al lit another Marlboro. 'Besides, friends of mine have seen him in Ventotene on Thursdays, partying.'

'What's wrong with that?' Rafi asked.

'Nowhere near Anzio,' said Al. 'Opposite direction.'

'Think he's supervising a pickup or a drop?' Holliday asked.

'Could be,' said Al.

'Tomorrow's Wednesday,' said Rafi.

'So it is,' said Al.

'Can you get us to this Santo Stefano by tomorrow night?' Holliday said.

'Sure,' said Al. 'Hookers is one thing, white slavery's something else.' The young man grinned. 'Kinda thing gives organized crime a bad name, *capisce?*'

22

Al's uncle Paolo, Mario the cousin's father, had a twenty-four-foot Toyo trawler named *Sofia* that he used for fishing when he wasn't busy raising rabbits for the hotels. Uncle Paolo was perfectly happy to rent Holliday *Sofia* for a price as long as he promised faithfully to bring the boat and his American nephew back to him in one piece – emphasis on *Sofia* rather than the nephew, Uncle Paolo being a practical man, after all.

Peggy would have called *Sofia* 'cute.' To Al she was 'smart.' To Holliday she seemed just a little silly, almost a toy. The plywood semidisplacement hull looked like a lifeboat with a telephone booth perched on the back and was painted white with a nice sky blue stripe down the gunwales.

The forward hold, lined with zinc, was big enough to carry a hundred and forty cubic feet or a little more than a ton of shrimp, caught using what Al referred to as a single Dutch seine rig towed behind the boat at a depth of about eighty to a hundred feet along the muddy and sandy bottom of the offshore area between the islands.

A ton of shrimp with its inevitable by-catch of hake and juvenile bluefin tuna during the high season was just about enough to keep the Ponza hotels going for a single day of the lunchtime trade, so the local *pescatori* switched their favorite fishing grounds and times to share the wealth. It took Al a few hours to negotiate the grounds between Ventotene and the prison island, but by midafternoon, properly attired in jeans, fresh T-shirts and sneakers, they chugged out of Ponza Harbor in *Sofia* and headed east at a steady eight knots, the old 35-horsepower Perkins diesel coughing and belching happily as they chugged their way onto the open sea.

Three hours later, with the falling sun turning the slightly ruffled ocean to a flashing bronze, they raised Ventotene on the horizon. As they closed on the island Santo Stefano appeared just behind it, the high-walled citadel of the old Bourbon prison rising like a fortress on the craggy summit.

They puttered into the tiny rock-hewn harbor at Ventotene just as the sun was going down. It was a smaller version of the waterfront at Ponza: eighteenth-century buildings in pastel colors clinging to cliff terraces, crisscrossing alley stairways zigzagging back and forth.

There was a place for ferries to dock, disgorging tourists coming for alcoholic getaways and baking sun for a few days, a week, or maybe two. There were more pleasure craft in the harbor here than at Ponza; day cruisers, motor sailers and full-out glistening yachts outnumbered fishing boats like the *Sofia* by two to one at least.

Al found an old iron mooring ring in the seawall that ran around the harbor, hitched *Sofia* to it, then went in search of the harbor master to announce his arrival and show his credentials. Rafi sat moodily in the bows staring down at the oily water that slopped between the boats at anchor while Holliday and Tidyman made a show of moving around the pile of seine net in the stern, readying the boat for a day's fishing the following morning.

'Your young friend looks unhappy,' said the Egyptian, glancing at Rafi as he worked.

'He's worrying about Peggy,' answered Holliday. 'So am I.'

'I hope he realizes that this cannot be a rescue

mission,' said Tidyman. 'This man Conti is sure to outnumber us. We can only do a reconnaissance, nothing more.'

'He's frustrated,' said Holliday. 'He feels as though he's not doing enough to help. I know what's going through his head, believe me.'

'That kind of frustration leads to foolish behavior,' cautioned Tidyman. 'It could get us all killed.'

'What are you suggesting?' Holliday asked.

'Perhaps you should talk to him,' suggested Tidyman.

'Why don't you?'

'Because I'm Egyptian and he's Israeli, among other things. There's too much history between our people, I'm afraid. A wall of mistrust.'

'Maybe it's time to tear it down,' replied Holliday.

Tidyman gave a brief, hollow laugh.

'Another day perhaps,' he said quietly. 'He doesn't strike me as being in the mood for reconciliation right now.'

Massimo Conti's cruise appeared later that evening, all 1,300 horsepower burbling powerfully as she shouldered her way into a preferred berth the harbor master gave her closest to the promenade stairway.

'Cute,' said Holliday, seated on deck with Al as the big boat docked.

'What's that?' Al said, smoking another Marlboro in the fading light.

'The name,' said Holliday. '*Disco Volante.*'

'Means Flying Saucer,' translated Al.

'Largo's boat in *Thunderball*,' said Holliday. 'Our boy has a sense of humor.'

As the evening spun into night Holliday watched as Conti and his friends from shore partied long and loud, the music swelling across the miniature harbor, intruding on the privacy of anyone within earshot, which likely meant the entire town. It seemed unlikely that anyone aboard would be in any shape for an early breakfast.

They left for the shrimping grounds at dawn, heading out of the narrow harbor along with half a dozen other boats, leaving the sleeping pleasure craft behind them along with the tightly shuttered sleeping town on the terraced heights above.

In the morning, with the sun no more than a hot

pink slash on the eastern horizon, Al ran the little trawler back and forth in the narrow strait between Santo Stefano and Ventotene, using his fish-finding gear to troll for likely shoals of shrimp big enough to grace the tables of the hotels and restaurants back in Ponza. Crammed into the tiny little day cabin-galley belowdecks Holliday, Rafi and Tidyman pored over the charts of Santo Stefano Al had found for them the day before in the Ventotene harbor master's office.

The island was a fortress in and of itself, a volcanic plug of dark basalt half a mile in diameter. Jagged cliffs rose five hundred feet to a broad plateau covered in an oddly sinister sea of wildflowers that broke on the yellow stone walls of the crumbling old prison like bright blue perfumed waves.

The prison was circular, four bleak tiers rising out of the volcanic rock, pierced with windows and doors, everything facing in to a central courtyard with a single guard tower in the middle, an elevated platform overseeing the inmates as they went about their business. There were no toilets, nor was there any running water. The only food was what the prisoners' families sent to them. There was no work or any kind of labor. Time was a wheel that eventually broke a man. Madness was a way of life.

The cells, each holding at least twenty men, were perpetually dark and the courtyard was in perpetual sun. If an inmate was stupid enough to try to escape there was nothing between him and the jagged cliff edge except the giant field of flowers and their sweet cloying scent. He could die in the darkness or die in the sun; the guards didn't care which. A life term on Santo Stefano was just a death sentence that took varying amounts of time to execute depending on how stubborn a man was.

Like the Château d'If in *The Count of Monte Cristo* there was only one way off the island for a prisoner: in a weighted shroud. There were two ways into the prison, however: a narrow switchback road that made its way up the slightly sloping western approaches to the plateau on which the prison loomed, or by following an almost impossibly steep goat track up the northern cliffs from a tiny gravel beach that all but vanished at high tide. The switchback road was visible from the prison if a guard was posted, and the goat track was virtually suicidal.

'There's no other way up,' said Holliday, peering

at the chart as they bobbed along in the lightly running morning sea. A seagull swooped and called, sensing the possibility of a meal. 'It's the cliff path or nothing. Even at dusk they'd see us going up the road.'

'What about the tide?' Tidyman asked. 'It says on the chart that the beach is covered at least half the time.'

'Al says he could drop us in the late afternoon, pick us up in the late evening, ten thirty or eleven. Next pickup wouldn't be until the following morning,' Holliday answered.

'In other words, we'd be on our own if there was any trouble,' grumbled Rafi.

'There is no fair play in this game, I'm afraid,' said Tidyman. 'Sometimes the cards are stacked against you.'

'What's that supposed to mean?' Rafi asked hotly. 'You backing out?'

'Not at all, Dr Wanounou,' said the Egyptian, holding up one placating hand. 'I'm just pointing out that whatever we do will be dangerous.'

'I'm aware of that,' said Rafi. 'But getting Peggy back is worth it.'

'She may not even be there,' cautioned Holliday. 'She could be farther down the pipeline by now.'

Rafi muttered something under his breath, then turned away and went back up on deck.

'You realize that your cousin may very well be dead,' said Tidyman. 'Especially if they have discovered who she is.'

'Yes, I know that,' Holliday said and nodded. 'I'm still trying to figure out why they took her on the expedition in the first place. If the expedition was just a cover for an attempt to find the German gold, why prejudice everything by taking along an outsider?' Holliday shook his head wearily and rolled up the chart. 'It doesn't make a hell of a lot of sense.'

'No, it does not,' replied Tidyman. 'Unless they had no choice.'

'Explain,' said Holliday.

'An expedition without a photographer would have been suspect perhaps. *Smithsonian* magazine suggests a story; how could they reasonably decline? Miss Blackstock becomes the sacrificial lamb.'

'I'm still not sure I buy it,' said Holliday. 'An American citizen held hostage by terrorists? That shines a pretty big light on these people. Would they have done that knowingly?'

Tidyman shrugged. 'There is only one way to find out.'

The hold of the *Sofia* filled to overflowing with tens of thousands of plump, squirming crustacea, Al swung the shallow-draft little trawler close in to shore, his actions hidden on the lee side of the island. As the carvel planking of the boat's almost flat bottom ground against the pebble beach, Holliday, Tidyman and Rafi dropped over the side and waded to the shore. Al would take his catch back to Ponza, a three-hour journey, off-load, and then return to Santo Stefano under the cover of night, returning to the little strip of inhospitable shingle with the next low tide, guided by a flashlight signal from Holliday.

Superficially it seemed like a simple enough plan, but as Holliday knew it was the simplest plans that often went the furthest astray. As the three men began to climb the near-vertical track up the cliff he found his thoughts turning to the thousand and one unknowns that could turn their little outing into an unmitigated and deadly disaster. The higher they climbed, clinging to the sheer rock wall, the more exposed Holliday felt, and the stiff breeze plucking insistently at his clothing was like a sour omen of skeletal fingers trying to pull him off his tenuous perch. He silently chided himself for being superstitious and continued to climb.

Calves in agony, knees buckling, Holliday reached the top of the cliff more than an hour later, sweat staining his T-shirt and running in rivers down his forehead, dripping in stinging torrents into his eyes. He fell to his hands and knees, breath coming in ragged gasps, the perfume of the immense field of blue flowers thick in the air. Finally he sat up and opened the binocular case at his hip, bringing out the powerful glasses he'd borrowed from Al.

A football field away the high walls of the horseshoe-shaped prison stood before him, windows and doorways peering blindly at him, empty holes in the old crumbling stone. The sun was level with the sea, turning the old ruins the color of old gold and deepening the shadows. There was no sound except the sighing of the breeze across the field, gently wafting the flowers and the dry screams of the pallid swifts that darted like flitting bats in and out of the ruins. Nothing moved and it seemed that for an instant the world held its breath. Hot and tired as he was, Holliday felt a sudden chill run down his spine.

He'd never thought of himself as being much of a believer in the paranormal, but every once in a while he found himself in places where he could have sworn the fabric of time and place had somehow worn thin and the past found itself uncomfortably close to the present and the future.

Each time he visited Paris and stood on the Champs-Elysées he inevitably heard the echo of Nazi boots goose-stepping on the cobbles, and standing on Burnside's Bridge in Antietam, Maryland, he swore he could hear the roar of cannons and the screams of twenty thousand dying men whose blood stained the muddy waters of the creek below, all in a single day.

'You feel it, don't you?' Tidyman said, flopping down beside him, panting.

'Yes,' answered Holliday.

'An evil place,' agreed the gray-haired Egyptian, peering across the open field to the ruins. 'Four hundred years of pain and suffering leaves its mark, I think.'

'I think you're right,' said Holliday.

'What are you two old men going on about?' Rafi asked, joining them.

'You're the archaeologist – you should feel it the most,' said Holliday.

'Feel what?' Rafi said.

'Time,' said Tidyman.

'Superstitious nonsense,' scoffed Rafi. A pair of darting swifts screeched like fishwives overhead and Rafi looked up, startled by the sudden sound.

'There's no one here,' said Tidyman quietly. 'It's empty. I can feel it.'

'We can't be sure,' said Rafi.

'Let's check it out while we've still got time,' suggested Holliday. 'If Conti comes, it'll be just before dark, guaranteed.

They walked across the empty field of wildflowers, listening and watching for any sound or sign of movement. There was nothing. They bypassed the ruins of an old wall marking the original prison dating back to Roman times and continued on in the dying sunlight, finally ducking through one of the empty arches into the Bourbon compound. Still nothing.

They climbed a few rough steps cut out of the

bedrock and reached the inner courtyard. It was laid out like an ancient monastery, three arched galleries running in a circle, each gallery with cell doors running off it, the fourth tier buried in the old foundations for prisoners doomed to solitary confinement for whatever reason. Four evenly spaced and enclosed square stairways connected one tier to the next around the horseshoe.

In the center of the courtyard the oddly ornate guard tower rose, looking like a belfry without a bell, its dome capped by an iron crucifix long bent and rusted to a shapeless chunk of crusted metal.

'The Mafia was born in places like this,' said Holliday, looking around. 'Communism, too.'

'How's that?' Tidyman asked, interested.

'The Bourbons put all their rotten eggs in one rotten basket,' said Holliday. 'Put that many Freemasons and revolutionaries together and you invariably get revolution. The Bastille gave you the French Revolution; Attica gave you the rise of Black Power. During World War Two the Germans put all their most dangerous prisoners into Stalag Luft Three P.O.W. Camp and you got the Great Escape.'

'I don't think there was ever any great escape from this place,' said Tidyman.

'None of which has anything to do with finding Peggy,' said Rafi.

The three men split up and began checking the cells, going from tier to tier. All Holliday saw were a few empty beer bottles, the remains of a small fire, and most bizarre, a red hot-water bottle missing its plug. As he searched, something niggled at the back of his mind and finally he figured out what it was: none of the cell windows still had their bars. They had been methodically removed, wrenched from their crumbling enclosures, leaving only gaping stone.

Half an hour later, with the evening light fading fast, Holliday met with Tidyman at the foot of the main gallery.

The Egyptian sighed. He picked up a pebble from among the weeds in the courtyard and tossed it against one crumbling wall.

'There's nothing here, no sign of anyone. We're wasting our time. Perhaps our American taxi driver was spinning tall tales.'

From the middle tier Rafi whispered harshly, his voice urgent.

'Somebody's coming!'

They ran across the courtyard to one of the enclosed stairways and climbed upward. They joined Rafi under one of the archways on the second-tier gallery and he led them into the musty interior of one of the old communal cells. Keeping well within the deep shadows they looked out through the empty cell window. They faced southeast, looking down the sloping length of the little island to the sea. At anchor, perhaps two hundred yards from the shore, was the sleek white shape of Massimo Conti's yacht, *Disco Volante*. On the zigzag path that climbed the cliff Holliday could see a little group trudging upward. He lifted the binoculars and fiddled with the focus.

'I think it's Peggy,' whispered Holliday, not quite believing it. His cousin was walking between two muscular-looking armed men. Conti and another man in conversation walked behind them. Conti was dressed in shorts and a T-shirt. The man with him was dressed in a dark suit with a stark white collar. A priest? Peggy appeared to be unharmed but she looked terribly tired, her usually bright features drawn and haggard.

'Let me see!' Rafi hissed. Holliday handed him the glasses.

Rafi swore.

'It *is* her!' he breathed. 'The bastard's had her on that boat all this time!'

'But why bring her here?' Tidyman asked.

'It doesn't matter!' Rafi said furiously. 'I'll kill the son of a bitch!'

'Those guards are both wearing shoulder rigs,' said Holliday. 'They'd kill you first.'

Rafi swung the glasses a little to one side.

'The man speaking with Conti. When they announced the expedition they had his picture in *Archaeology* magazine. That's Charles-Étienne Brasseur, the expedition leader, from the Biblical Archaeology School in Jerusalem.'

'The man who went after the gold?' Holliday asked. He took the glasses back from Rafi and focused on the group again. 'What on earth is he doing here? And what is he doing with Peggy?'

'Listen!' Tidyman said. In the distance they could hear the distinct whickering sound of an approaching helicopter. A big one.

'What the hell is going on?' Holliday said. He watched as the group reached the top of the zigzag track and paused. The helicopter came in low out of the west and thundered over the top of the old prison enclosure. Dust blew up in swirling clouds as the big machine came in over-head.

It settled slowly onto the broad, slightly slop-ing field like some giant insect, the flowers bending beneath the powerful downdraft of the five-bladed rotors. It was a big Sikorsky SH-3, the one they called the Sea King. The livery was white with a broad blue stripe around the mid-line. There were patches taped over the places where the roundels and service name would ordinarily be but the bird was clearly military. There was no visible weaponry; it was a VIP transport. But where was it from and where was it going?

The Sea King had a range of more than six hundred miles; not far but enough to put it down from the coast of Spain to the Black Sea and all of continental Europe in between. With a long-range fuel tank a chopper like that could take you halfway to Moscow. A needle in a hundred hay-stacks.

The engines cycled down to an idling whine and the rotors continued to whirl lazily. A door-way opened in the hull just behind the cockpit and someone inside lowered a short set of stairs. Massimo Conti and his group came forward a few paces, then stopped again. Peggy looked around blearily as though she was trying to get her bearings. Holliday felt a lurch in his stomach, his heart going out to her, but he knew there was nothing he could do.

Beside him Rafi made a small sound in his throat and tore the binoculars out of Holliday's grip. Someone stepped down from the helicopter and waved at Conti, standing a few yards away. The man was tall and completely bald. Rafi swung the glasses away from the group, focusing on the new arrival. Suddenly he dropped the glasses away from his eyes and stared blindly out through the dark opening of the cell window. The blood drained visibly from his face.

'What's wrong?' Holliday said.

'It's him,' whispered Rafi, real horror in his face. 'The bald one. I'd recognize him anywhere. The guy who stole the Crusader scroll from us. The one who had me beaten half to death a year ago in Jerusalem. It's him. He's here.'

Rafi handed over the binoculars. Holliday looked, seeing the man for the first time. Rafi's beating had come at the hands of the same people who'd tried to kill Holliday and Peggy in a back alley in Old Jerusalem on the same night a year ago. Call them what you wanted, Black Templars, La Sapinière, Sodalitium Pianum, Organum Sanctum, the Instrument of God, it was all the same, and then and there he knew where the big white helicopter had come from and where it was going: its destination was Rome. The Vatican.

23

The three men arrived in Rome after an hour-long train ride up the coast from Anzio. They reached the Roma Termini station in the late afternoon, almost exactly twenty-four hours after first seeing Peggy on the prison island of Santo Stefano. Stepping off the train, Holliday spotted a man in a Marine Corps service uniform greeting a friend on the platform and immediately braced him. The Marine turned out to be a West Point graduate, although one well before Holliday's time there. The Marine also turned out to be part of the security detail at the U.S. embassy, and he gave Holliday directions to the old palazzo on the Via Veneto as well as a few contact names to smooth the way.

At the embassy Holliday went through security while Rafi and Tidyman waited at a table under the awning at the Café de Paris across the street. Almost an hour later, Holliday reappeared and joined his companions at the café. Acting on the advice he'd been given at the embassy, they took another taxi through the hectic downtown area and headed northwest. Skirting the high walls of the Holy See, they were eventually dropped off in front of the Alimandi Hotel at Viale Vaticano, 99.

The five-story building, once a police station and then a police association retirement home, had been refurbished into a four-star hotel complete with a roof garden restaurant that looked directly across at the ornate main entrance through the high walls to the Vatican Museums and the Sistine Chapel.

'So how exactly is this going to work?' Rafi asked as they settled into their suite of rooms. Holliday stepped out onto the balcony and looked out onto the Vatican rooftops. Part of the church since the time of Constantine more than fifteen hundred years ago, it was exactly what it appeared to be, a fortress state guarded by high stone walls and two thousand years of tradition – as well as being the single largest corporate entity in the world. And he was about to take it on. *I must be out of my mind*, he thought.

Holliday let out a long breath and felt an itch at the back of his throat – a sense memory of a

time when he'd smoked two packages of unfil-
tered Camel cigarettes a day. Standing there in
the warm afternoon light he knew he could start
again in an instant, even though it had been
almost twenty years. He glanced down at the
cobblestone plaza in front of the high arched
entrance through the wall. Souvenir carts and ice
cream vendors were parked in front of the entrance
like remora cleaning the teeth of a cruising shark.
He sighed again and turned back into the room.

'So how is this going to work?' Rafi asked
again.

'Maybe it's not,' answered Holliday.

'You really think Peggy is in there?' Rafi said.

'Probably not, but the way to get her back is.'

'And how are we to work this act of magic?'
Tidyman asked, dropping down into a silk-covered
armchair.

Holliday turned back to the view out the doors
leading to the balcony.

'First we have to find the right bird, then tempt
it out of its cage so it can sing.'

'So how do we find the bird?' Tidyman asked.

'Call it,' said Holliday.

In the end it turned out to be remarkably easy.
An initial telephone call to the Pontifical Institute

of Christian Archaeology on the Via Napoleone III and mentioning his own name, the name of Sodalitium Pianum and Walter Rauff all in the same sentence elicited a polite callback, which in turn led to a second call from the Second Section of the Vatican Secretary of State's office thanking Holliday for his interest and suggesting that in furtherance of his interests a visit to the Gregorian Egyptian Museum on the following day at noon might be in order. It wasn't stated in the conversation but the implication was clear: he should come alone if he had any expectations of 'furthering his interests.'

'Are you actually going alone?' Rafi asked.

'Of course not,' answered Holliday. 'I want you to tail me and Emil to tail you. They'll almost certainly have me under surveillance, but let's see just how deep it goes.'

Rafi went down to the souvenir stands on the other side of the Viale Vaticano and purchased floor plan guides of the Vatican Museums for all of them. The Gregorian Egyptian Museum was located one floor above the main entrance and was reached by climbing the famous spiral staircase used in the final murder montage in *The Godfather: Part III*. The three men would enter the museum at five-minute intervals and stay well apart at all times. It wasn't foolproof but it was the best they could do.

At eleven thirty the following morning Holliday left the hotel, crossed the street and went through the high arched entrance in the high stone wall. He purchased the required tickets for the museum, then climbed one flight up the broad winding stairway. Reaching the main floor, he turned to his left and went down a short hallway, following the signs to the rooms containing the Egyptian Museum. He found a bench across from a display case of funerary urns and sat down to wait.

A few minutes later a man in a dark suit sat down beside him. He was dark-haired and dark-eyed with cheek and chin grayed with five o'clock shadow. His English was flat and without accent. His shoes were black, highly polished, and looked very expensive. Why was it that he'd never seen a priest in cheap shoes?

'You're Colonel Holliday?'

He hadn't used his rank when he'd called on the telephone.

'You know I am.'

'What is it that you want?'

319

'You know exactly what I'm after,' answered Holliday.

A younger man walked in front of them, another priest, this one carrying an attaché case, which was a bit strange since any kind of backpack or parcel had to be left at the coat check downstairs on the admissions floor. As the younger man passed he shook his head briefly and continued on. The older man on the bench beside Holliday seemed to relax. He nodded his head toward the display of funerary jars in a glass display case across from where they sat.

'An odd people, don't you think, Colonel? Dividing up the body into its separate parts before burial.'

'Like the Nazis separating Jews into their separate parts to get the gold from their teeth,' said Holliday.

'A cumbersome analogy, but I presume you're referring to Colonel Rauff,' replied the man beside him on the bench.

'Standartenführer Rauff, you mean,' said Holliday. 'He wasn't regular army – he was S.S.'

'I suppose you would be able to make such distinctions,' murmured the other man.

'Just who are you?' Holliday asked.

'You can call me Thomas,' said the man.

'Doubting Thomas?' Holliday said.

'If you like,' answered the man, smiling lightly. 'Now, how can the Church be of help?'

'The church can give me back my cousin.'

'Your cousin?'

'Peggy Blackstock. The photographer who accompanied your expedition into Libya led by a man named Charles-Étienne Brasseur. They were supposed to be looking for the tomb of Imhotep. They were actually looking for a shipment of bullion flown out of Germany in 1944 on a captured American bomber named *Your Heart's Desire*.'

'Your information seems very detailed,' answered Father Thomas, still smiling blandly.

'The answers are always in the details,' said Holliday.

'As I understand it from the newspaper reports Father Brasseur and the rest of the expedition are being held hostage by a terrorist group known as the Brotherhood of Isis.'

'The Brotherhood is a crock and neither Peggy nor Brasseur is being held hostage by them. Two days ago they were seen getting into a helicopter on Santo Stefano Island about fifty miles south of here.'

'Seen by whom?' Father Thomas said.

'Me,' Holliday answered bluntly.

'Really?' Father Thomas said. 'You are a resourceful man, Colonel Holliday, to know such things.'

'You don't know the half of it,' said Holliday. 'Peggy and your man Brasseur were in the company of a thug named Massimo Conti. He works for a criminal organization known as La Santa. The same people who were apparently transporting the Rauff bullion out of Libya and into Marseille. Your hirelings, in fact, just like Pesek and Kay, the husband-and-wife team who took out Valador.

'It took us a while but my friends and I finally figured it out. Alhazred found the gold that the Vatican ratlines lost in 1944. He got in touch and you did a deal, but you betrayed him. The only trouble is Alhazred had already hidden the gold again. Now Alhazred's disappeared and so has the bullion.'

'A fanciful tale, Colonel.'

'But pretty close to the truth, I'll bet.'

Father Thomas let out a long-suffering sigh. 'So, you have a proposition?'

'Give us Peggy, we give you the gold. About three tons of it, by my calculations. That would finance a lot of your nasty little group's operations for a while.'

'And what nasty little group are you referring to?' Father Thomas asked mildly.

'You've had a lot of names over the years,' said Holliday. 'During the time of the Templars you were known as Organum Sanctum, the Instrument of God. During the twenties and thirties you were called Sodalitium Pianum, the Brotherhood of Pius. During the Cold War it was Propaganda Due. The Church has always needed plausible denial, like Nixon's Watergate plumbers. You're it, whatever you call yourself, the Vatican's version of an arm's-length CIA. Bullyboys answerable to no one. In the twelfth century Henry the Second said, "Who will rid me of this troublesome priest," and four guys just like you went out and murdered Thomas à Becket, the Archbishop of Canterbury. Ax men. Every big corporation needs them. You're up to your ears in it. Holy crap, as Peggy would say.'

'Why would an extraordinary organization

such as the one you suggest have any interest in kidnapping a news photographer like Miss Blackstock?' Father Thomas replied.

'Ask the bald guy who was on the helicopter, the one who almost beat my friend Rafi to death a year ago. Ask the dead guy in that back alley in Jerusalem, the one who tried to kill me and Peggy because of the Templar sword. You knew what the real secret of the Templars was even then: the secret was their continued existence, the secret contained in that little book Helder Rodrigues gave me as he lay dying. Ten thousand connections to a trillion dollars in assets. A great deal of power for anyone who could wield it. *That's* why you kidnapped Peggy when the opportunity fell right into your laps. Bait. You knew I'd come looking for her and you were right.' Holliday stood up. 'Well, here I am,' he said. 'Make your play.'

'Do you have proof of any of these peculiar allegations?' Father Thomas asked calmly, staring up at him.

'I don't need proof,' said Holliday. 'I've got the gold.'

Father Thomas stood. 'You're at the Alimandi Hotel?'

'Just across the street.'

'We'll be in touch shortly,' said Father Thomas. 'A pleasure to meet you, Colonel Holliday.' The priest turned on one expensive heel and walked away.

'Did they buy it?' Rafi asked when they met back at the hotel.

'Some of it,' said Holliday. 'I think they were worried that I was wired.'

'The man with the attaché case?' Tidyman asked.

'I think so,' Holliday said and nodded. 'Carrying a bug detector in the briefcase.'

'They're being careful,' said Rafi.

'They could stonewall till the cows came home,' said Holliday. 'That's what worries me. They know we've got more to lose than they do. They don't have to play along at all.'

'I'm not sure of that,' mused Tidyman, sipping a cup of excellent room service coffee. 'These people are greedy, just like others of their kind. Like Alhazred. Like the unfortunate Mr Valador of Marseille, the one smuggling the gold.'

'Which makes them very dangerous,' reminded Holliday. 'Our Czech assassins Pesek and Kay put a hatpin through Valador's brain, remember?

They tried to kill me and Peggy once – they'll try again, I guarantee it.'

'Certainly,' agreed Tidyman. 'Greed makes people dangerous. It also makes them vulnerable. And that is how we win this game, my friend; we play to their vulnerabilities.'

24

Father Thomas called the following morning to arrange another meeting.

'We were on your turf before,' said Holliday. 'How about somewhere else this time?'

'Where do you suggest?' Father Thomas asked. Holliday could hear the muffled sound of traffic in the background. Thomas was on a cell phone, probably sitting in a car.

'You could come here,' said Holliday.

'I think not, Colonel,' the priest replied with a laugh.

'You're welcome to bring along your techno-geek with the attaché case. We've got nothing to hide,' said Holliday.

'As the Beatles were so fond of saying, Colonel Holliday, everyone's got something to hide except me and my monkey.'

'All right then,' said Holliday. 'How about a restaurant? They've got a nice roof garden here.'

'Again too close for comfort,' said the priest.

'And too well known. Somewhere a little more discreet, perhaps.'

'There's a pizzeria around the corner,' suggested Holliday. 'On the Via Candia. It's called Piacere Molise, a little family place.'

'You know Rome, Colonel?' For the first time the priest seemed surprised.

'We ate dinner there last night,' explained Holliday. 'The concierge at the hotel suggested it.'

There was a moment's silence. Holliday could hear the up-and-down wail of a siren coming over the phone. He could also hear it coming through the open balcony doors. The priest was close by. They were being watched.

'All right,' said Father Thomas. 'When?'

'Early,' replied Holliday. 'It gets crowded quickly. Five okay?'

'Of course,' answered Father Thomas.

'How many do I make reservations for?'

'I shall be bringing a colleague,' said Father Thomas.

'The techno-geek?' Holliday smiled.

'Yes, but only briefly. The other man will be a principal in our discussions.'

'You mind if I bring a friend along?' Holliday said.

'The more the merrier,' answered the priest. There was a smile in his voice again. 'It's always wise to know one's enemies.'

Via Candia was a nondescript street of old apartment blocks with shops and restaurants carved out of their ground floors over the years. Piacere Molise was located in a salmon-colored building at number 60, across from a knockoff perfume store and a knockoff sportswear store. It was late summer, and by five o'clock, with the exception of the restaurants and coffee shops, most of the stores had drawn their gates and rolling shutters. The cars parked at the curb were uniformly small and relatively cheap; Via Candia appeared to cater to the middle class; the men and women on the streets were all dressed like secretaries and clerks. There didn't seem to be many children.

Once upon a time Piacere Molise had been the building concierge's apartment, located beside an old-fashioned porte-cochere that ran through to a courtyard in the back. Now it was three narrow rooms and a kitchen painted a friendly yellow with perhaps a dozen tables inside and four more on the sidewalk outside. The décor was made up of framed prints of famous impressionist painters scattered everywhere interspersed with decorative plates. The rooms were lit by a few modern chandeliers. The tablecloths were yellow and the place mats matched the rust and yellow marble checkerboard tiles on the floor. As the name suggested the restaurant was clearly informal, *piacere* – come as you are.

Not surprisingly Father Thomas was already there when Holliday and Rafi stepped into the little pizzeria. He was sitting at one of the double tables in the middle room along with two others. One was the bald man they'd spotted getting out of the helicopter on Santo Stefano; the other was the young priest with the attaché case they'd seen at the Egyptian Museum the day before.

'I don't know if I can sit at the same table with that bastard,' said Rafi softly.

'Baldy?' Holliday said. 'Imagine him in his underwear.'

'Imagine him dead,' grunted Rafi.

As they approached the table the young man with the attaché case stood up. He had a small wandlike device in his hand and a single-button headphone in his ear. He waved the wand in their direction, passing it up and down their bodies, concentrating on the sound from his earpiece.

After a few moments he shook his head, opened his attaché case and tossed the wand inside.

'*Qualcosa?*' Father Thomas demanded.

'*Nulla,*' said the young man, shaking his head again. '*Sono polito.*' They're clean.

'*Andar via,*' ordered Father Thomas, making a little brushing movement with his hands. The young man nodded and snapped the attaché case closed.

'*Come desideri, Padre.*'

The young man picked up his attaché case and left the restaurant. Holliday and Rafi sat down across from the priest and his companion.

Holliday got his first good look at the bald man from the helicopter. Big, muscular even in a plain dark suit. Big-knuckled hands like hammers. He wasn't bald at all; his head was shaved clean without a hint of stubble. The face was hard and Slavic, maybe Russian, the cheekbones high, the cheeks themselves slightly cavernous and the chin sharp. The eyes were a pale cornflower blue, the pupil on the right eye with a cast that made it look as though a black tear was staining the glittering iris. The man was staring at them like a butcher-bird deciding which spiky thorn it would impale them on. The stare of a true believer; the stare of a wild animal tugging at its leash. Holliday knew exactly why the priest had brought him to the meeting: he was a hound being given the scent of its prey.

Father Thomas smiled across the table at Holliday.

'I gather that Dr Wanounou and Father Damaso have already met,' said the priest.

The bald man looked at Rafi with an expressionless stare. Then his lips twitched, briefly revealing a double row of surprisingly white teeth. Rafi looked back.

'We were never formally introduced,' said Rafi.

'Father Damaso was very pleased to discover that you had come to Rome. He tells me the two of you have some unfinished business.'

'We're not here for a pissing contest,' said Holliday.

'I'm not entirely sure what we're here for,' said the priest.

A young waiter in a long apron appeared with a dish of olives and a basket of bread. He put them both down on the table, then brought a large pepper grinder out of one of the apron's deep pockets and a scratch pad from another. He put the pepper grinder on the table, then asked for their order in very broken English. The priest immediately questioned the waiter in Italian and the young man responded with a list of things that sounded as though they could be dinner entrées.

The priest turned back to Holliday.

'Molise is a very poor region of Italy but it is known for a dish that is a specialty here: *zuppa di pesce alla Termolese*, a sort of Italian bouillabaisse. They also carry a rather good vintage of a local white wine, Falanghina Del Molise 2005, very nice with the fish.'

'We didn't come here to eat,' said Holliday.

'An Italian never needs an excuse to eat,' answered the priest. 'There is no reason why we cannot share a meal.' His smile flashed moment-arily. 'On me, of course,' he said. Father Thomas turned away briefly and spoke to the waiter. The young man scribbled on his notepad, repeated the order back to the priest and then scurried away, heading towards the rear of the restaurant.

'Can we get down to business now?' Holliday asked, the irritation clear in his voice.

'I wasn't aware that we had any business,' said Father Thomas. He spent a few seconds preparing himself a little side plate of olive oil and balsamic vinegar from the little vinaigrette decanters on the table, then tore a piece of bread in half and wiped it through the mixture. He popped the chunk of bread into his mouth and followed it up with an olive.

'You have my cousin Peggy. We want her back.'

'Ah, yes,' the priest said and nodded. 'Dr Wanounou's paramour.' He smiled at Rafi, then dipped another piece of bread into the oil-and-vinegar mixture.

'We're offering the gold for her return,' said Holliday. 'You get Rauff's bullion in exchange.'

'How do I know you have the gold?' Father Thomas asked.

'I never said we had it. I said we knew where it was.'

'How do you know we haven't found it already?'

'It wasn't in the camp. If you'd managed to take Alhazred alive after your little raid he would have told you by now and you wouldn't be sitting here bargaining with us.'

'The Church has plenty of money, Colonel Holliday. Why should we need your so-called bullion?'

'Number one, I'm not so sure that the Church has as much money as you'd have us think; you're much the same as General Motors, Ford and Chrysler; you're trying to sell an inferior product and people just aren't buying anymore. Number two, even if the Church has money, I'm willing to bet your budget isn't what it once was. And number three, if any word of the Church's involvement with Rauff and that gold became public it would put the last nail in the coffin of your continued existence. You have to get that gold back before it starts leaking onto the open market. That's why you had Pesek and Kay kill Valador in Cannes; he was skimming. You need to get those bars re-smelted and erase any connection between Rauff and the Church. A German Pope who was in the Hitler Youth is bad enough; the Church in bed with the man who invented the modern gas chamber would be a disaster.'

'As you suggest, Colonel Holliday, gold is probably the easiest currency to launder. Yesterday's gold incisor is tomorrow's wedding band. But the question is irrelevant; Standartenführer Rauff made an agreement with us in 1944. Through our organization he received aid and documentation allowing for his escape from prosecution. In return he promised us his hoard of Tunisian gold. We kept our part of the bargain and even posthumously he will keep his. The gold is ours by right.'

'Release Peggy and you'll have it,' said Holliday.

There was a pause in the conversation as the waiter reappeared with the wine, followed by a man in a chef's high hat carrying two large flattish bowls piled high with clams, mussels and seafood in an aromatic broth. The waiter set down the wine, the man in the chef's hat put down the bowls and a few seconds later a plump, pleasant-looking woman in a flowered dress appeared carrying two more bowls of the *zuppa di pesce* and then withdrew with a beaming *Buon appetito!*

The priest lifted his fork, picked out a mussel on top of the pile in his bowl and surgically removed the meat from its dark shell. He savored the morsel, then washed it down with a little wine. Nobody else at the table had touched either food or drink. Father Thomas gave a little sigh and put down his glass.

'I think perhaps you should disabuse yourself of any thought that our meeting is in any way a negotiation, Colonel Holliday. You are out-gunned, outnumbered and outmaneuvered. You have nothing to bargain with. Should you decide not to tell me about the whereabouts of the gold I shall have Father Damaso here defile your cousin in ways you could not imagine in a thousand years. Should you continue to guard the secret of the bullion's whereabouts Father Damaso will execute Miss Blackstock, slowly and painfully. And he will enjoy himself doing it, Colonel.

'Father Damaso, I might add, has been trained by some of Augusto Pinochet of Chile's most experienced torturers, and they of course were trained by the man of the hour, Standartenführer Rauff. From what Father Damaso leads me to understand, Herr Rauff's methods would even have impressed the tribunals of the Spanish Inquisition.'

Father Thomas picked up another clam between his fingers, sucking the muscle wetly out of the shell and into his mouth. He chewed and swallowed.

'So there you have it, Colonel Holliday. Not a negotiation, an ultimatum.' The priest took a small square card and a Mont Blanc fountain pen from the inside pocket of his suit jacket. He unscrewed the cap of the pen and wrote briefly on the card, then handed the little square of cardboard across the table to Holliday. It was a phone number.

'Call me,' said Father Thomas. 'You have twenty-four hours to make up your mind.' He glanced meaningfully towards the bald man, who still had neither moved nor said a word. 'After that things will no longer be within my control.' The priest smiled pleasantly. 'Now eat up before your food gets cold.'

'I think I'm going to puke,' said Rafi. He pushed back his chair, the legs scraping noisily on the tile floor. He stood, glared down at the bald priest Damaso, who had begun to eat his *zuppe*. 'I'll kill you if you so much as touch her.'

Damaso looked up from his bowl, a little juice dripping down to his sharp chin. His lips barely moved when he spoke.

'You could try, Jew boy,' he said quietly.

Rafi stormed out of the restaurant.

'Your friend appears to have lost his appetite,' said Father Thomas. 'Perhaps your Egyptian colleague watching us from across the street would like to finish Dr Wanounou's meal; he must be hungry by now.' He pointed his fork towards

Rafi's place at the table and the steaming bowl of aromatic seafood soup. 'It would be a shame to see it go to waste.'

Holliday stood up.

'I'm not hungry, either,' he said.

'As you wish, Colonel Holliday, but you're missing a culinary treat.' He took a sip of wine. 'Twenty-four hours.'

Holliday followed Rafi out of Piacere Molise.

The priest watched him go, then turned his attention back to the food before him.

Half an hour later Rafi sat fuming in one of the armchairs in the sitting room of their suite at the Alimandi Hotel. On the other side of the small elegant room Holliday sat waiting by the telephone. Through the open doors leading out to the balcony came the buzzing sound of the waspish little Vespa scooters whizzing through the traffic on the Viale Vaticano.

'Did it work?' Rafi said.

'Hold your horses,' said Holliday. 'We'll know in a few minutes.'

'We should have heard by now. And why hasn't Tidyman called?'

'Relax,' said Holliday.

'How am I supposed to relax? That bastard

was talking about torturing Peggy,' said Rafi hotly. 'If this plan of yours doesn't work, we're screwed.'

The phone rang. Rafi jumped. Holliday picked up the receiver and listened.

'Thank you,' said Holliday. 'Send him up.' He hung up the phone and turned back to Rafi. 'He's here.'

'It's about time.'

Holliday rose and went to the door of the suite. A few moments later there was a knock. Holliday opened the door. It was the waiter from Piacere Molise, minus the long apron and carrying a paper bag in his hand. He was grinning broadly. Holliday led the young man into the room.

'You two haven't been introduced. Rafi, this is an old student of mine, Lieutenant Vince Caruso, class of '06. I gave him a C minus, if I remember correctly. He works for the military attaché here.' Caruso sat down on the couch and put the paper bag on the coffee table.

'Pleased to meet you,' said Rafi.

The young lieutenant opened up the bag and took out the tall pepper grinder he'd left on their table in the restaurant. He unscrewed the bottom of the grinder and eased out a flat FM microphone with a dangling wire. He reached into the bag and put something that looked like a small cassette player on the table alongside the little microphone.

'My boss would have a fit if he knew I'd borrowed his stuff,' said Caruso.

'How'd we do?' Holliday said.

'They kept talking for half an hour after you guys left,' said Caruso happily. 'All sorts of good stuff. Kind of thing that the media eats up. These are serious bad guys.' The young man shook his head. 'Talk about wolves in sheep's clothing.'

'The most dangerous kind,' said Rafi.

'Any trouble with the owners of the restaurant?' Holliday asked.

'Are you kidding?' Caruso laughed. 'He calls those people *corvos nero*, black crows. He was only too happy to help his amici Americano.'

'Then we've got them,' said Holliday, clapping his hands together with satisfaction.

'But we still don't have Peggy,' said Rafi.

The phone rang on the other side of the room. Holliday got up and answered it. He listened for a few moments, then hung up.

'That was Emil,' said Holliday, grinning from ear to ear, his eyes sparkling happily. 'The GPS tracker you gave us worked perfectly, Vince. We nailed it.'

'Where is she?' Rafi said.

'A place called Lido del Faro – Lighthouse Beach, less than twenty miles from here at the mouth of the River Tiber. They've got her stashed in some kind of old fishing shack there.'

25

'I'm surprised that it worked at all,' confessed Holliday, sitting in the roof garden of the Hotel Alimandi and eating breakfast. It was only nine thirty but the day was already hot, the summer sun shining down from a cloudless sky. Across the Viale Vaticano Holliday could see the top of the Sistine Chapel and the ranks of tiled rooftops within the Holy City.

'I'm not,' said Emil Tidyman, eating a very Western meal of sausages and scrambled eggs. 'Perhaps you have to live in a religious place like Egypt to understand it. A place that has bred fundamentalist thought for a thousand years.'

'I was born and raised in Israel,' snorted Rafi. 'What would you call that?'

'Israel is a democracy; church and state are separate. In Egypt the ulamas, the religious leaders, still control the heart and soul of the nation. The only thing the average Jew does not do is eat these,' said Tidyman, waving a chunk of sausage on the end of his fork. 'I'm talking about how these people *think*.'

He ate the sausage, then reached out and poured himself another cup of coffee from the shiny silver pot in the middle of the starched linen tablecloth. He nodded towards the Vatican rooftops. 'Jews have turned independent thought into a virtue. To Catholics and Muslims it is virtually a sin. Catholic fundamentalists and Muslim fundamentalists are very much alike in that they share a common fundamental belief: there is no individual, there is only Faith with a capital *F*. Everything is the will of God or the will of Allah and that's all there is to it. The ordinary man is powerless. Free will is for the Gods alone, interpreted by various popes and mullahs. It is their strength as well as their fatal flaw.'

'History is full of that,' agreed Holliday. 'They took interpreting prophecy very seriously in the old days. The Macedonian kings had less power than the Oracle at Delphi. Troy fell because Cassandra's prophecy went unheeded. Caesar died because he failed to heed his soothsayers about the Ides of March.'

'I still don't see what all of this has to do with our killer priests,' said Rafi.

'I was just getting to that,' said Tidyman seriously, putting a generous layer of honey on a thick slice of toast. 'According to their dogma, Man cannot change history – history can only change Man. They have the absolute arrogance of infallibility; they are the Church, after all; how could a few outsiders presume to overpower them? It never occurred to Father Thomas or whatever he calls himself that we would act offensively against him.' The Egyptian shrugged. 'As I said before – we must take advantage of their vulnerabilities.' He bit off a piece of toast and smiled.

'Then again,' said Rafi sourly, 'for all your philosophy, maybe we just got lucky.'

'That, too,' said Tidyman, washing his toast down with a mouthful of coffee.

'According to their schedule,' said Holliday, 'we've got about twelve hours left.'

'Then you should make the call,' responded Tidyman. 'I'll go down to the desk and get the package your friend from the embassy left for us earlier.'

Back in their suite Holliday called the telephone number written on the card the priest had given him. It was answered promptly on the first ring.

'Colonel,' said Father Thomas. 'You've come to a decision?'

'I've changed the rules,' answered Holliday.

'Really,' said the priest. He didn't sound impressed.

'Listen.'

Holliday held the speaker of the digital recorder Vince Caruso had used the night before. He pressed the On switch.

'Yesterday's gold incisor is tomorrow's wedding band,' said Father Thomas on the recorder. Holliday switched off the little machine.

'Remember that?' Holliday said.

There was a long silence. Finally the priest spoke. His voice was strained.

'I told you that you were resourceful, Colonel Holliday, but clearly I didn't know just how resourceful you really were. Someone else was obviously involved.' He paused and thought for a moment. 'The waiter?'

'You told me I had nothing to bargain with,' answered Holliday, ignoring the priest's question. 'Now I do.'

'We could simply deny it,' said Father Thomas. 'A fake, a fabrication created by our enemies. No one would believe you.'

'Not everyone, but a few would believe it. There'd be an investigation. It's like Watergate, Father Thomas. It's not the crime that gets you – it's the cover-up.'

There was another long silence.

'What are you suggesting?' Father Thomas said finally.

'Just what I offered last night, except now you get a bonus. The gold *and* the tape. A twofer.'

'How will I know you didn't make copies?' queried the priest.

'You don't,' said Holliday. 'But I'm not a fool. I'll keep my side of the bargain. We're well aware of your organization's long arm.'

'You'd do well to remember it,' warned Father Thomas.

'A trade and a truce,' offered Holliday.

'That would require an exchange.'

'I'll call you,' said Holliday. He hung up the phone.

'Will he actually do it?' Rafi asked.

'Not in a million years,' said Holliday.

Tidyman reappeared a few minutes later carrying a heavy-looking rectangular box wrapped in brown paper. He sat down on the couch, took a penknife from his pocket and opened the box with a few deft slices through the paper. Inside the plain covering was a medium-sized blue Tupperware container, and inside the plastic box, packed in foam peanuts, were three automatic pistols, three boxes of ammunition in plastic strip-clips, a GPS unit and five black Nokia cell phones.

'Will the lieutenant get in trouble if any of this surfaces?' Tidyman asked.

'We're supposed to toss the weapons and the phones when we're done – they're clean, untraceable. The GPS unit he wants back if possible,' replied Holliday.

'The boat?' Tidyman asked.

'Leaves the dock at the Marconi Bridge at noon,' said Holliday. 'It gets to Ostia Antica at one thirty.' He glanced at his watch. 'We've got an hour and a half to set up.' He looked across to Tidyman. 'You know what to do?'

'There is a big potted plant by the doorway next to the pizzeria with the green awning at Santamaura Street and Via Candia,' recited the Egyptian. 'I plant the phone there, call you when I'm done and then get to the bridge in time to catch the boat.'

'Rafi?'

'When you call me I get to the Castro Pretorio stop on the Metro and then I call the priest. I make sure he hears the announcer on the PA system give the name of the stop.'

'Then what?' quizzed Holliday.

'I get on the subway and go in the opposite direction to the Marconi stop. Then I get myself to the bridge and the boat.' The Israeli paused. 'If any of us are being followed we'll know by then. We hope.'

'Good,' said Holliday. He could almost feel the blood rushing through his veins. 'That's it. Are we ready?'

'Ready,' said Tidyman.

'Ready,' said Rafi.

Holliday smiled to himself, a little surprised at the depth of his emotions.

He hadn't felt this alive in years. This was who he *was*.

'Let's saddle up then,' he said.

'Not "lock and load"?' Rafi grinned.

'Different generation,' said Holliday. 'I'm from the John Wayne era, but yeah, that too.'

For Holliday it was a simple exercise in applied tactics: when faced with a superior numerical force the primary objective was to distract the enemy and split his forces; divide and conquer. The Normandy invasion was a classic example: make Rommel's forces believe that the invasion was coming at Pas de Calais, the obvious choice, then attack somewhere else, in that case the beaches at Normandy.

For Rafi and Tidyman it was a bit too obvious, like a high school football play: fake left, go right. Distract the priest and his thugs and send them on a wild-goose chase to the north on the subway line, but attack them with a much smaller force to the south, into the heart of enemy territory.

Using a map of Rome and Vince Caruso's familiarity with the city, they concocted a Robert Ludlum-Jason Bourne, cat-and-mouse, hither-and-yon, hares-and-hounds game across the city that would supposedly lead the priest and his men to where the exchange of Peggy for the location of the bullion would take place. In fact, it would all be a figment of their collective imaginations, the moves and countermoves orchestrated with generic, throwaway cell phones and overseen by Lieutenant Caruso driving his Italian girlfriend's Dragon Red Vespa GTS-250 scooter. With the paper chase concentrating Father Thomas and his colleagues, Holliday, Rafi and Tidyman would meet at the Marconi Bridge on the downstream River Tiber, then board a river sightseeing cruiser down to the old ruins at Ostia Antica, Rome's original port, now two miles inland after the deposit of three thousand years' worth of accumulated river silt.

If things went according to plan they would discover a speedboat left for them by Vince Caruso at the marina where the sightseeing boat docked, which they would then use to reach the fishing shack where Peggy was being held hostage.

Like most rescue plans it looked perfect on paper, and like most rescue plans, as Holliday well knew, it would be anything but perfect in its execution. Still, it wasn't bad for something put together in a hurry. In every theater of war Holliday had fought in, he'd seen much worse plans generated by entire committees of so-called experts, and over the years he'd developed a basic rule of thumb: in war, just like cooking, too many cooks just screwed things up. In his own mind it was all pretty straightforward. Find Peggy, kill anybody who got in their way, grab her and get the hell out of town as quickly as possible.

The Ponte Guglielmo Marconi crossed the Tiber River south of Rome in a surprisingly rural area, especially on the southern side. The dock for the sightseeing boats was located a little downstream of the wide modern bridge on the bank of the river, squeezed in between a junior league rugby field and some fenced-off public tennis courts. The only way to get to it was down a dirt road that seemed to peter off the farther along you went. If it hadn't been for Lieutenant Caruso's detailed directions none of them would have ever found it. On the other hand, it was the perfect spot for a rendezvous; if anyone was following you they could be spotted a mile off. The boat was a small converted passenger ferry named, not surprisingly, the M.V. *Horatio*. She had three wedding-cake decks outfitted with restaurant-style booths set beside large tinted picture windows.

Holliday arrived first and waited on the dock, receiving updates from Caruso on his cell phone every few minutes. As far as the young lieutenant could see everything was going according to plan. Father Thomas had successfully retrieved the cell phone left for him in the potted shrub by Tidyman and had begun his wild-goose chase.

According to Caruso there was no sign of the bald Father Damaso.

At eleven forty Emil Tidyman arrived, improbably dressed as a tourist in a Hawaiian shirt, a straw hat and big sunglasses with both binoculars and a camera hung around his neck. Ten minutes later Rafi appeared on the dock. As far as Holliday could tell neither man had been followed. He waited until they were about to pull in the gangplank before he boarded the broad-beamed, top-heavy ferry, and shortly afterward the M.V. *Horatio* eased out into the turbid green water and began making its ponderous way downstream.

They made their way along the sinuous snaking river for an hour. It wasn't very exciting as sightseeing trips went; the great buildings and monuments of Rome had been built farther upstream, centered on the city's seven hills. For the most part all there was to see was the pastoral weed-choked banks of the river and the spans of various modern bridges. The advantage to Holliday and his companions was that taking the sightseeing boat made pursuit unlikely, if not impossible.

The *Horatio* eventually turned in towards shore and docked at a comfortably ramshackle pier at Ostia Antica. The ruins, an entire city of them, were spread out over hundreds of acres. The buildings, no more than crumbling walls and tiled floors, were silent testament to the ancient port city's violent end.

In A.D. 67 bands of roving pirates had descended on the city in ragtag fleets, burning everything as they went, eventually leading to the enactment of the Lex Gabinia, the law of Gabianus, its creator, giving the emperor of Rome far-reaching and completely arbitrary powers that were reminiscent of the panicked regulations enacted after 9/11.

Power corrupts, Holliday reminded himself as he stepped off the boat, and absolute power corrupts absolutely; Father Thomas and his minions were proof enough of that. The pastoral teachings of a wandering prophet had been perverted into a tool of war.

Instead of following the rest of the passengers up the path towards the ruins, Holliday, Rafi and Tidyman turned right, taking a barely visible dirt track that ran beneath the old trees along the riverbank.

'This is like something out of a really bad Disney movie,' said Tidyman. '*Tales of the Riverbank* or something. You expect Bambi to come out of the trees or bluebirds singing a merry tune and dropping daisies on our heads.'

'What do you know about Disney movies?' Holliday asked.

'I used to run home from school every day just to watch Annette Funicello's breasts grow on the Mickey Mouse Club,' said Tidyman. 'Zorro. Davy Crocket.'

'Thumper,' added Holliday. 'Bambi.'

'Just remember what happened to Bambi's mother,' cautioned Tidyman, laughing.

'You've got a very strange sense of humor for an Egyptian,' said Holliday.

'What are you old men mumbling about now?' said Rafi, bringing up the rear of the little procession filing through the trees.

'I think it is called whistling in the dark,' said Tidyman. 'Smiling in the face of adversity.'

A hundred feet farther along the low bank they came upon an old man fishing with a long pole, just as Vince Caruso had described. The man had white hair as fine as a baby's over a spotted skull, white stubble on his chin. Probably one of the army of relatives that Caruso seemed to have just about everywhere. There was a plastic bucket of squirming silver-bellied eels beside the man.

'*Qual è il tranello?*' Holliday asked, carefully repeating the phrase just the way Caruso had told him. 'What's the catch?'

'*Oggi c'è la pesca del salmone,*' the old man answered with a gap-toothed grin. 'Salmon is the catch of the day.' It was the correct response.

'*La barca?*' Holliday asked. 'The boat?'

'*Li,*' said the man, pointing with his sandpaper chin.

They found it a little farther along the bank, half hidden by artfully concealing shrubbery and weeds. It was a sixteen-foot classic drift boat with a high pointed bow and a narrow transom fitted with an oddly shaped outboard motor.

The boat was filthy, with a pile of rancid-looking throw net in the bow and half a dozen long bamboo poles hanging off the sides. The seats were covered in fish scales and the paint on the sides was peeling. There was a pair of scruffily painted oars shipped along the gunwales and a variety of tackle boxes, boat hooks, gaffs and other equipment littering the flat bottom. The boat smelled of dead, rotting fish left too long in the sun.

'Is this somebody's idea of a joke?' Rafi asked, staring at the boat tied up to an overhanging willow branch. 'Because I don't think it's very funny.'

'It's not a joke,' said Holliday. 'It's protective coloration. My course in the history of camouflage was the only thing Vince ever got an A in.' He grinned broadly. 'I always knew the kid would go far even though he got such lousy marks.' Holliday shook his head. 'It's perfect – what do you do on a river? You fish. That's an electric outboard, a trolling motor, which means it'll be silent. Look at the current out there: the tide is going out; we'll be sucked down the river like a freight train.' As if to prove his point a waterlogged tree limb went swirling by in the rushing center of the river.

'How far?' Tidyman asked.

'According to Vince, two miles,' answered Holliday. He undid the line from the willow branch. 'Climb aboard, gents, this is the endgame. Let's go get Peggy.'

26

'How will we know the place?' Rafi asked, sitting in the bow of the drift boat as they slid rapidly down the ever-widening river.

Tidyman answered the question.

'It's called a *chiesetta*, a chapel. They're like little fishing cottages on stilts. There's dozens of them built on the breakwaters at the mouth of the river. They've got these purse seine nets they hang into the water at the end of huge pole cranes. The *chie-setta* we want is the last one nearest the open sea on the left bank. It's bright red with a brand-new sheet-aluminum roof.'

As the river broadened the color changed, going from a silty brownish green to a deeper blue as they neared the sea. The terrain on both sides of the river was mostly reclaimed marsh, the land divided into neat fields of grain. The banks of the river were lined with long rows of sailboats and small sport cruisers moored against short-piered docks. There were fishermen in boats like theirs everywhere, mostly following the gentler currents closer to shore. No one paid the three men the slightest bit of attention.

The Tyrrhenian Sea was visible now, a darker shimmering blue against the cloudless sky directly ahead. The banks of the river were lined with huge tumbled rocks used as breakwaters to prevent erosion, the ramshackle *chiesetta* fishing shacks standing like shabby long-legged insects poised above the boulders. They all looked much the same, standing closely together, each one with a rickety decklike balcony fitted with one, two and occasionally three of the fifty-foot-long cranes dangling over the water, cantilevered, braced with long guy wires connected to the roofs of the shacks. Now, with the tide rushing out, the cranes and their nets had been hauled up. As the tide reversed itself and the water flowed upriver once again the poles and nets would be lowered into the water.

'What do they catch?' Rafi asked.

'According to Vince, mostly mullet and eel, like the old man back there.'

'Gross,' said Rafi, making a face. 'Who eats eels?'

'Eel pie,' murmured Tidyman wistfully. 'What a treat. Jellied they are very good, too.'

Seated in the narrow stern, Holliday started up the little outboard and silently eased the boat out of the main current and to the northern bank of the river, now more than a hundred yards wide.

'Drop the anchor,' said Holliday.

Tidyman hauled the pile of netting to one side and uncovered the heavy little Danforth anchor. He eased it overboard, letting out the nylon line slowly and steadily until the anchor flukes bit and held in the silt. The boat swung around to face the current and they were at the mouth of the river, the sea behind them. A thousand feet away across the river was the red *chiesetta*, its shiny roof flashing in the sun, a red spider with twin pole cranes swung inboard like long antennae.

Tidyman took the binoculars from around his neck and passed them up to Rafi, who handed them on to Holliday.

'Look busy,' said Holliday. 'I'm going to check the place out.'

'Aye, aye, Captain,' said Tidyman. He and Rafi pulled long bamboo poles out of the bottom of the boat and they both dropped their hooked and unbaited lines over the side.

Holliday raised the binoculars.

The fishing shack was about twenty by thirty, the narrower end facing the river. There was a wide opening in the front leading out to the balcony deck where the swinging pole cranes were set up. The flat corrugated aluminum roof sloped front to back. The only proper entrance appeared to be from the rear of the shack via a walkway that crossed the boulders to the unpaved street behind. Half hidden by the building Holliday could see part of what appeared to be a compact closed-sided white van parked at the end of the dirt road. The opening facing the sea was lost in shadow. No one appeared to be watching.

He shifted the glasses to look beneath the building. There seemed to be a homemade ladder that dropped down from the floor of the shack to the boulders below, probably used when the net was snagged or there was some other problem that needed attention. He shifted the glasses again. The nearest neighbor was fifty feet away. On the other side of the shack was the stone breakwater and then the open sea.

'We either go in through the trapdoor in the

floor or from the back,' said Holliday. 'I don't see much in the way of options here.'

'Why not both?' Rafi asked, trying to keep his attention away from the shack where Peggy was being held. 'Why not split up and come in both ways?'

'Too dangerous,' said Holliday. 'That kind of two-pronged attack almost never works. You wind up shooting each other. Go in that way and it's going to be difficult to tell who is who.'

'All of this is dangerous,' argued Rafi.

'I'm afraid I agree with our young friend,' said Tidyman. 'Whatever we do will be dangerous. If we come over the walkway we will lose the element of surprise. If we climb to the trapdoor there will be a bottleneck.'

'We have to do *something*,' said Rafi. 'We can't stay out here much longer.'

Holliday thought for a moment, then looked back over his shoulder.

'There was a little marina back there,' he said. 'Did anyone notice if it had a gas pump?'

Holliday crouched in the shadows under the fishing shack next to their objective. An onshore breeze thrust in from the sea, making the big pole cranes above him creak and moan. Water lapped against the boulders all around him and the air was full of the rich scent of the sea.

The drift boat had moved on silently and disappeared beyond the end of the breakwater. Holliday checked his watch, frowning. The whole thing was going to depend on perfect timing. If he or Tidyman and Rafi screwed it up, Peggy was as good as dead. Both of the other two had done compulsory military service, Tidyman mostly to get more hours as a military pilot and cement his Egyptian citizenship status, Rafi because that was simply what you did if you were a Sabra – a native-born Israeli. Holliday on the other hand was a professional; he'd react on instinct born of years of experience in hot zones all over the world. He wasn't too sure about his companions.

There was Peggy to consider as well. If she froze up at a critical moment they *all* would be as good as dead. Hopefully she'd figure out what was happening and put her head down and get herself out of the line of fire in the first few seconds of the action. Holliday closed his eyes for a second and sent up a silent prayer to all the gods of war. Worst of all, they were going in blind;

they had no idea how many men were guarding Peggy in the fishing shack a few yards away.

He looked at his watch again, then leaned down and picked up the five-gallon gas tank of outboard fuel mix he'd bought at the little upstream marina. It was time to go. He listened, his senses at full alert, nerves tingling. He swallowed, feeling his mouth go dry and his heart begin to pound.

The feeling was a familiar one: part fear, part anticipation and part rising bloodlust. It always surprised him that he felt so comfortable with the desperate feeling deep in his gut, and every now and again he wondered if there was a pathological need for it with soldiers – junkies for battle and the dangerous game of jousting with death. He'd known a few like that in his time, soldiers who re-upped again and again because they simply couldn't deal with the sudden withdrawal into the passive routine of life out of the kill zone.

Holliday forced all conscious thought out of his mind, tuning his senses to the world around him, willing every part of himself to fuse his actions into a slow-motion psychedelic dreamscape where everything he did was perfectly synchronized with everything else.

He heard the muffled sound of a man and woman arguing in the fish shack directly overhead, heard the squeak of a cable shifting in the breeze, saw the riffled feathers of a kite as the giant bird soared above the estuary water, heard the chatter of a motorboat far away and the constant pulsing whisper of the sea.

There were no windows on the side wall of the shack, only a rudimentary ventilation grille. If the workers in the shack fished through two turns of the tide per day it probably meant the catch was stored somehow, most likely in galvanized steel tanks. On a hot day like today the tin-roofed huts would be turned into ovens. The stink would be awful.

Carrying the gas can Holliday stepped out of the shadows and made his way between the two *chiesettas*, moving quickly but carefully beneath the stilts of the last shack in the row. Looking out across the breadth of the river mouth he could see the squat shape of the gray-and-white-striped octagonal lighthouse that gave the rocky beach its name.

The red-walled *chiesetta* was supported on a

total of six stilts, three long, three short. The stilts were made of four-by-fours clewed together to make foot-square columns to support the weight of the floor above. Looking upward Holliday could see that the floor itself was nothing more than sheets of plywood laid over widely spaced fir rafters that were really only two-inch planks turned on end. Flimsy didn't begin to describe it.

He unscrewed the top of the gas can, reversed the spout and screwed it down again. He divided the contents between all three front columns, then set the empty can down beside the center post. He checked the time. Two minutes.

Holliday took out a package of matches and lit the posts one after the other without pause, leapfrogging across the boulders. He watched as the flames took hold, barely visible, little more than rippling heat vapors in the clear air. He turned away, scrambling up the rocks, then started to climb the makeshift ladder up to the trapdoor in the floor.

He reached the top of the ladder a few moments later and suddenly, blindingly, had a terrifying thought. He cursed himself for a fool. What if the trapdoor was bolted from above? It was the kind of stupid oversight that got men killed. He turned on the ladder. The flames had reached the tops of the columns and were starting to lick across the underside of the floor. Any second now. There was a quick, sharp detonation as the vapors in the empty gas can exploded. There was a second or two of almost deafening silence, then the sound of running feet overhead. Black smoke began to billow. A cry went up.

'*Cazzo merda! Fuoco! Fuoco!*'

One last time check. Thirty seconds. It didn't matter; the flames were rolling his way in long consuming tongues; if he didn't move now he was going to fry. He pulled the Tanfoglio 9mm out of his belt. The Italian weapons Vince Caruso had provided were commercial grade, mostly used for target practice and self-defense. Simple to use with sixteen in the magazine. A total of forty-eight rounds between them. Any second now and there was going to be a hailstorm of bullets upstairs. Holliday winced, thinking about it, then forcing himself not to. Like sticking your head into a hornet's nest. He took a deep breath, then pushed up on the trapdoor.

To Holliday it was like a series of snapshots taken at a billiard table, stuttering stroboscopic images connected like the cars on a freight train. It went far better than they had any right to expect.

There were five men in the shack and the call of *Fire!* had split them almost evenly, two men running towards the balcony and into the choking cloud of smoke and two men turning towards the sound of the crashing door as Rafi and Tidyman burst in through the rear, rolling left and right as Holliday had instructed. The fifth man, the bald Father Damaso, stayed exactly where he was, seated in a comfortable stuffed chair with a clear field of view towards their hostage, who was chained to an iron U bolt in the corner of the room.

The shack was divided into two areas separated by a flimsy plywood wall, the tank room in the forward area and the living and cooking area in the back. The trapdoor was set into the floor between the two and opened looking forward. Coming through the floor Holliday was facing back towards the river. Partway into the room he leveled the automatic and squeezed off half the clip without aiming, simply swinging the muzzle from right to left in a rapid arc. He hit both men, one in the face, the other in the chest. They both fell without a sound, thrown back into the smoke and flames.

Holliday pushed himself up and out of the opening in the floor, turning away from the fire, then rolled to his left, bringing his weapon to bear but not firing. Rafi was already up on his knees, his body between the guards and Peggy, who had flung herself down on the mattress she had been given by her captors. He had his pistol in one hand and the steel-pointed fish gaff he'd used to pry open the door in the other. Tidyman was directly opposite him on the other side of the room, creating the angled cross fire Holliday had suggested to them.

Both men fired a steady stream of fire into the two guards, both armed with some kind of compact machine pistols they were still struggling to remove from their sling holsters as Rafi and Tidyman began to fire.

Rafi, his clip empty, lunged towards Father Damaso with the fish gaff. The bald priest was unarmed except for what appeared to be a cricket bat balanced across his knees. He brought the bat up defensively as Rafi lunged, screaming obscenities. Damaso swiped at Rafi one-handed, clubbing the younger man aside as he rose out of the chair. Grasping the long flat instrument in both hands, the priest was about to bring it down like an ax on the back of Rafi's skull when Holliday shot him, putting half a dozen rounds into his chest, shredding flesh and bone and sending the dead man tumbling back over the stuffed chair.

The front half of the shack was an inferno and it was getting closer with each passing second. The first two men had been completely consumed and the flames would reach the rear half of the shack in an instant. Holliday rushed forward, retrieving the steel fish gaff, heading for Peggy, who was now curled up on the mattress, arms crossed above her head.

As Rafi groaned and pushed himself to his hands and knees, Holliday got the gaff through the U bolt shackling Peggy to the floor and started to pry it up. He got a good look at his cousin. Her face was streaked with grime and her short dark hair was matted, but under the circumstances she looked better than he'd expected.

'Peg?'

'Doc?' Her voice was parched and cracked.

He pushed the hair gently off her face.

'It's okay, I'm here now, kiddo.'

Peggy laughed weakly. 'What the hell took you guys so long?'

'Love you too, Peggy-o,' Holliday said and grinned. She smiled up at him wearily. Suddenly she looked terribly fragile. Then Rafi took her in his arms and the tears began to flow. A few seconds later Holliday managed to get the U bolt out of the floor and she was free. Tidyman appeared out of the smoke and haze. He had a ring of keys in one hand and his pistol in the other. Suddenly there was a sound like a gunshot going off and the front of the *chiesetta* lurched and sagged. The flames roared towards them.

'Our chariot awaits,' said Tidyman. 'Better hurry up unless you want to be part of the fish fry.'

They followed the Egyptian out of the burning shack and into the sunlight. There were no sirens yet, and except for the roar of the climbing flames at their back and the cloud of greasy smoke rising into the salt air everything seemed normal. Rafi brought up the rear, supporting a still wobbly Peggy, his arm around her shoulders.

She staggered a little as she walked, leaning

into Rafi's side, her head bent to his shoulder. Tidyman unlocked the doors of the old Fiat Ducato van and they climbed in, Rafi and Peggy in the back, Tidyman and Holliday up front. The interior of the van was baking hot, the air close and suffocating. As Tidyman started the engine they heard the first warbling of the fire trucks in the distance ahead of them.

'Bug-out time,' said Holliday. Behind them the flames burst through the roof of the shack and boiled into the air. Holliday leaned back in his seat, feeling the adrenaline and the sudden sag of fatigue in a single instant. 'They start finding bodies with bullets in that barbecue behind us and we'll be in trouble.'

He glanced out the window on Tidyman's side of the van and saw people coming out of their shacks to gawk at the rising flames. Some busybody would take down the license plate number and there'd be an all-points alert on the airwaves in minutes.

Holliday's cell phone vibrated in his pocket. He dug it out. Tidyman put the van in gear and swung the steering wheel around. They headed up the dusty road, gravel crunching under the wheels. The approaching sirens were getting louder.

'Text message from Caruso,' said Holliday.

'What does it say?' Tidyman asked.

Holliday frowned, not understanding. He read out the message.

'Termini Station. Seven forty-five sharp. Dress formal. RSVP.'

27

'You've got to be kidding me,' said Holliday to Vince Caruso, standing on the platform for Track 11 at the central Rome train station. Beside the two men, Rafi, Peggy and Emil Tidyman waited, staring at the long line of old-fashioned railway cars on the track beside them. Each of the gleaming, freshly washed coaches was painted a deep rich blue and bore an ornate crest with the letters *V.S.O.E.* entwined and picked out in gold. Just below the curved, cream-colored roof of each coach, also in gold, was a banner that read *Compagnie Internationale des Wagons-Lits*.

'Last night you asked me for an exit strategy, Colonel, sir; this is it,' said the young man proudly. 'Gets you out of Rome in style.'

'But Vince,' said Holliday, 'the Orient Express? Come on!'

'Beg your pardon, Colonel, but it makes pretty good sense from a tactical point of view. Actually, it makes a lotta sense. According to my sources half the cops in Rome are looking for you. Apparently you were involved in the suspicious homicides of a priest who worked for the Vatican and a bunch of mobbed-up La Santa types from Naples. Am I right, Colonel? That a fair assessment?'

A brake valve hissed loudly and there was an incomprehensible announcement on the PA system. A piercing whistle blew.

'Close enough,' said Holliday.

'Which means they'll have the airports sewn up, and knowing the cops they'll have roadblocks everywhere. There's more surveillance cameras in Rome than there are in New York. They've been dealing with domestic terrorists for a lot longer than we have, right?'

'Right,' said Holliday.

'There you go,' said Caruso. 'So who's going to expect you to bug out of town (a) on a train, and (b) on a train full of rich people and bigwigs? It's like trying to escape from Sing Sing on the *Queen Mary*.' The young lieutenant frowned. 'Much as I'd like to, sir, there's no way I could stash you at the embassy, either. You and your friends here are red-hot right now.'

'I appreciate everything that you've done,

Vince. Believe me, we couldn't have pulled this off without you,' said Holliday.

Peggy, still looking a little the worse for wear, stepped forward. Caruso was easily six feet three in his bare feet and Peggy had to stand on tiptoe to kiss him gently on the cheek.

'Me too, Lieutenant,' she said quietly. 'You saved my life.'

Caruso blushed like a schoolboy out on his first date. Peggy stepped back and took Rafi's hand. Tidyman, still a little dumbfounded, stared up at the exotic livery of the train car beside him.

On a track farther over a much more modern train pulled out of the station, the deep hum of the electric locomotive echoing loudly as it gathered speed. Through the open roof the newly risen moon shone down.

'What about documents?' Holliday asked.

Caruso pulled himself together, blinking.

'Uh, right here, Colonel.' He took a thick envelope out of his pocket and handed it over. 'Passports for all of you, well used, new names. Some credit cards, some cash. When you get to Paris, go to the embassy and we'll take it from there.'

'We're going to Paris?' Peggy asked dreamily.

She yawned and leaned sleepily against Rafi. He didn't seem to mind at all.

'You're booked on the train all the way, Venice, Vienna, and then west to Paris. I've arranged for a shepherd to meet you in Bologna at around midnight. His name is Paul Czinner – he knows all about you.'

'How do we know him?' Holliday asked.

'He dresses like a slob and he'll be wearing a ring from the Point,' said Caruso. 'He's one of us.'

'Good enough for me.' Holliday nodded.

A railway security officer in blue slacks and a blazer weaved through the pedestrian traffic on a humming Segway transporter, looking distinctly out of place beside the elegant old train. Holliday looked away, his heart rising into his throat. The railway cop cruised by, heading down the platform, and Holliday relaxed.

'Weapons gone?' Caruso asked softly.

Holliday nodded. 'Into the Tiber.'

The platform around them was crowded now; last-minute buzzing swarms of well-dressed people speaking half a dozen languages were milling around, followed by attendants in blue uniforms hauling overloaded luggage dollies piled high with designer suitcases.

'I don't think we're dressed for this,' said Holliday, looking around at the obviously upscale passengers.

'All taken care of,' said Caruso. 'Suitcase for each of you already in your compartments.' He paused and pulled a second folder out of his pocket, this one secured with a rubber band. 'Tickets.' Holliday took them.

'How'd you know my size?' Peggy asked.

'Uh, the colonel described you, ma'am,' said Caruso, blushing furiously again. 'I used to work summers at my uncle Ziggy's place in the garment district. He ran a fashion knockoff shop and sold stuff on Canal Street. I used to hang out with the models. You sounded like a size six to me.'

'You're a sweetheart,' she said, smiling. Caruso reddened yet again. He looked at his watch. 'Time to get aboard, sir.'

Caruso led them up into the train. There was a bit of a crush in the narrow corridor, but they eventually reached a doorway midway down the car. The door was made of some sort of burled exotic wood veneer. The fittings were brass. The carpeting in the corridor was a dark paisley pattern, the corridor lights above them soft and muted. Everything looked expensive. The effect was like stepping into an old photograph. Next thing you knew a Russian princess would appear, draped in jewels and smoking a cigarette in a long ivory holder.

Caruso opened the sliding door and stepped aside. There was a drawing room with a long couchette, a folding screen drawn back to reveal two bunk beds in the next room, more wood veneer, more brass trim, more paisley carpet and matching upholstery.

There were four small black nylon suitcases stored under the couch and on a brass-trimmed overhead rack. Holliday could see a black dress and several suits on hangers stored in a narrow little cupboard next to the door. Neat, compact and elegant.

'It's a double stateroom, a suite they call it,' the young lieutenant said nervously, his eyes on Peggy. 'Ten single compartments in each car. These are number six and seven. There are three dining cars, a bar car and three sleepers behind us, four sleeping cars and the baggage car forward.

Everything's completely private. Bathrooms at either end of the car. Except for that you don't have to leave the compartment until you get to Paris. The cabin steward will bring you your meals if you want. His name is Mario.' Caruso shrugged. 'I guess that's it then, sir.' He held out his hand. 'Do I get an A, Colonel?'

'A plus, Cadet Caruso,' Holliday said with a laugh, taking the young lieutenant's hand. They shook.

'Good luck, sir.'

The soldier stepped back, gave Holliday a smart, crisp salute and backed out of the compartment.

Holliday closed the door and threw the latch. He turned back into the little room. Peggy was already sprawled on the couch, her legs across Rafi's lap. Tidyman was seated closest to the window, looking out onto the platform. For the first time since the morning he realized that everyone in the room smelled like a hickory barbecue.

Holliday felt a hesitant lurching movement beneath his feet. There was the deep bass note of a generator gearing up, and then, almost imperceptibly, the train began to move, sliding silently forward so smoothly there was the brief illusion that it was the platform moving, not the train.

'We made it,' said Rafi.

'I could sleep for a week,' sighed Peggy, her eyes already closed.

'Being taken captive and held hostage by Tuareg terrorists will have that effect on you,' said Rafi, smiling fondly at her. Holliday felt a tug in the pit of his stomach, remembering his time with Amy, so long ago now, before the awful tide of all-consuming cancer swept her away. He and his wife must have looked like Peggy and Rafi looked now.

There was a quiet knock on the door behind him. Holliday turned around and unbolted the door. He opened it a crack. A handsome thirty-something man in a blue uniform with brass buttons stood in the passage. He was actually wearing white gloves.

'I am Mario, *signore*, your cabin steward for the duration of your journey. For your pleasure cocktails are being served in the bar car at the moment. There is also a late buffet in the forward dining car.'

'Thank you, Mario,' said Holliday.

'*Prego, signore.*' Mario gave a little bow. Holliday nodded, smiled briefly and shut the door. He threw the bolt again and turned back into the room.

'What do you think?' Holliday said. 'Anyone up for it?' He shrugged. 'I've got to stay up to meet this Czinner character at midnight.'

'Pass,' mumbled Peggy, already half asleep.

'Me too,' said Rafi.

'I'll join you,' said Tidyman.

'From the look on Mario's face when he saw how I was dressed, I think we'd better change first,' said Holliday.

The suits were Zegna and Armani, the shirts were Enrico Monti, the ties were Cadini, the shoes were Mirage and everything fitted like a glove.

They'd taken the clothes out of the narrow closet and closed the connecting panel of the screen. Peggy was fast asleep on the couch and Rafi was snoring sitting up. Holliday hadn't the heart to wake them for Mario to make up the bunks.

'I feel like an impostor,' said Tidyman, grimacing at his reflection in the little mirror over the sink on their side of the compartment. He raked his fingers through his shoulder-length gray hair.

'You look like something out of GQ maga-zine,' Holliday said with a grin, knotting his red-and-blue-striped tie.

'GQ for old men,' grunted Tidyman. 'After today's adventures I feel a million years old. I'm too old to be James Bond.'

'Roger that,' agreed Holliday. 'Let's go get a drink.'

The bar car was a comfortable arrangement of small tables and tapestry-upholstered wing chairs, with a bartender at the ready and a piano player noodling show tunes and Scott Joplin numbers on a baby grand. The bartender looked bored and the smile on the piano player's face looked completely and utterly insincere. There were only a few people in the car. Apparently if you had enough money to travel on the Orient Express, you were too old to party.

They sat down at the table farthest from the piano. A waiter in a short white jacket took their order and both men leaned back in their chairs. The wheels rattled and roared over the sleepers and the landscape was nothing more than flicker-ing lights and shapes in the darkness, smeared through the heavy glass by the slanting rain that had begun to fall as they left Rome. The waiter reappeared with Holliday's Martini & Rossi on the rocks and Tidyman's brandy.

'Truly astounding,' said Tidyman after taking a small sip from the large tulip-shaped snifter. 'This morning men die at my hand and this evening I sip calvados in the bar car of the Orient Express wearing a two-thousand-dollar suit. The world is an amazing place, Colonel, wouldn't you agree?'

Holliday swirled the fluid in his glass, blunting the sharp edges of the ice cubes. He shrugged.

'We did what we set out to do,' he said. 'We rescued Peggy. The men that died today, the bald bastard priest in particular, were going to rape, torture and then kill her. People like that live in a different world, Emil, a darker world with darker rules. I just played by them.'

'No remorse, no feeling?' Tidyman asked curiously.

'No more than they would have had killing you or me, or Peggy.'

'A beautiful young woman,' said Tidyman. 'She and the Israeli truly seem smitten.'

'Don't they just?' Holliday laughed. He took a slug from his glass, savoring the taste.

'She is small, your Peggy, petite,' said Tidyman,

his voice softening. 'My wife was very much like her as well.' The Egyptian's voice snagged and he turned away, staring blindly out through the dark window.

'I'm sorry, Emil,' said Holliday quietly. 'I know how it hurts. I lost my wife as well.'

'Does the pain lessen?' Tidyman asked.

'A little,' said Holliday. 'It fades like an old photograph over time, but it never really goes away.'

'Good,' said Tidyman. 'I don't want to lose her in my heart.' His voice suddenly hardened and his eyes grew black as coal. 'Nor do I want to forget what I will do if I ever find that *Kekri Gahba*, the desert pig, Alhazred.'

The Egyptian smacked his right fist lightly into his open left palm and hissed a curse.

'*Alaan abok, labo abook, yabn al gahba, okho el gahba, yal manyoch kess, ommek, o omen, yabetek!*'

'Sounds very unpleasant,' commented Holliday.

'You have no idea,' murmured Tidyman. He stared out the rain-swept window, peering into the black night as though it might have answers for him. They sat that way for a long time, silently. Finally Holliday spoke.

'Tell me about your daughter,' he said, and Tidyman turned away from the window, his face filling with light and life again.

They sat together in the bar car until they were the only ones remaining. The piano player eventually signed off with 'Kiss Me Good-Night, Dear,' then wandered away while the bartender ostentatiously began polishing crystal glasses that were already gleaming. Outside there were more and more lights flashing by as they reached the suburbs of Bologna. Holliday checked the time. Almost midnight.

Tidyman stood, a little unsteadily, exhausted by the day and feeling the effects of several brandies.

'Time to sleep, I'm afraid,' said the Egyptian. 'Mario must surely have made up the beds.' He smiled. 'I'll take the bottom bunk if you don't mind; I don't think I could face a ladder right now.'

'No problem,' said Holliday.

'Many thanks for the conversation,' said Tidyman. 'This is a hard time to be left alone with your thoughts.'

'My pleasure,' said Holliday. 'Good night, Emil, sweet dreams.'

'Or perhaps no dreams at all,' said Tidyman. 'Good night, Doc.'

He turned away, stumbling a little and swaying with the rhythm of the train. He pulled open the door, the sound from the vestibule between the carriages rising to a roar. Then the door swung shut and the Egyptian disappeared. The bartender gave Holliday a long, steady, meaningful look. Holliday ignored him and gazed out the window into the rain.

Fifteen minutes later the train pulled into the Bologna Centrale train station.

28

'How long do we stop for?' Holliday asked the bartender. He took fifty euros of the cash Caruso had given him and put it down on the cherry-wood bar. The man looked down at the folded bill disdainfully, his polishing cloth scouring the inside of a perfectly clean old-fashioned glass.

'Twenty minutes, *signore*, to change crews only,' the man responded. 'Be careful or the train will leave without you, *signore*.' The man looked as though that was exactly what he would like to happen.

'Thanks,' said Holliday. For a moment he thought about putting the fifty-euro note back in his pocket, but in the end he let it lie. He left the bar car and went back three cars until he found a vestibule door that was open onto the platform. He went down the steps. The platform was dry but the air was still full of the sharp, clean taste of rain.

The platform was like every other train platform

in the world: a long strip of stained concrete, a yellow line warning you that you were too close to the edge, bright industrial lighting turning night into day. Overhead there was a humming spider-web of wires for the catenary electrical system that powered most European locomotives.

There were four other people on the platform with him, a young couple with backpacks lip-locked on a narrow bench that was advertising something called Zaza, a maintenance worker in a low-brimmed baseball cap and blue coveralls pushing a heavy broom, and a man alone in a trench coat who looked like a young Peter Falk in the TV series *Columbo*. He was carrying a bat-tered, old-fashioned clasp briefcase and wore a rumpled brown suit. Seeing Holliday, he gave a little wave and trotted down the platform. Holli-day stayed where he was. The man approached him, raising one hand in a little salute. The man's shoes were black and highly polished.

'Colonel Holliday?' said Columbo. He had a sandpapery voice of the kind that usually meant a lot of booze and cigarettes. It was obviously American with the flat tones of the Midwest. Illi-nois or Kansas maybe, but with an odd twang. His expression was tense and wary.

'You must be Czinner,' answered Holliday.

'In the flesh,' the man in the grimy trench coat said. He held out his hand. There was a fat signet ring on the third finger. A West Point graduation ring. Holliday shook the extended hand.

'What a cool jewel you got from your school,' said Holliday, looking down at the chunky gold ring and the large ruby-colored stone in the center. The man looked puzzled for an instant. Then he got it.

'Oh, yeah, you mean the ring,' he said and nodded. He twirled the heavy gold band loosely on the finger. 'Lost quite a bit of weight since then.'

'How are we doing?' Holliday asked.

'Could be better,' said Czinner. 'Those Czechs, Pesek and his wife, arrived in Venice today. We spotted them at Treviso Airport coming off a SkyEurope flight from Prague. They don't know they've been made by us, but we're not taking any chances. We're assuming there's a contract out on you and your people. We're getting you off the train early.'

'Where?'

Czinner looked around, clearly nervous.

'We can't talk here,' said Czinner. 'Let's get you

back on board the train.' Czinner looked around the platform again uneasily. The couple on the bench were still completely self-involved. The janitor had gone. Nothing else moved. Brake lines vented. There was an echoing laugh far away and then silence.

They climbed aboard at the first available set of stairs. Already blue-uniformed train men were coming down on the platform to look for stragglers. Czinner and Holliday walked down the train, going from car to car.

They went through all three of the ornate, empty dining rooms, already laid out for the à la carte breakfast, crown-shaped and crisply starched linen napkins marking each place, silver gleaming in subdued light, the crystal bud vases in the center of each table waiting for their fresh flowers. Checking his ticket, the man in the trench coat eventually found his compartment.

'Here we go, old man,' said Czinner, sliding open the door. He stood aside to let Holliday enter.

'After you,' said Holliday, deferring to the rumpled man. Czinner shrugged and stepped into the small room. Holliday followed.

The compartment was a half-sized version of

the suite Caruso had arranged for them. A single bunk had been made up from the couchette and a folding table was set up beside the window. Czinner slid between the bunk and the table, then reached up and pulled down the roller blind. He turned back to Holliday.

'Can't be too careful,' he said. He sat down on the bed and patted a place beside him on the tightly tucked-in blanket. 'Have a seat,' said Czinner. He dug around in the pockets of his trench coat and pulled out a Trenitalia schedule and a folded map. He laid both out on the little folding table.

Holliday sat down beside him. Caruso was absolutely right; there was actually an honest to goodness mustard stain on the man's Windsor-knotted tie and the trench coat smelled of mothballs. His cologne on the other hand was Roger & Gallet. Holliday would have expected something like Old Spice.

Czinner took a fat, expensive-looking ball-point pen out of his inside pocket, then flipped open the schedule to a turned-down page. He found what he was looking for on the map.

'This is Bologna,' he said, pointing with his pen to a dot on the map. 'And this is the main line to the Po River, about fifty kilometers north of us. There is a town called Pontelagoscuro, about six thousand people, a nothing place but it has a railway bridge across the river.' Czinner paused, looking over at Holliday.

'Are you with me, Colonel?'

'I'm with you,' Holliday said and nodded.

There was a piercing whistle from outside and the train began to move and gather speed. Czinner went back to the map.

'At the speed we travel it'll take us about forty-five minutes. The bridge is for high-speed Eurostars and slower locals like this one. We fixed the signals at the bridge to read double red so the train will stop to let the Eurostar go by first, coming from the opposite direction. It will take them at least ten minutes to figure out that the Eurostar isn't coming and that the signal is wrong. That gives us all time to get off the train.'

'What then?'

'There's a footpath down to the river. The terrain is quite flat and the banks aren't steep. Under the bridge there will be a boat waiting. The boat will take us upstream to the town of Ferrara. From there we've got a plane laid on to get you into Switzerland.'

'Very efficient,' said Holliday. 'I'm impressed, especially on such short notice.'

'It's what we do,' said Czinner with a shrug. He clicked the ballpoint pen. Something flashed. The lights flickered and went out for a second as the train slid under a faulty catenary wire and Czinner made his move. Holliday moved first.

He'd been tensed and waiting for it. As Czinner backhanded the pen around in a sweeping arc Holliday lifted his left arm to block the lunging thrust to his throat. At the same time his right hand came around, palm up, the heel of his thumb catching Czinner under the chin.

The man's head snapped back and his legs came up, smashing into the underside of the table. Holliday twisted around, caught Czinner's right arm under his own elbow and wrenched it back until he heard bone snap. Czinner screeched and Holliday used the same elbow to crack him across the mouth and nose, silencing him with a gout of blood and broken teeth.

Barely pausing, Holliday gripped Czinner's right wrist and bent it backward at an impossible angle. Bone snapped again and the lethal pen dropped from the killer's nerveless fingers. Holliday scooped it up as Czinner struggled beneath the trench coat with his left hand.

The false agent finally managed to extract a flat automatic pistol from the coat, fumbling clumsily with the safety. Holliday didn't hesitate. Using exactly the same kind of backhanded sweep that Czinner had tried on him, Holliday drove the needle tip of the hypodermic pen into his attacker's throat. Czinner instantly began to convulse. His feet drummed on the floor and his arms began to flap and jerk.

His eyes bugged and stared as his throat went into spasm. He foamed at the mouth, making horrible gagging sounds. Finally his back arched and his swollen tongue thrust out between his lips. His entire body fluttered on the bunk in a final spasm and he died, the skin of his face flushed in a grotesque parody of rosy health, his eyes wide open, staring into eternity. Curare or strychnine or something like it. Just like the killer who'd attacked him at West Point. Holliday looked down at Czinner. If his reflexes had been a fraction of a second slower, it would have been him instead.

Holliday reached out and took the automatic out of Czinner's dead grip, then put it in the pocket of his own jacket. He slipped the West Point ring off the dead man's finger and dropped it into his pocket along with the gun.

'You won't be needing this where you're going.'

There was a discreet tapping at the door. Holliday jumped.

'*Biglietto, signore,*' a voice outside the door said quietly. For some reason the conductor assumed he was Italian.

'*Momento,*' said Holliday. He turned and dug frantically in the pockets of the dead man's trench coat. He found the blue and green folder and turned back to the door. He switched off the overhead light and cracked the door an inch or two, then slipped the ticket folder through the opening.

'*Prego,*' said the conductor. There was a tearing sound as the conductor ripped off the appropriate flimsy, and then it was slipped back through the crack. '*Conserva il biglietto fino alla fine del viaggio, signore,*' he added.

Keep your ticket until the trip is over? Something like that.

'*Prego,*' answered Holliday.

'*Buona serata, signore,*' the conductor said politely. Brain frozen, Holliday took a guess.

'Buona serata,' he answered.

Holliday slid the door closed, squeezed his eyes shut, then held his breath, praying hard.

The conductor moved off down the passage-way. Holliday began to breathe again. He stayed that way for a long moment, back against the door, standing in the darkness, Czinner's corpse a dark shadow on the bunk. According to the schedule the train got into Venice at about three in the morning. The passengers wouldn't be awakened until the calls for breakfast beginning at seven, before they began their day of sightseeing in the ancient city of canals and gondolas. Seven hours or so between then and now. Not enough of a head start but it would have to do. He flipped the light on again. Gritting his teeth, he went through Czinner's pockets more carefully, looking for anything he could use.

He had two passports, one a black and gold U.S. passport in the name of Peter Paul Czinner, forty-two, born in Chicago, Illinois. The picture had been overstamped and was clearly out of date, but at a quick glance the body on the bed would have passed.

The other one was a Vatican Diplomatic Passport for someone named John Pargetter of

Toronto, Canada, which explained the odd twang. According to the passport Pargetter was an official Vatican photographer. The face in the photo definitely belonged to the dead man on the bed. Father Thomas again. It made sense. They seemed to be everywhere, so why not in the U.S. embassy? Somehow they'd found out about Caruso's operation and the John Pargetter character on the bed had been dispatched to intercept Czinner and take his place. It had almost worked.

In addition to the passports there was a billfold with ten thousand euros in large-denomination bills, a single key on a worn leather ring, a folding Buck knife with bone handles and a brass tang, and a Gemtech suppressor for the Walther P22 semiautomatic. The dead man wore a religious medal around his neck. A bald, bearded and emaciated St Nicholas in gold. Holliday smiled sourly. Someone had a sense of humor. St Nicholas was the patron saint of military intelligence.

Holliday took the Buck knife, the silencer, the key and the billfold. He left the medal where it was. He stood and looked at his watch. They'd reach the bridge in less than twenty minutes. He had to wake the others quickly. They were running out of time. He stood, turned out the light a second time and went to the door. He slid it open and looked out. The passage was empty, the overhead lights glowing dimly. He slid the door open fully, slipped out of the compartment, then closed the door firmly behind him.

He headed down the train, moving softly down the corridor, then went through into the next car. A steward was dozing in his little alcove across from the toilet. Holliday eased by and continued on. The next car was his. The door to Mario's little cubicle was closed. Holliday went down the corridor to bedroom seven, praying that Tidyman had remembered to leave the door unlocked. He tugged the brass handle and breathed a sigh of relief as the door slid open easily. He stepped into the room, turning to shut the door behind him.

Time stopped.

The violet-colored night-light in the ceiling of the compartment was on. A figure in dark blue coveralls was crouched on the floor, rummaging through a suitcase. The janitor with the broom on the train platform in Bologna. Emil Tidyman lay on the bed, eyes shut, a rubbery, gaping wound in his slit throat still seeping blood into the already soaking sheets. Murdered in his sleep by a thief in the night. He never had a chance.

The man in the coveralls rose up, turning, a heavy rubber-handled commando knife in his hand. Holliday stared, horrified. It was Rafik Alhazred, haggard and drawn, a wild, desperate look in his eye. He lunged forward.

'*Wad al haram!*' Alhazred hissed, the big knife flashing down.

Years before, a Ranger drill sergeant and instructor with the unlikely and unfortunate name of Francis Marion had told Holliday that only an idiot talked in the middle of a knife fight and only an idiot would try to stab you like Anthony Perkins in *Psycho*.

Holliday reacted exactly the way Francis Marion had trained him. He kicked Alhazred in the kneecap, kneed him in the groin and used the flat of his palm to crush the cartilage of his nose.

Alhazred's knife glanced off Holliday's forearm, gashing through the fabric of Holliday's suit jacket, drawing blood, and then Alhazred was on the floor, facedown. Holliday barely noticed, continuing the attack.

He stamped hard on Alhazred's wrist, disarming him, then dropped his knee across the back of Alhazred's neck, breaking it with a distinct wet cracking sound. Holliday stood up, his breath coming in ragged gasps, blood dripping from his arm.

'You cowardly son of a bitch,' said Holliday slowly. 'You killed my friend.' He sagged against the wall, struggling to catch his breath.

The train slowed and then came to a lurching halt. They had reached the railway bridge across the Po.

Holliday tried the latch on the partition door between the two compartments. It was locked. He hammered on it.

'Rafi!'

There was a pause and then a groan.

'Who is it?' Rafi's voice.

'It's Doc! Open up!'

'What time is it?' Peggy's sleepy voice this time.

'Open the damned door!'

There was a sigh and then another groan and finally the sound of movement. The partition door bolt slid back and the door opened. Rafi stood there, bleary-eyed, but still dressed. Peggy, tousle-haired, was sitting up on the couchette behind him. Rafi's face was full of sleep but he finally took in Holliday and the blood dripping from his arm.

'What the hell?' And then he saw the scene in the other compartment. 'Dear God,' the archaeologist whispered. 'What happened?'

'It's a long story,' said Holliday. He stepped into their compartment and shut the door. 'Tidyman's dead. We have to get off the train. Now.'

'But . . . ,' Peggy began, still not understanding.

'Don't argue, kiddo – there's no time.' He opened the passageway door and looked out. Empty. Everyone was asleep. Through the passage windows he could see yellow arc lights glowing, reflecting off the dark still waters of the river just ahead. Farther upstream, past a sleeping little industrial park at the edge of a small town, there was a low-slung bridge for cars and trucks. The river looked about a thousand feet across. He turned back into the compartment.

'Come on,' he said.

Still half asleep, Rafi and Peggy followed as Holliday went down the corridor to the door between the cars. He pulled it open and stepped out onto the little platform. Mario had awakened as the train halted and come out to see what was happening. He'd put down the steps and climbed down to see why the train had come to an unscheduled stop.

Mario saw Holliday and then Rafi and Peggy crowd in behind him. The steward shook his head and came forward, making a little pushing gesture with his hands as his shoes crunched on the gravel roadbed.

'No, no, please, *signore, prego*. Remain on the train. There is no cause for alarm. We have only stopped for the *segnale di ferroviario*, how do you say, the train signal, yes? Back on the train, *signore*, please.'

Then he saw the blood dripping down from Holliday's arm and paled.

Holliday fished the Walther out of his pocket and pointed it down at the uniformed man.

'*Signore?*' the steward whispered.

'Back up,' said Holliday, keeping the gun up as he came down the steps. The steward did as he was told, his eyes glued to the flat black pistol. Holliday waved Rafi and Peggy down with his free hand. He lowered the gun, keeping it at his side as they descended.

Holliday looked left along the train. The bridge was built with two side-by-side spans, each with its own track, the two tracks converging at a switch point and signal just in front of the waiting locomotive. The signal showed two red lights, one above the other. Suddenly the top light went out and the bottom light changed to green. The riverbank was two hundred feet beyond that. The train whistle blared.

'Mario, I want you to listen to me,' said Holliday, his voice firm but calm.

'Yes, *signore*.'

'I want you to get back on the train and go to your compartment.'

'Yes, *signore*,' Mario said and nodded.

'Stay there. If I see you again, or if the train stops or if anyone comes after us, I will kill you, *capisce*?'

'Yes, *signore*.'

'Good. Do it.'

'Yes, *signore*,' agreed the steward fervently.

Holliday stood aside and let Mario pass. The whistle screamed again. Mario pulled in the steps and slammed the door. Holliday looked up at the train. Right now Mario was probably making a beeline for the conductor.

'What do we do now?' Rafi said.

'Run,' said Holliday.

He led the way, pelting down the roadbed, heading for the river, trapped in the yellow glare of the industrial lights beside the twin bridge spans. Beside the running figures the train began to move. The whistle sounded for a third time and directly ahead Holliday saw the signal change to double green. Still no alarm. The train began to gather speed and Holliday felt a surge of hope. Maybe they were going to get out of this after all. The locomotive reached the bridge and the train began to thunder over it.

They reached the first bridge supports and Holliday saw the narrow footpath in the dirt between the twin spans, just as the false Czinner had described it. Holliday paused, hands on knees, panting as Rafi and Peggy caught up with him.

'What are we doing?' Rafi insisted. 'I thought you were meeting Czinner. Now Tidyman's been killed.'

'Czinner's dead, too, or at least a man posing as Czinner. He was one of the priest's crew. He was an impostor.'

The train rumbled past, leaving them beside the empty track. Mario had taken his threat seriously, thought Holliday. He popped the magazine on the Walther and checked. Fully loaded. He pushed the magazine back into place, feeling it lock with an efficient Teutonic click.

'What are we doing out here?' Peggy asked wearily.

'This was Czinner's escape route,' explained Holliday. 'Now it's ours.' He dug around in his pocket and found the suppressor. He screwed it onto the tapped muzzle of the short-barreled pistol.

Rafi stared at the weapon.

'Expecting trouble?'

'You never know,' answered Holliday. 'Czinner's ride is down there. Maybe it comes with a driver.'

'I don't want Peggy hurt,' cautioned the Israeli, putting his arm around her shoulders. She shook it off.

'I can handle myself, Rafi,' she said, annoyed.

'Nevertheless, stay back, both of you. And *keep* back until I whistle Dixie.'

'Dixie?' Rafi asked.

'"*Hava Nagila*" for Southern crackers,' explained Peggy. Rafi looked confused.

'Just stay back until I whistle,' said Holliday.

Leaving them behind, he followed the path

down between the bridges, turning under the low left-hand span. A dense row of willows and alders stood at the top of the bank, screening the path along the river edge. The arc lights beside the train track were behind Holliday now and the way ahead was lost in gloomy darkness. He could hear the water, a light lapping noise against the soft earth of the muddy riverbank and a different sound with it – the river slapping quietly against the hull of a small boat.

A lanky figure rose out of the darkness directly in front of him. A man in a dark sweater with something slung over his shoulder. The shape was familiar enough: an old Colt Commando from the Vietnam War, the short version of the M-16. The dark figure unlimbered the old assault rifle.

'*Padre?*' the man whispered harshly. He was less than fifty feet away.

Holliday didn't wait for the sound of the rifle's slide as a round popped into the chamber. He lifted the Walther in a two-handed grip, pointed the pistol at the man's chest and fired six times in quick, evenly spaced succession, the silenced rounds sounding like someone snapping dry twigs.

Whatever else Czinner had been, he was a

professional when it came to his job. To be that quiet the rounds had to be subsonic. Given that they were in Italy that probably meant Fiocchi Super Match. The man with the rifle turned into an empty bag of flesh and slid to the ground, face in the dirt.

'No,' said Holliday. 'Not your murdering padre.'

Holliday waited. Nothing stirred. The only sounds came from the river's movement. He approached the fallen man, keeping the Walther pointed at the back of his head. He checked the pulse. Nothing, which was as he'd expected at that range. He stood up.

Behind the man a sleek-looking old-fashioned wooden speedboat was tied up to a crumbling concrete dock that looked as though it might have been cast off during construction of the bridge piers. Holliday had seen one just like it in the ruins of Milosevic's summer home on the Danube years before.

The boat was an Italian Ravi Aquarama, the so-called Ferrari of cabin cruisers, a mahogany dream from the sixties built to challenge anything ever made by Chris-Craft. The twenty-eight-foot boat was fitted with Cadillac engines and could plane through the water at close to fifty knots.

First things first. He unscrewed the silencer from the pistol and put both back into his pocket. He slid the rifle out from under the body and pitched it into the river. That done, he grabbed the dead man by the armpits and dragged the corpse across the shingled beach, then rolled him into the underbrush. Peggy had seen enough death; she didn't need another body to add to the toll.

When he was satisfied he turned back to the path and whistled the first few bars of the old minstrel tune that had somehow become the anthem for a losing army, long ago. As he whistled he felt the weight of the world settle on his shoulders and the strange sense of loss felt when a battle ends. He whistled another few bars then turned and went out to the boat.

He stepped over the curving deck and took the leather key tag out of his pocket. He sat down behind the white Bakelite wheel, put the key into the ignition, then twisted the port starter to the On position. There was a coughing sound and then a deep-throated rumbling as the massive engine came to muttering life. He twisted the starboard starter and the second engine echoed its mate.

He tugged the throttle just a little and the muttering became a muted roar. Holliday smiled. It was like having two tigers tugging on a leash. *Emil Tidyman would have enjoyed this,* he thought, his heart sinking a little. Then Rafi and Peggy appeared out of the darkness and, seeing them, Holliday's heart lifted once again.

Rafi stared at the speedboat.

'Good Lord,' he said.

'Neat,' said Peggy. 'Can I drive?'

'No,' said Holliday. 'Unhitch the line and climb in. We're going home.'

And that's what they did.

29

Holliday sat behind his desk in the study of the little house on West Point's Professor's Row. There was early snow on the ground outside and he had a fire burning in the grate. It was the day before Thanksgiving and once again West Point was almost empty. Anyone who had anywhere to go had gone. Home for the holidays. He looked around the room.

The floor was stacked with boxes ready to go into storage and all the bookshelves were empty. The house was well on its way to becoming a barren shell of naked walls and vacant rooms, no longer anyone's home.

The inquiry into the death of the killer who'd attacked him on the same day Rafi had arrived at his door seeking help was done and Holliday had been completely exonerated.

His term as the head of the History Department at the United States Military Academy was formally complete, papers signed, position resigned, re-up declined. As the old science fiction writers used to put it, life as he knew it was over. He was unemployed and homeless. Peggy was in Jerusalem with her new husband and he was alone.

The funny thing was, he didn't give a damn. In fact, he was looking forward to whatever was coming his way. His time tracking down Peggy halfway across Africa had taught him at least one good lesson: friends were precious, life even more so and time was the only real treasure.

He sat in the firelight, remembering. They'd parted ways in Paris after taking the big speed-boat downriver to the Adriatic coast and then south, away from Venice and down to Ravenna. From there getting to Paris had been easy.

During a farewell meal in the Terminal R brasserie at the Radisson SAS hotel at Charles de Gaulle Airport, Rafi had asked him how he'd been tipped that the man posing as Czinner was an impostor. Holliday pulled the big West Point graduation ring out of his pocket and laid it down on the table.

'What a cool jewel you got from your school,' said Holliday, smiling.

'*Pardonnez-moi?*' Peggy said in an atrocious French accent.

'That was Czinner's reaction,' said Holliday. 'He recovered very quickly, but not quickly enough. A West Pointer would know. I knew then that he wasn't Czinner. I was ready for him.'

'I don't get it,' said Rafi. He picked up the big signet ring and looked at it closely, an archaeologist at work, trying to decipher the artifact.

'It's a ritual, a poem,' Holliday explained. He quoted the whole thing:

> *Oh my gosh, sir, what a beautiful ring.*
> *What a crass mass of brass and glass.*
> *What a bold mold of rolled gold.*
> *What a cool jewel you got from your school.*
> *See how it sparkles and shines.*
> *It must have cost you a fortune*
> *Please, sir, may I touch it,*
> *May I touch it, please, sir.*

'Not the greatest poetry I've ever heard,' said Peggy.

'I still don't get it,' said Rafi. He put the ring back on the table.

Holliday picked it up and slipped it back into his pocket. The ring was engraved with Czinner's names and dates, and eventually he'd send it to

Vince Caruso at the embassy so he could get it to where it rightfully belonged. He finished his explanation.

'Like I said, it's a ritual. A hazing thing for freshman cadets. Back in the day every plebe at West Point had to learn that verse by heart, on pain of death, or at least a severe dressing-down and some punishment duty. When he saw a student from that year's graduating class wearing his ring the plebe had to salute, fall to his knees and recite the poem. If you remembered any piece of poetry at West Point, that would be it. They still do it, only now you don't fall to your knees.'

'Your West Point is a very strange place,' said Rafi, grinning. 'Its first commandant your country's greatest traitor, assassination attempts, now young men falling to their knees and reciting awful poetry. It's a wonder you've won so many wars.' He shook his head in mock consternation.

'Yes,' agreed Holliday, 'but there's no place like home.'

And now home was a thing of the past.

Speaking of things from the past.

Holliday smiled to himself, staring into the crackling fire and listening to the November wind rattling angrily at the windows. At least he'd know how to find his way to the new one. And to find his way back to Alhazred's hidden gold. Gold that he'd find again and make sure got back to its rightful inheritors.

He opened the drawer and pulled out the only memento he had of his terrible time in the desert. Two shaped strips of wood, dark with age, both eight-inch squared rods carved with tiny symbols, numbers from thousands of years before. One of the strips was drilled with a square hole that exactly fitted the dimensions of the other.

Put together it formed a slightly mismatched cruciform with the inner arm able to slide up and down within its mate. The same cruciform the figure of Imhotep held in the boat fresco on the wall of his hidden tomb. The cruciform object he found, forgotten within the huge stone sarcophagus.

He'd realized instantly what the little wooden objects were and somehow he'd managed to keep them with him and hidden for the rest of his journey. Two strips of ancient wood more valuable than the tons of bullion on the underground chamber floor.

Two strips of wood that would have given the archaeologists from Jerusalem, or Rafik Alhazred, almost unlimited fame. Two strips that gave the ironic lie to the old name for Father Thomas's covert organization, Organum Sanctum, the Instrument of God.

Holliday fitted the two little squared rods together and slid them up and down. Almost as elegant as Imhotep's translation of the beehive tomb design of his native land into the gigantic pyramids of his adopted home. As simple and perhaps almost as brilliant in its own way as the most famous equation in the world: $E = mc^2$.

The two little sticks, brought together in the correct way, its symbols read as degrees of angle when pointed towards the sun, was the first navigation instrument that allowed men to leave the shore and travel the ocean. A true Instrument of God to a man like Imhotep, whose greatest god was Ra, the sun, and whose private god was knowledge.

Effectively the two sticks joined were a simple version of a Jacob's Staff, named for the man who had invented it, Jacob ben Machir ibn Tibbon, a Jewish astronomer living in Provence in the thirteenth century. Except Tibbon had *not* invented it – Imhotep had, approximately four thousand years before him. The invention, and the fresco in the hidden tomb, brought up another possibility:

What if the landscape in the fresco wasn't the near-mythical land of Punt? What if the island in the fresco was Manhattan and the river was the Hudson, flowing a few hundred yards from where he sat, down to the invisible Atlantic, hidden beyond the hills? What if Imhotep had sailed his long-keeled boat across the Ocean Sea three thousand years before Christ, let alone Columbus, and claimed the land for his great pharaoh, Djoser?

Only a year or so ago they'd found funerary boats buried in the sands near the Tomb of Ramses in the Valley of the Kings, boats twice as long as any Columbus sailed to the West Indies. The pieces put together made it quite possible. Now wouldn't that turn history on its complacent ear?

He picked up the wooden cross and put it back in the drawer along with the Templar notebook with the bloodstained cover he'd inherited from the old monk Rodrigues. He watched the fire in the hearth die down as the room grew cold. He thought about Imhotep, about the gold and about the past. And then he thought about the future.

Emil Tidyman had been right: gold and power brought out the worst in almost everyone. A lot of people had died because of Rauff's bullion and Holliday could bet it wasn't over yet. He was fairly certain that Father Thomas wasn't finished with him. That battle would almost certainly go on, wherever he went. There were scores to settle.

And letters to write.

He took a few sheets of paper from his drawer along with a felt pen and a brand-new moleskin notebook he carried. It had taken some time and a lot of phone calls, but he'd eventually discovered the names of the four men who made up the crew of the ill-fated B-17, *Your Heart's Desire*:

Major-Fleigerstabsingenieur Johann Biehl, the pilot; Captain-Fleigerhauptsingenieur Hugo Dahmer, the co-pilot; Lieutenant-Fleigerobersingenieur Gerhard Fischer, the flight engineer/navigator; and, finally, the radio operator, Lieutenant-Fleigerobersingenieur Willi Noller.

He'd also discovered the names of their nearest relations, all surviving sons and daughters, and he'd decided to write them each a letter telling them of the plane's discovery and the fate of their forgotten fathers. It was the least that he could do.

And then there was Tabia, Emil Tidyman's daughter. It had taken even longer to discover her whereabouts, but he'd pulled some strings and called in some markers and eventually he had the name and address of a cutout who would eventually get the letter to the people taking care of her.

Perhaps someone would read Tabia the letter now, or perhaps she'd read it herself somewhere far in the future. It didn't matter. Since coming back to West Point he'd had a lot of time to think about what he'd say and now the words came easily.

In the dark of a chilly New York night he began to write, his pen moving easily across the blank paper, forming letters and words that told a story of friendship and family love, a story of a rogue but a rogue redeemed, and the story of a friend who believed in friendship at any cost. Above all it was the memory of any child's hero, her father, a man she could be proud of. Holliday wrote for a long time and when he was done he smiled. He put down the pen and leaned back in his chair. Perhaps, for Tabia at least, the bad times were over.

Outside, the winter wind shook its fist at the moaning eaves and the frost-rimed glass, reminding the world of things to come, like cold bad dreams. Holliday's smile slipped away and became a thoughtful frown. Sitting there with the fire no more than dead ash in the hearth, he knew that while Tabia's troubles were done, his own were just beginning.

READ ON FOR A SPECIAL SNEAK
PREVIEW OF THE NEXT
PAUL CHRISTOPHER THRILLER

THE TEMPLAR THRONE

AVAILABLE SOON FROM SIGNET

Colonel John 'Doc' Holliday, U.S. Army Rangers (retired), most recently a professor of Medieval Military History at the United States Military Academy at West Point (and retired from that, too), sat on the glassed-in terrace of La Brasserie Malakoff, an upscale café in the prestigious 16th arrondissement of Paris. His companion was Maurice Bernheim, director of the Musée national de la marine, the National Maritime Museum of France.

Both men were eating a lunch of salad and croque monsieur, the Parisian version of a Reuben sandwich that might as well have come from an entirely different universe. The Parisians looked down their noses at everyone else on the planet, but when it came to food they were right. Even a *Royale avec Fromage* at a Paris McDonald's was vastly superior to a Big Mac sold anywhere else in the world. Bernheim had been lecturing him on the subject for the better part of an hour, but a good lunch on a spring day in Paris made up for a lot of things.

Holliday had crossed paths with Bernheim previously when he was in the midst of tracking down the secret of the Templar sword. The chubby little historian who smoked the foul-smelling cigarettes called Boyards had helped him then, and now Holliday was hoping he'd help him again.

'I must say it is too bad that your charming niece could not be with you today,' said Bernheim. He finished the sandwich and hailed a waiter, ordering crème caramel and coffee for both of them.

'Cousin,' corrected Holliday. 'She's too busy being eight months pregnant in Jerusalem.' Peggy and the Israeli archaeologist Rafi Wanounou had married last year shortly after their adventures in the Libyan desert. The same adventures that had eventually led Holliday to his high-cholesterol lunch with Maurice Bernheim.

'Such a pretty young woman,' sighed the middle-aged man.

'Her new husband thinks so,' Holliday said with a smile. 'Speaking of which, how's your wife and kids?'

'Pauline is well, thank you. Fortunately for me her dental practice keeps me in the style to which my little hellions and I have grown accustomed. The twins of course must also have the latest running shoes. *La vie est tres cher, mon ami.* Life is very expensive, yes? Soon it will be makeup and matching Mercedeses.' Bernheim flicked an invisible bit of fluff off the lapel of his very expensive Brioni suit.

The crème caramel arrived and the museum director stared at it reverently for a moment, as though it was a great work of art, which, to Bernheim, it probably was. Holliday ignored the dessert and tried the coffee. As with everything else at Malakoff's it was excellent. At least with the ban on smoking in Paris restaurants he didn't have to endure Bernheim's Boyards.

'So,' said the nautical expert. 'What brings you to Paris and my humble little museum?' He took another bite of the crème caramel and briefly closed his eyes to savor the flavor.

'Have you ever heard of a place called La Couvertoirade?' Holliday asked.

Bernheim nodded.

'A fortified town in the Dordogne. Built by the Templars, I believe.'

'That's right,' Holliday said and nodded. 'A while back an archaeologist, a monk named Brother Charles-Étienne Brasseur, discovered a cache of documents from there relating to the Templar expedition to Egypt.' Holliday paused, trying to remember it all. 'The texts were written by a Cistercian monk named Roland de Hainaut. Hainaut was secretary to Guillaume de Sonnac, the grand master who led the Templars at the Siege of Damietta in 1249.'

'Of course. The Seventh Crusade,' said Bernheim. 'They couldn't get upriver because of the Nile flooding, so they sat around for six months and had their way with the Egyptian women.'

'They also played at being tourists,' added Holliday. 'Guillaume de Sonnac's personal ship as grand master was a caravel called the *Sanctus Johannes* chartered out of Genoa from a ship owner named Peter Rubeus. De Sonnac provided his own captain, a fellow Frenchman named Jean de St Clair.'

'A common enough name in France, I'm afraid,' said Bernheim. 'Rather like John Smith in America.' He smiled. 'A name used to sign hotel registers with.'

'Well, while this particular St Clair was in

Damietta he traveled a little way to Rosetta, where the famous stone was found a few hundred years later by Napoleon's archaeologists.'

'And stolen by the British, I might add,' snorted Bernheim.

'Take it up with the Queen,' said Holliday. 'Anyway, while St Clair was on his little visit to Rosetta along with de Sonnac's secretary, they stumbled on some old Coptic documents in a monastery there. The documents described something they referred to as an Organum Sanctum.'

'An Instrument of God,' translated Bernheim. 'It generally refers to a person. Moses was an instrument of God, for instance.'

'Not this time,' said Holliday. He opened the floppy, old-fashioned briefcase on his lap and took out two ten-inch-long strips of wood. One of the strips was slightly thicker than the other and had a square hole halfway down its length. The narrower of the two pieces was clearly meant to fit into the hole, forming a cross. Both strips were notched at regular intervals.

'A Jacob's Staff,' Bernheim said with a nod as Holliday passed them over. 'A sixteenth-century navigational instrument.'

'Except the documents were discovered by St Clair and de Sonnac's secretary two hundred years before that,' said Holliday. 'Stranger still, the documents described the device from which that model was made as being even older – from the time of the pharaohs, in fact.'

'Ridiculous,' scoffed Bernheim.

'I found the original of the device you hold in your hand in the mummified hand of the pharaoh Djoser's vizier. The mummy was entombed at least twenty-five hundred years before the birth of Christ and four thousand years before Jean de St Clair was in Rosetta. The original is now in the safekeeping of the Metropolitan Museum of Art in New York. The copy you're holding is an exact duplicate made by their model department.'

'There can be no mistake about the age?'

'Spectroscopic analysis is accurate with a margin of error less than ten percent for African juniper. There's no doubt about it, Maurice; the instrument is forty-five hundred years old.'

'Merde,' breathed the man, his crème caramel forgotten. 'You know what this does to the basic paradigm of modern nautical history?'

'Destroys it,' answered Holliday flatly.

'This device would be as much a secret weapon as the atomic bomb,' said Bernheim. 'A seafaring nation which had it would have an incredible advantage over a nation which lacked it.'

'At least for the two hundred years or so between St Clair's discovery and the Jacob's Quadrant being invented in the fifteen hundreds,' said Holliday.

'Columbus goes out the window.'

'And it almost certainly means that those fairy tales about the Templars going to America are true. Or could be,' said Holliday.

'St Clair, Sinclair,' mused Bernheim. He ran his thumb along the notches along the sides of the two strips of wood, then fitted the two pieces together. He held up the cruciform instrument. 'Have you ever seen the ancient coat of arms of the St Clairs?' Bernheim asked.

'No,' answered Holliday.

'*La Croix Engraal*,' said Bernheim. 'An "engrailed" cross.'

'Which means?' Holliday asked.

'In heraldic terms *Engraal* means protected by the Holy Grail, the Grail being indicated by what in that silly *Da Vinci* book was referred to as the V of the sacred feminine. But what if, on the

St Clair crest, the *Engraal* notches on the cross referred to something else? Something much more practical.' Bernheim ran his thumbnail along the notches in the wood.

'The gradation indentations on a Jacob's Quadrant,' said Holliday, grinning. 'The simplest explanation is most often the truth. Occam's razor.'

'*C'est ca,*' said Bernheim happily. 'The mystery is solved.'

'Not until I find out more about this Jean de St Clair, whoever he was.'

Bernheim had gone back to his crème caramel. He put down his spoon and wiped his lips with a napkin. He shrugged.

'Historically the Sinclairs of Scotland came from a little place known as Saint-Clair-sur-Epte. The Epte River once served as the border between Normandy and Ile de France; that is, between the English possessions and the rest of the country. It is also the river diverted by Claude Monet to create his famous water-lily pond.'

'What on earth does any of this have to do with maritime history?' Holliday laughed, impressed by Bernheim's fund of knowledge on such an obscure subject.

'Your interest, your expertise is in medieval warfare, correct?'

'I'd like to think so.'

'Mine is ships and the sea. Before ships there must be wood, before wood there must be trees. Have you ever heard of the Beaulieu River in England?'

'No.'

'Then you've never heard of the village of Buckler's Hard.'

'Not a name I'm familiar with,' Holliday said with a smile.

'Anyone involved in French maritime history would be,' said Bernheim. 'HMS *Euryalus*, HMS *Swiftsure* and HMS *Agamemnon* were all built there, ships which were key during the Battle of Trafalgar in which the British defeated the French fleet in 1805. It was wood from the surrounding New Forest which built Nelson's entire fleet.'

'You're saying the Epte River had the same function?'

'Since the time of the Vikings,' Bernheim said, nodding. He scraped the last of the crème caramel from the sides of his dish. He smacked his lips and sighed. 'If the St Clair you seek was a seaman he almost certainly came from Saint-Clair-sur-Epte.'

He stared mournfully down at his empty dish and sighed again. 'There is an old abbey nearby, the Abbaye de Tiron. Speak with the librarian there, Brother Morvan. Pierre Morvan. Perhaps he will be able to help you.' He glanced over at Holliday's untouched crème caramel. 'Not hungry?' Bernheim inquired hopefully.

He just wanted a decent book to read ...

Not too much to ask, is it? It was in 1935 when Allen Lane, Managing Director of Bodley Head Publishers, stood on a platform at Exeter railway station looking for something good to read on his journey back to London. His choice was limited to popular magazines and poor-quality paperbacks – the same choice faced every day by the vast majority of readers, few of whom could afford hardbacks. Lane's disappointment and subsequent anger at the range of books generally available led him to found a company – and change the world.

'We believed in the existence in this country of a vast reading public for intelligent books at a low price, and staked everything on it'
Sir Allen Lane, 1902–1970, founder of Penguin Books

The quality paperback had arrived – and not just in bookshops. Lane was adamant that his Penguins should appear in chain stores and tobacconists, and should cost no more than a packet of cigarettes.

Reading habits (and cigarette prices) have changed since 1935, but Penguin still believes in publishing the best books for everybody to enjoy. We still believe that good design costs no more than bad design, and we still believe that quality books published passionately and responsibly make the world a better place.

So wherever you see the little bird – whether it's on a piece of prize-winning literary fiction or a celebrity autobiography, political tour de force or historical masterpiece, a serial-killer thriller, reference book, world classic or a piece of pure escapism – you can bet that it represents the very best that the genre has to offer.

Whatever you like to read – trust Penguin.